SAVING EVA

THE EVA SERIES, BOOK 3

JENNIFER SIVEC

To my family who knows me completely and loves me anyway, I'll love and appreciate you forever and always.

1

Saving Eva

~Brynn

I wasn't dead.

I knew that after all I'd been through, I should be, but I wasn't. I'd wished for death, but I was alive in some strange existence I didn't understand. Living had taken on a dream-like state, presumably from the medication they had me on that dripped through the tubes that were connected to me and into my veins, a result of the accident that nearly took my life. But even though I yearned for the peacefulness of death, a small part of me was grateful that I survived at all.

The scene plays before me repeatedly.

The big F150 headed toward me with no time or space to move. My reaction time slowed by my swollen, pregnant belly, and disbelief as to what was taking place before me. I was so excited for the trip I was taking and on my way … somewhere important. I was headed somewhere life-changing …

But I didn't make it.

Instead I ended up in the hospital for months, or years, I'm not even sure. I know the time I lost would never be regained, but I was grateful to be alive because it all simply could've ended at impact. From the appearance of my car, a mangled and twisted mess of blue metal, it should have.

But being alive after the accident was lonely, and the existence I thought I should have has eluded me completely. Time passes like a movie that's set on slow motion and only the time I'm able to spend with my daughter, Eva, makes sense. When I'm with her, it's as though the world is bright with every single color of the rainbow. The world is alive with beautiful music. With Eva, I am awake and alive and my life unfolds before me, exactly the way it should.

I remember the day she was born as though it was yesterday, with Adam by my side, begging me to push. After the accident, he was terrified that I would die, but I knew that I needed to live for Eva. I knew that I had to hold on so she could breathe her first breath and take her first steps. She needed my body for her own life, and I didn't have a choice but to keep breathing. I knew that I wouldn't let her go, even though the pain was sharp and endless, and the effort was excruciating. I held on tight long enough to hear her cry for the first time. When I heard the sound of her tiny cries, like the mewing of a small kitten, I let myself go into the bright light that absorbed me with warm comfort.

For the first time I could remember, I was at peace.

I knew that I had to be dead and I accepted it, but when I opened my eyes again, I was alone in Eva's nursery and somehow I had been spared. The pain from the accident was gone and as I picked her up, gently and carefully, she fixed her large blue eyes on me. She knew that I was her momma and I held her close, breathing in the smell of her fresh, soft skin. This was the moment I had waited for my entire life. This was the brief moment I had with my first-born, Sophie, before she died. With Eva, I knew there would be so many more moments like this and I reveled in the thought of living a life where nothing mattered except absorbing her sweetness and watching her grow.

The years have passed by quickly with no sign of Adam or anyone else that had been important in my life. I don't know where they've all gone. The accident took them away and I wish I had gotten a chance to say good-bye. They have abandoned me, and my heart aches for a day when they might return. Nothing makes sense other than Eva, not even this house that I put so much of my heart and soul into. When I look through the rooms there are no windows or doors and no way in or out of this place that I loved so much. Even my sweet half-brother, Noah, who I was entrusted to care for, has gone, and so has my beloved grandmother. I'm sure Adam has moved on and so have my best friends, Kelly and Jane. The only person I get to see is Eva, but there is no one in the world I would rather be with than her.

Though it's lonely when she is gone, I'm thankful I get to live in this strange and disjointed existence. The world is a different place than I imagined it would be, but I can't complain because I should have been killed.

Every day, I realize that I'm exactly what I've always wanted to be. I'm awake and alive and able to be what I've always wanted more than anything.

Eva's mother.

Saving Eva

3

The Bride
~Eva

I awaken slowly to see Eva standing at the end of my bed, dressed in white and beautiful, even in the haziness of sleep. She is small and breath-taking, her long, dark hair soft against the whiteness of her dress. Her blue eyes are bright and she instantly brightens when she sees that I'm wake.

I rub my eyes, waiting for the drowsiness to fade as I take in her floor-length gown and long veil. Her outfit doesn't make sense to me and I strain to remember what I must have forgotten.

At age ten, the thought of Eva getting married is ridiculous, yet the dress seems to fit her perfectly with its long train and fitted bodice. It seems that her age never matters because her personality is always the same, her mind mature, as though she is the adult and I'm the child.

"What are you doing, Love?" I ask, sitting up slowly so I won't get dizzy.

"I'm practicing, Momma," Eva says, smiling with her beautiful, full lips and perfect, white teeth.

"What are you practicing for?" I ask, confused.

"I'm practicing for when I get married. I want to make sure that I look good in all white and that my dress fits me well." Eva looks at me as though this makes perfect sense as she stands up slowly and makes a few twirls around the room.

I sit up completely, my back screaming, and swing my legs over the side of the bed. I rub my neck trying to ease the painful tightness that never goes away. The accident has left me broken and suffering in ways I never imagined, but I'm determined to get up every day for Eva.

"Well, Love … by the time you get married you're going to need a larger dress because you'll be much older and this one will be too small," I say, aching to reach out and touch her long dark hair.

Eva stares at me, her cheeks turning red with embarrassment. "Oh … well, I thought I would practice. I mean … I've never worn a long dress before and … I just thought I would practice so I wouldn't look silly."

I look at her small. dainty feet in her clean, white shoes. "I don't think you'll have to worry about that, Love. You're beautiful and will always look good in anything."

Eva smiles at me, a strange expression on her face that is a mixture of sadness and something else that I can't decipher. Unexpectedly, I watch as tears well up in her beautiful eyes.

"What's the matter, Love? Why are you crying?" I grab her and pull her in as close as I can, enjoying the soft fragrance of flowers that seems to emanate from her silky hair.

"I miss you, Momma. I just … want you to be here when I get married."

"I will always be here for you, Love. Don't miss me. I'm here for you now." I take in her sadness and am confused by her words.

Eva is quiet as she continues to cry, wiping the tears from her face., She never takes her big blue eyes from mine.

"Momma ... but ... you aren't always here," Eva looks at me earnestly as she says the words gently.

"I know that the medicine makes me confused and tired, Love, but I'm doing the best I can. I can't help it sometimes, but I promise that I will be here for you when it matters the most."

Eva sniffles and looks as though she wants to continue crying, but she pushes back her tears for my benefit. "I know, Momma. I know that you could've died and left me. I know that. Sometimes, I just want to be selfish and be like the other kids ... and ..."

Eva is quiet as she looks at me shyly.

"And what ... Eva?" I ask, unsure of where she is going.

"Never mind, Momma. It's okay." Eva sniffles again as she wipes the tears from her eyes. "I'm happy you are with me now."

I reach for her and she falls into my arms and I know that nothing in the world will ever stop me from being there for her every day of her life. Nothing will stop me from being at her wedding. Absolutely nothing.

4

The Wedding
July 15th, 2016

The young woman sat at her vanity slowly brushing her long, dark hair. She stared into the mirror for a long moment, her pretty face a mixture of excitement and sadness.

She tried to hold the tears back, but she couldn't no matter how hard she tried. *This is a happy day!*

She reminded herself that it was supposed to be a joyous day; the happiest day of her life. Sadness didn't belong, although, she knew that it would be there no matter how hard she tried to fight it. It had been there her entire life. It was there on her first day of school, when she got her first bra, when she left for her first date, at her senior prom, at both of her graduations, and it was here now. The sadness was a part of her no matter where she went or what she did. And she knew that it would be there on her wedding day, alive, and as palpable as ever.

Will it ever go away? She sighed.

She had asked to be alone. Too many people were milling about, in and out of her room, trying to be too helpful. There was too much noise and no time to think. She needed to think. She needed to reflect. She needed to feel *her* here.

She knew that she couldn't do that through all the noise.

She walked to her window and looked out into the garden. There were a lot of people, mostly her family, friends and those who were obligated to be there because of her name, but there were none of his. This was part of their bond … their loneliness. She held her breath. *So many people!*

I just want to get through this without crying, without ruining my makeup.

There was a gentle knock on the door.

"Eva, Are you ready?"

"Almost," she said straightening up. She reached up and felt her floral headband to make sure it was still firmly in place. She took a deep breath and opened the door.

It was Aunt Jane who had come back for the big day. Eva was happy that she was there, but sad that she would have to leave immediately after the wedding. Eva missed her so much, but knew that Jane had her own family to take care of now.

Jane's eyes immediately filled. "Oh sweetheart, you look so … so …"

"It's okay, Aunt Jane," Eva smiled. She knew what she was going to say because Eva had been thinking the same thing, too. Except for the color of her eyes, she was nearly the spitting image of her Brynn. "I look like my mother."

Jane nodded, choking back the tears. "Yes."

"Shall we?" Eva said motioning toward the door where she knew the staircase was waiting to take her to her groom.

"Oh, yes," Jane said trying to compose herself. "I told myself that I wouldn't cry, but I just couldn't help myself. I'm so sorry."

"It's okay." Eva hugged the older woman who had been so much like a mother to her. Eva had begged her father from the time she could remember to let go of her mom and find another wife. She desperately wanted a mother, but he refused. Even now he just said that he was too old, even though he wasn't. She just wanted to see him happy once in her life.

They started down the long, winding staircase. Daddy was standing at the bottom of the stairs waiting for her.

"I'm going to sit down, Sweetie. I'm sorry that I can't stay after the ceremony, but I have to get back home. Call me after you settle in." Jane hugged Eva firmly but gently, planting a soft kiss on her forehead like she used to when she was a little girl. "I miss you and I love you."

Eva blinked back tears and whispered, "I love you." She had promised herself that she would do her best to only cry happy tears today.

"Oh, Eva," Adam whispered, his deep, blue eyes sparkling and wide. He was seeing what she had seen in the mirror. "You're a vision, you know that, right?"

Eva nodded. *I wish she were here with me!*

Eva had never known Brynn, but yearned for her with an endless ache. Even though she visited her every day, she had never heard her voice or looked her in the eyes. Her mother had been taken from her in a violent car accident with a drunk driver. It had been a horrific accident, and Brynn had been kept alive for a couple of months afterward solely for the purpose of allowing Eva to continue growing in Brynn's womb. Eva had been told many times that she was lucky and easily could have been killed in the accident. But being without a mother was so lonely that there were days she wished she had.

Nobody understood the emptiness she felt without her mother.

Nobody. Until she met Chris.

"It was a miracle that you lived and were healthy after all that you went through," Daddy had been telling her for as long as she could remember. He wanted her to understand how lucky she was and to live her life to the fullest. The mangled picture of Brynn's car was burned into her brain. The twisted blue metal, the shattered windshield, and the bloodstains that nobody thought she could recognize. They stayed with her like a bad memory, haunting her when she closed her eyes, reminding her that she should feel lucky even though she didn't.

Nobody understood the echo that resounded deep within her without her mother there to guide and love her. She loved Adam, but living with him was like living with a ghost. She grew up in the big, empty house virtually alone with Daddy, and for a short time, Uncle Noah.

She knew that she had loved Uncle Noah even though she could barely remember him. Adam told her that he died so that he could be with Grandma Amy, who had died of a broken heart after Brynn's accident. Eva hadn't known Grandma Amy, but she hoped wherever they were now that they were together and no longer lonely without the ones they loved.

Now that she had Chris in her life, she wasn't lonely anymore. He had come into her life out of nowhere and pulled her out of the depths of darkness, truly sweeping her off her feet. He hadn't even pushed her into sleeping with him and was always a gentleman, keeping a respectful distance. He knew she was an inexperienced lover. The first time they had given into their longing for one another, he had seemed almost embarrassed about it afterwards. They had fallen in love quickly, and Eva was a mess of emotions when she realized she was pregnant. The baby bonded their rapidly growing relationship and, within a couple of months, they became engaged, with an entire life planned out for them. Eva was relieved not to be alone any longer and she seemed truly happy for the first time in her life.

"Are you ready to do this?" Eva said looking at her dad who looked handsome in his tuxedo. For a moment, she could see him as he had been as a younger man and sadness crept into her heart. The gaunt, aged man who stood in front of her reminded her that she hadn't been the only one who had lost. She took a deep breath and gave him the biggest smile she could.

"I'm ready," Adam said, smiling back at her. It was a rare, but genuine smile that made her want to cry with happiness. He had suffered so much and it hurt her heart to see the permanent sadness etched into his face. His smile was like seeing the sun for the first time, and she felt herself instantly lighter as she gripped his arm tightly.

Normally, she thought he resembled Eeyore from her *Winnie the Pooh* stories, his hair more white than the dark hair of his youth, his blue eyes lost and unfocused, and his words slow and often dismal. But today, she saw a little bit of the man he must've been, the one who had captured Brynn's heart as he stood in front of her, combed and polished in a tuxedo that fit his slender build, his blue eyes bright with excitement. As they stood, prepared to make the walk down the aisle, she took a deep breath, trying to exude enough joy and happiness for the both of them.

The walk down the aisle was breathtaking. The backyard of The Harper House had been transformed into a beautiful scene for their wedding, the sweet smell of orchids in the air. Many of the elite had come to wish her well, even though she had never met most of them. It was the cost of being a descendant of James Harper, founder of Harper Enterprises, and heiress to a very large fortune. She felt beautiful, like a princess with her handsome prince waiting for her. Chris was wonderful and she tried to imagine that her mother would approve of him. Eva often talked to Brynn, telling her about Chris just as she had spent her entire life, telling her mother every detail and secret, even though she didn't know if her words were ever heard. It made Eva feel better to tell Brynn anyway because nothing seemed real until the words had come out of her mouth and fallen into Brynn's ears.

The moment that Eva met Chris, her loneliness began to disappear. He was larger than life and filled her days and nights with laughter and happiness. She couldn't believe how lucky she was to have met him and she hoped that the child growing inside of her would have her blue eyes and his beautiful blonde hair. She envisioned a house full of tow-headed children running around creating chaos and joy, finally bringing The Harper House to life the way it deserved; the way James Harper had hoped it would one day be. As she walked down the aisle she thought about those things, happy to have met someone to spend the rest of her life with, promising her that she would never be alone again.

The ceremony was as beautiful as Eva hoped it would be. Their kiss was full of affection and passion, and everyone in attendance stood up and cheered as they walked down the aisle Mr. & Mrs. There had been whispers about how quickly Eva had fallen for her handsome, young gentleman, but when anyone saw the love between them, there was no question that they were meant to be. Chris was clearly smitten with Eva, holding her, touching her, and taking care of her every chance he got. He was the perfect, doting young husband, and it was clear that they were deeply in love.

As they walked up the long staircase preparing to dress for the reception, Eva held Chris' hand and told him that she needed to make a stop.

"I'll be quick," she said kissing him sweetly on the cheek.

He nodded at his beautiful bride knowingly. "Do you want me to come? I don't mind at all."

"No, later," she said kissing him gently once more, her lips lingering on his as she allowed herself to bask in the love that passed between them.

He smiled at her, his beautiful hazel eyes sparkling as he gazed at her, his lovely bride. She felt special and cherished in his eyes and she hated being apart from him even for a few moments.

Eva walked down the quiet hallway to the room at the end.

She opened the door and peered in. Kelly looked up at her and smiled. "Are you official now?"

Eva nodded and Kelly hugged her tight, a guilty look passing over her pretty face as she pulled the bride to her. "Congratulations! I'm sorry, Honey. I wanted to come down, but I would have felt guilty leaving her all alone."

"I know." Eva smiled. Kelly had been there nearly every day of her life for as long as she could remember. She had taken care of Uncle Noah, and then after Brynn's accident, she had stayed to take care of her. Even though Kelly was married, she was devoted to the Michaels family as though it was her own. With a husband she rarely talked about and children who were grown, Kelly had become more family than she was an employee. Before the accident, Brynn and Kelly had become close, and Kelly was as devastated as everyone else. Eva couldn't remember a day without Kelly in it, and loved her almost as much as the mother she missed every day. "How is Mom today?"

Kelly looked down at the bed. She shrugged and gave Eva a small smile.

"She's the same ... as every day," she said sadly.

Eva sat on the side of the bed, careful with her long gown. She kissed Brynn's scarred cheek as she held her lifeless hand. "I did it, Mom. Chris and I are married now. The ceremony was beautiful and you would've loved it. I wish you could have been there and seen it."

Brynn's body was still except for the up and down of her chest rising from the breathing machine. Eva hated that she had to live like this, but Daddy refused to let her go. Brynn had never changed him from being her Power of Attorney when they divorced, and he always had the final say. Eva hated watching her lie so still and helpless like this. She had never known her mother, but she knew enough about her to know that she would hate this existence! Aunt Kelly and Aunt Jane had told her that she would rather have just died, but neither of them could convince Daddy to let her go.

"She's a shell, Daddy! She shouldn't have to live like this. Why can't you just let her go?" Eva had begged him time and again, the frequency of her pleas increasing as Eva grew older.

"I can't let her go! I need her and what if there's a small chance that she'll wake up one day? I can't let her go, Eva. It's not that easy! You just don't understand what we've been through!" Adam argued with her and anyone else who fought him. "She could come back. It happens! There's activity on the brain monitor from time to time, which means she's in there somewhere. I've abandoned her before, and I'm not going to do it again!"

They had nearly lost her on several occasions, her body and organs atrophying with lack of use, but every time Adam made them bring her back, hoping she would fully return to him, though it was clear to everyone but him that she never would.

Brynn's body lie small and motionless on the bed. Her muscles had deteriorated in her arms and legs with lack of use, even though Adam insisted that Kelly massage and exercise her limbs daily. Although the scars on Brynn's face had faded over the years, her cheeks were sunken in and she was barely recognizable against the pictures that Eva had seen of her. Eva was proud that her mom had been breathtakingly beautiful and was thankful that she resembled her.

Brynn was full of tubes for feeding and monitoring, the big machine next to the bed taking every breath for her, but Eva had learned to tune the noise out. She had been coming to talk to her nearly every day of her life, even though there was a part of her that knew it wasn't really her mom lying there. Brynn's body was simply an empty shell, a faded vision of the beauty that she once was in a lifetime Eva had never known. Eva was ashamed to admit that all her life, part of her wished that Brynn had just been taken away permanently when the truck hit her car. Watching Brynn lying in the bed, wasting away and helpless, was sometimes more than she could bear. It was torture to have her mother there beside her, but not with her.

"I wish that he would just have let her go," Eva said quietly, more to herself than anyone, as she had so many times. Kelly thought about how beautiful Eva looked in her wedding dress and how Brynn would've been so proud of her. She tried to ignore the pain in her own heart as she gazed at Eva, her big, blue eyes overwhelming the face that reminded Kelly so much of Brynn's beauty.

"I know. I do, too," Kelly said, trying to disguise the anger from her voice as she always did when Eva brought it up.

The monitor hooked to Brynn's brain waves blipped and both women looked at the same time.

"That's why," Kelly said shaking her short blonde bob. "He thinks she is still in there, waiting to come out at any moment."

"What do you think?" Eva asked again, a question she often asked Kelly, even though she already knew the answer.

"She's been gone since the moment that truck hit her," Kelly said soberly. "You know that, Eva. We've talked about that many times before. You've got to let go, too, Honey."

They sat in silence, the world outside of the doorway moving rapidly without them, preparing for the large reception.

"Don't you have to get to your celebration?" Kelly asked finally shaking herself out of her reverie, and shuddering deeply as though trying to dismiss a sad memory.

"Yes," Eva sighed, slowly getting up but wishing that she could stay. It made her feel morbid, but she liked sitting here. She liked hiding with her mom. She hated it every time she had to leave and this time was no different. "I suppose that I should go now and get ready for the reception.

"Bye, Mom. I'm going to my reception now. I'll stop back and visit before we leave for Europe. I know that I've said this before, but we'll be gone for two weeks," Eva said, bending over to kiss Brynn's forehead. She smoothed Brynn's faded brown hair across her forehead gently, allowing her fingers to graze her skin.

She hesitated for brief moment and then leaned over and whispered something in her ear so that Kelly couldn't hear. Kelly thought it was strange that Eva would feel the need to whisper when she knew that Brynn couldn't hear her. Eva usually told Kelly everything and she felt the slightest pang of jealousy. She shook it off, reminding herself that Brynn was Eva's mother and not her. Kelly had children of her own that she adored, but she smiled softly, thinking not for the first time, that she would've loved having Eva as a daughter.

Eva stood holding Brynn's hand, unaware of Kelly's admiration for her in that moment. She hated leaving Brynn like this, but she knew that she had to ... she had been leaving Brynn all her life, but this time when she left, she knew that it would be for good. She was a married woman and would have a life of her own waiting for her when she got back. She knew she should be happy, but something about it seemed empty without her mother.

Eva walked slowly toward the door and opened it.

"I love you, Mom," Eva said trying to make her voice sound happy. *If there is a chance she can hear me, I want her to know that I am happy.*

She closed the door behind her and leaned against it for a long moment as she took a deep breath.

She heard the music playing down the hall and knew that her guests would be waiting patiently and wondering where she was. Eva didn't want to keep them waiting, but she felt guilty walking away from the room. With a heavy heart she forced herself to do it.

Eva turned around and walked toward her new groom, her new life, and her new happiness. She knew that is what Brynn would have wanted.

Kelly watched the door close behind her and sighed. Her heart hurt for Eva every day. It was sad watching her grow up without Brynn. She had tried to help as much as she could, but she knew that she could never fill the void in Eva's heart. Kelly could've left a long time ago, but she couldn't leave Brynn. She spent hours with Brynn, talking to her, reading to her, watching the lines on the monitor and praying for a miracle. But she had given up on miracles a long time ago.

She stood up and cracked her back feeling every bit her age. The room was too dark and she walked over to the curtain to let some light in. "Well, Brynn, your baby is married. You should be very proud," she said staring out the window wishing her friend understood what she was saying.

Suddenly, Kelly froze.

She could tell that someone was in the room with them. She could feel it.

The hairs went up on the back of her neck and she turned around slowly. She scanned the room, feeling as though someone was watching her. She stood stock still, not daring to move. Time passed slowly and the sensation eventually disappeared.

She chuckled at herself for her foolishness and sat back down in the chair next to Brynn's bed. *This house is getting old and I'm getting old.*

"Brynn, we're getting old, girl," she said glancing over at the lifeless body of her friend, knowing that she wasn't going to answer. She looked at Brynn not believing what she was seeing.

"Oh my God, it can't be!" she whispered, jumping up out of her chair, her heart racing wildly in her chest.

When Kelly looked at Brynn, all she could see were her huge, brown eyes staring right into hers.

5

The Flashback
~Nick
April, Ten Years Earlier

Nick had never been able to get Brynn out of his mind completely no matter how hard he tried. Even his therapist couldn't explain it or help him, and he had all but given up on the idea that he would ever be able to forget her.

The night he was supposed to meet with Brynn ten years prior continued to haunt him, even in his dreams. Even years after he had moved on past that tragic night, divorced his first wife, Melanie, and then remarried once again he was never able to purge Brynn from his mind. He couldn't forget how he had waited for hours at the winery where they had their first date, anxiously watching for her to arrive. When she never did, he called her phone repeatedly, getting nothing but her voicemail. And when he finally drove to The Harper House at eleven thirty that night, knowing in his gut that something was wrong, he was alarmed to see that most of the lights in the main house were on. He rang the doorbell, a knot in the pit of his stomach, and was greeted by a sweet housekeeper who introduced herself as Beth.

He noticed immediately when the older lady opened the door that her eyes were puffy and rimmed with red, which filled him with immediate dread.

"Yes? Can I help you?" she had asked politely, seemingly unfazed that it was 11:30 at night.

"I-I-I was hoping to see Brynn," Nick said, barely able to get the words past the huge lump in his throat.

"And you are ..."

"Nick. I'm Nick. I'm a friend ... of Brynn's."

At the mention of Brynn's name, Beth let out a quiet sob and backed away from the door, putting a well-used tissue up to her face as she let Nick in.

He walked in the door and immediately felt sick to his stomach.

"Please, sit," Beth said, leading him into the kitchen and pouring him some tea without bothering to ask if he wanted any.

"Where is Brynn?" Nick asked, anxiously waiting for Beth to talk. He thought about the last time he had been with Brynn, both of them holding one another, healing each other, and barely able to let the other go.

"I'm s-s-sorry," Beth said, sniffling and wiping the tears from beneath her glasses, reminding him of his favorite aunt. "It's just that ... I'm not good at this, and I don't even know if I'm supposed to be telling you anything ..."

"Please, tell me. She was meeting me tonight and she never showed up and I've been calling her cell phone all night, so please ..."

"Oh, *you're* Nick!" Beth said as though seeing him for the first time. "Oh, goodness. I'm so sorry."

Beth tried unsuccessfully to stop herself from crying.

"Please," Nick grabbed the older woman's hands. "Please tell me, where can I find Brynn?"

"Brynn is in the hospital. It was a horrible car accident ... and she m-m-may die, her and the baby ..." Beth continued to cry. She didn't notice when Nick released her hands.

"The baby?! What baby?" Nick said, his voice barely audible as the words sunk in.

"Oh. You didn't know about the baby?" Beth said, her gray eyes wide with alarm. "Oh, I'm so sorry. I didn't realize you didn't know that she was pregnant ..."

"Should I know? I mean ... do you know if I should know? Is the baby mine? Did Brynn say anything about the baby being mine?"

"Please, you have to talk to Kelly, or to John Palmer. I shouldn't have said anything about the baby." Beth was even more upset now than she had been when Nick rang the doorbell. He worried that she might pass out.

Nick sat down in a chair at the kitchen counter with a thud, his head spinning with a thousand thoughts that he couldn't put into words.

Beth's voice was suddenly close in his ear as she leaned toward him, concerned about the expression on his face. "Are you okay?"

"Yes ... I just ... I ... need to get to the hospital. I need to see Brynn."

"Oh ... Okay, but ... I don't know if that's a good idea. I mean, you're welcome to go if you'd like but ..."

"But what?" Nick was running his hands through his hair in frustration.

"Well ... it's just that ... Adam ... her hus ... ex-husband will probably be there," Beth said, her face red.

Nick had never met Adam. All he knew was that Adam had broken Brynn because, before him, Adam had been her only love. Nick wanted to pummel Adam for hurting Brynn the way that he did, but he knew that confronting him in the hospital wouldn't help anything. He wasn't even sure if Adam would know who he was and what he meant to Brynn. Telling him in the face of such tragedy would be cruel.

Nick debated about whether or not he should go to the hospital, and while he did that, he realized he felt more lost than he had ever been, even in his own disastrous marriage. Ever since he had met Brynn, she'd changed him and he found himself thinking about doing things that he never would've imagined doing before.

He looked at Beth for a moment, unsure of what to do and hoping that the kind, older woman would be able to give him some kind of answer. Her face was full of only sadness and no wisdom. Nick hugged Beth quickly and walked out the door. He sat in his car for a long moment. He was unsure about which direction he should go and tried to decide if he was brave enough to go to the hospital and make his claim over Brynn, even during the worst moment of her life.

Determined, he drove toward the hospital, remembering how he had passed it on his way to The Harper House. He knew that if he didn't go to her now that he may never. As he drove he imagined facing Adam and an uncertain future with Brynn, and he felt his resolve waver as he tightened his grip on the steering wheel. As the exit for the hospital began to appear he suddenly switched lanes, his car careening dangerously off the opposite side of road, his heart pounding in his ears. As he sped toward the airport, he picked up his phone and booked a flight home, his voice shaking as he felt a strong sense of self-loathing and disgust for his cowardice.

A week later, unable to think of anything else, he called The Harper House and asked for Beth who eagerly told him about Brynn's coma. Even though she knew she was giving him far more information than she should, the older woman had seen how heartbroken Nick had been. He made it a monthly habit to call and talk to Beth who was always willing to tell him as much as she could until one day, there was nothing new to tell. The story became the same month after month, and he finally stopped calling altogether.

His decision to walk away from Brynn haunted him day after day.

After his disastrous divorce from Melanie, and then losing Brynn, Nick met and married a sweet woman who loved him more than life itself. Despite the fact that he was never able to return her affection at quite the same level, his sweet wife, Fiona, loved him with all of her heart, even giving him a beautiful daughter, Amanda. Nick gave it every effort to completely love his wife and daughter, but he couldn't escape the coward that stared back at him from the mirror.

He could never truly forgive himself for abandoning Brynn and hiding inside a life and a love that he never felt he deserved.

6

Waiting
July 15th, 2016

The years passed slowly and painfully for Adam Michaels. There were moments when he ached for the courage to end it all so he could finally have the peace he longed for. If it hadn't been for Eva, it would have been easier, but he knew he couldn't leave her.

He had raised her the best way he knew how, though he was admittedly lost and unsure of himself in every way. But he had made a difficult decision a long time ago to be there for her and he knew he had to do everything he could. He owed it to Eva and to Brynn. Adam knew he would've made a complete mess of it if it weren't for the help of Brynn's best friends, Jane and Kelly. *Thank God for them* was his daily mantra as they were always available at a moment's notice to help with any womanly crisis that Adam didn't know how to handle.

Jane had raised two daughters of her own, and ran the restaurant that had been Brynn's. She had done it so well, expanding it into a mini-chain, each restaurant unique, each one successful and bearing Brynn's signature passion for food and hospitality. Brynn had saved

Jane when Jane was a single, young widow with two young girls and nowhere to go. And in turn, Jane had saved Brynn when Adam had left all those years ago and Brynn had nobody else to turn to. Jane was still saving Brynn, by helping to raise Eva while building a thriving business that continued to grow. Jane knew that Brynn would have been so proud of her and she missed her friend daily. As Eva grew, Jane saw more and more of her in the little girl, which pleased her. Jane loved Brynn like a sister, and had developed a soft spot for Eva, the girl who had fought her way out of the womb to live. She loved Eva nearly as much as she loved her own daughters.

Kelly had been the one Adam called when Eva started to become a woman and had questions about boys and her body. A nurse and care-giver, Kelly was gentle and nurturing, and was able to ease Eva's fears. Kelly was like family, agreeing to stay on in the huge Harper House to take care of Brynn, even long after sweet Noah, Brynn's half-brother, had passed away.

Ellie, Brynn's birth mother, had reappeared in Brynn's life and urged her to meet and care for Noah, but Brynn had been reluctant and untrusting. Ellie had abandoned both of her children on separate occasions, replacing her love for them with her incessant need for the drugs and alcohol that consumed her. Ellie finally succumbed to the drugs that ultimately destroyed her, leaving Brynn to care for Noah.

Noah had been slow to develop from birth, but had the heart of an angel and Brynn had instantly loved him. He had the sweetness of a child in a grown man's body and they formed an immediate connection. The adjustment to life in The Harper House had gone surprisingly well, brother and sister bonding as though they had known each other all their lives. Noah had not lived a long life, but Brynn had filled it with happiness until the accident. She filled the void in his life that Ellie never could.

With Ellie, the sole heir to the Harper fortune, gone, The Harper House was passed down to Brynn, as well as the majority of the fortune from Harper Enterprises. Run by a trusted family friend, John Palmer, Brynn was free to rebuild her relationship with Noah and her grandmother, Amy.

But after the F150 plowed into Brynn's car and Brynn was left in a coma, Amy and Noah's health deteriorated as well. Brynn had been their rock and their purpose and without her, neither was able to hold on for very long. Amy died first, followed a few years later by Noah. Adam felt guilty, knowing that Brynn would be disappointed in him for not being able to save them, just as he hadn't been able to save her.

Daily, Adam recalled the last time he had spoken to her. Brynn had been pregnant with Eva, and had refused to acknowledge that the baby she was carrying was Adam's. He had been angry as he stared into Brynn's dark eyes, more strange and distant from him than he had ever seen. He knew that he had betrayed her trust and love so many times that he no longer had any right to expect her to love him, though he desperately prayed for it every day.

Brynn had even gone so far as to try and convince him that she had slept with someone else, but Adam hadn't believed her at the time. He was convinced that Brynn had never been with anyone other than him. Adam had been her love since they were fifteen years old and there had never been another. Adam had done the math and knew that the timing worked with the last night they had been together. Their passion and pain had fueled their need for one another like nothing they had ever experienced together before, but when it was over, she had pushed him away, this time for good.

He knew the baby had to be his and he was excited and desperate for her to acknowledge it. He knew that he should've admitted to her that he'd never signed the divorce papers, but he was afraid. He had been the one to initiate the divorce. He'd been the one who left her, after he swore to her that he never would again. His drinking had changed him into a man he never imagined himself to be, but even after they sat at the lawyer's office and divided everything up, signing most of the papers, he hid the last paper that he was supposed to sign, refusing to make it real.

When he realized Brynn was pregnant, he knew it would be a good time for him to finally admit it, but he couldn't. Her big, beautiful eyes had always disarmed him. That time had been no different, even as she stared at him coldly and told him the child she carried wasn't his.

Adam couldn't blame her for her fear. After they lost their first child Sophie as a newborn, Brynn was never the same. She separated herself from him almost completely. He had gotten lost in his drinking until Brynn was completely out of reach. The drinking had been a deal-breaker in their marriage, the love between them dissipating because of it. Adam knew that no matter how much he drank, or what he did, he could never get Brynn out of his heart.

Adam had been walking down the stairs to Eva's reception when he heard Kelly shrieking from the hall. His heart froze and he wondered for the hundredth time if he was about to lose her forever. He raced back up the long staircase, nearly barreling Kelly over outside of Brynn's doorway. Kelly grabbed his hand and dragged him down the hall to Brynn's room where she suddenly froze.

"I-I-I'm sorry, Adam. I don't want to ruin the reception. If it's not true, don't tell me I'm crazy, but I swear … I saw it." Kelly stammered, her sweaty hands making Adam feel uncomfortable.

"Saw what?" Adam asked, his head spinning and his heart pounding wildly in his chest.

"Her eyes, Adam. Her eyes …" Kelly struggled to form a clear sentence.

"What about her eyes?" Adam was growing impatient, trying to walk into the room, but held in place by Kelly's strong nurse's hands.

"They were … open." Kelly's voice was nearly a whisper and Adam's blue eyes grew wide.

"W-w-hat do you mean?" Adam said, struggling to get the words out.

"Her eyes were open," Kelly said, trying to decide if she could believe it herself. "They were staring right at me … Brynn was staring right at me."

Adam froze, wanting to believe her, but also terrified that it might be true. He had dreamt for years that she would awaken, but he lived in fear that if she did, she wouldn't love him and would ultimately send him away. He was used to having her with him even if she was lying motionless in bed, unaware of the world around her. He always knew where he could find her and that was his comfort.

Adam knew that he hadn't always done right by her. The drinking had separated them and Adam knew that Brynn would never be at peace with it after what Thomas had done to her. Brynn hadn't told him *everything,* but he knew that her adoptive father had been cruel to her. The nightmares she suffered through for so many years hinted at some of the horror she had experienced as a young girl. Adam cringed with guilt at the memory of how he had almost hurt her in his own drunken stupor until ultimately, there was nothing else between them and they had agreed to divorce. But he always dreamt that he would win her back even though he knew he didn't deserve her.

He stepped cautiously into the room and walked to Brynn's bed. He looked down at her small, frail body, the feeding tube trailing from below her gown and the ventilator connected to her mouth. She had been nothing but an empty vessel for so many years and Adam felt the familiar weight crushing his heart every time he looked at her. The whooshing of the ventilator was the only noise in the room, and Adam found comfort in the familiar sound of the machine that breathed for the woman he had loved for nearly four decades.

His heart was pounding wildly in his chest as he tried to decide what to do next. He looked down at her face, at the scars left by the broken glass of the windshield that had faded with time. He thought she was just as beautiful as she had been so many years ago, and he tried to imagine that she was merely sleeping.

His heart stopped as he realized she was looking right at him, her big brown eyes beautiful, but blank.

"Brynn?" he said, his voice barely audible. "Brynn? Are you there?"

Brynn's eyes continued to stare at him, not blinking, not moving.

Adam was afraid to breathe, his mouth dry as he tried to say her name again. "Brynn ... Brynn."

He thought that if he stared hard enough she might blink at him, but she didn't. Her eyes were fixated on him, yet empty, her body still tiny and motionless on the bed.

He was unnerved as he felt a shiver run down his back. Seeing her stare at him was eerie, and he hated himself for wanting her to close her eyes again.

"Kelly, call the doctor. We need her to be seen right away. This can't wait!"

Kelly nodded slowly and stepped out of the room to make the call.

As Kelly stepped out, she thought she heard Adam stifle a cry. She sighed in pity for her friend. It wasn't the first time she had ever heard him cry for Brynn and she knew in her heart that it would unlikely be the last.

7

Sandcastles
~Brynn

"**Y**ou stupid bitch! You don't know anything. You're a complete idiot." I lie huddled on the floor, waiting for the boots to kick me in the side. He was never one to use a belt or a paddle. He liked to use his feet and his hands because he liked the feel of my flesh as he struck me. He liked to watch my face screw up in pain as his words tore deep inside of me, leaving a permanent mark. I tried not to show him how much his ugly words hurt me, but they always shredded me to the core. The pain cut as deeply as his blows would sting, even though I'd learned to just lie still until he was done, when he finally thought he had hurt me deeply enough.

"You stupid bitch, you stupid bitch." I don't know how many times he'd said that to me during my childhood, but it never seemed to be enough to satisfy him. He didn't ever seem to tire of tearing me down and I felt my insides begin to shrink until there was nothing.

I knew that is what he thought, that I was truly nothing. The look on his sour, ragged face told me so every day when he was alive.

Even now I try to move away from him, but I can't. And even

though I know that he's been dead for decades, I can still see him in my mind as though it was yesterday. His watery, blue eyes full of venom and hatred toward me for stealing the love he thought that only he deserved are burned in my brain. He thought my adoptive mother, Rose, would somehow learn to love him, yet he didn't realize that beating and abusing her would never inspire love. I could still see his ragged fists going at her, punishing her for not loving him until he was finally too sick to even go near her at all.

I try and release myself from the memory, but my mind won't let go. I think desperately about the only person who can save me at a time like this and I invoke the vision of my little Eva with her long, dark hair and big, blue eyes. I know that Eva can save me from the misery of the past that I have tried to let go of without success. Even though I tried to hide from him, Thomas always seems to seek me out. It's as though he knows that I am helpless against him.

"You stupid bitch, you stupid bitch." Thomas haunts me, his words echoing cruelly in my head.

Like magic, Eva appears out of nowhere, almost as though she knows exactly when I need her, and in an instant, Thomas has disappeared and she is solid in my arms at just the right moment.

"Momma," she says hugging me close. I hold her tiny body in my arms and I feel my heart rate begin to return to normal. "Momma, why are you upset? Don't be upset. Let's go to the beach."

In what feels like an instant, we are on the beach and I look down to see my feet buried in the warm, soft sand. The sun is hot and bright and I wonder how many times we've been here together before. Eva is only about five, but she seems to be so much older, guiding me to a spot where our blanket, umbrella, and lounge chair are already set up and waiting for us. "Momma, sit."

I obey.

I always listen to Eva because somehow she seems to know exactly what I need and when I need it. I look down at her dark, shiny hair and lean over to kiss the top of her head, absorbing the warmth of it on my lips.

"I love you, Eva," I say, lingering close.

"I love you, too, Momma." Eva smiles up at me, her blue eyes bright. "Sandcastle?"

I follow her to a spot in the sand where an entire landscape waits for us to build something magnificent. We toil for hours in the hot sun, shoveling and shaping, careful to preserve our hard work with our meticulous fingers. We work in silence, and every once in a while, I catch her staring at me with a look that I can't quite read, so I smile at her and then she smiles back. She has my face nearly down to every detail, only slightly more delicate, with eyes as blue as the sea. She is beautiful and I can't believe that it's possible to love someone so much. Sophie, my first daughter, lived for only a few hours. I loved her, but my love for Eva is crushing and heartbreaking, and I can't even begin to explain the gravity of it.

We build for hours until the sun begins to fade and the sky begins to dim. The sandcastle is a masterpiece and she works with the patience of someone far beyond her short five years. I don't know how the day has passed so quickly without food or water, but somehow it has. The beach has been empty all day except for the two of us, but I can't complain. I've had Eva to myself all day and any day with her is so much more than I could've ever hoped for.

"Momma," she says, her voice musical and tiny as it always is. "Do you love me?"

"Of course!" I respond to her, shocked that she would even ask me something so obvious. I reach out and tuck a strand of her windswept hair carefully behind her ear, the smoothness of her sun-kissed cheeks mesmerizing me as my fingers sweep over them. "Of course I love you, Eva."

"Then why are you still here? Why can't you just let go of me and move on?"

I don't understand her question.

I look at her lovingly but something about her question creates a sudden emptiness in the pit of my stomach.

"I'm here for you, Love. I'm here because I've been spared so that I can live this life with you." She leans and puts her forehead against mine and closes her eyes.

I stare at our sandcastle and it's a masterpiece, intricate in every detail and far more beautiful than anything I'd ever built before. I am amazed that we are able to create something so massive and beautiful in one short afternoon.

Most of all, I marvel at her.

I don't know how she grew to become so beautiful and so incredible, but I know that it can't be all me.

"Momma, I want to go home now. I'm tired," Eva says, standing up and wiping the sand off her bathing suit.

"Yes, Love. We can go home." I'm tired, too. I look around once again for another living soul, but there is no one to be found. I should be used to this by now, but I always look anyway, hoping there will be someone else so that I will know that this isn't just a dream.

"Daddy must be waiting for me," Eva says, smiling at me sadly.

"Yes, I'm sure he is." I give her a quick squeeze. "We don't want to worry him."

"We did good, Momma," Eva says, surveying our castle, her eyes bright and full of pride.

"Yes, Love. We did very good."

I stand up and Eva grabs tight to my hand. We walk toward the sun and the bright light nearly blinds me. I'm not quite sure where we are going, but somehow, we always seem to be walking toward the light.

"Momma," I hear Eva's tiny voice. "I love you."

"Yes, Eva Love. I love you, too."

8

The Visit

September, Ten Years Earlier

For years, the memories became stronger and Nick realized that he could no longer live with himself and the day that he had driven away from Brynn after her accident.

Even though he had gone on to start a new life, Nick still drove to the scenic Harper House year after year and sat outside of the large gate, punishing himself for his cowardice. He sat for days simply waiting and watching out of morbid curiosity to see if he could catch a glimpse of Brynn. Something twisted within him looked forward to the annual pilgrimage toward the love that he had never claimed, yet mourned as though it had been his for a century. Something about his life had never felt as complete as the moments when he had held Brynn in his arms, inhaling her sweet smell and stroking her thick, soft hair, her beautiful brown eyes seeking his out.

Even though he told himself he would, Nick couldn't find the courage to walk up to the front door of the house and ring the doorbell, asking to see her.

It wasn't until during the tenth year of his pilgrimage and years of sleepless nights that he found it within him to walk up to the front door and finally attempt to see her. In all his visits, he had never seen a car leave the gates of the house and he often wondered throughout the years whether she ever left or was even able to. When he knew that he could no longer live without seeing her, he decided that he didn't have a choice—Adam or no Adam.

Even though the gates were usually closed on previous visits, it was almost miraculous that they were open on the day he decided that he would finally see her. He drove down the long driveway lined with trees and woods, marveling at the beauty that surrounded the large house. He took a deep breath and, for a moment, he wasn't sure that he could go through with it. The house was intimidating and beautiful and he thought about how much it reminded him of Brynn. He knew that he would never again be able to live with himself if he drove away now. After standing on the large, wraparound porch for fifteen minutes fighting the urge to run, Nick reached up and rang the doorbell. The door opened immediately, startling him, as though someone had been expecting him. He found himself staring down at a younger version of Brynn with the bluest eyes he had ever seen.

"Hello?" the girl said cautiously.

"Hi," Nick said, clearing his throat.

"Hi ..." The girl moved backward a step.

"I'm Nick ... I uh ... was a friend of Brynn's many years ago, and I was hoping I could visit with her."

The girl looked at him strangely and Nick suddenly realized he was staring at Brynn's daughter. His mind began to race. He'd imagined meeting her many times and couldn't help but stare, searching her out for any sign of himself.

"If Beth is here, she can confirm who I am." Nick added, nervously.

"Beth died," the girl said simply, lingering with the door half-open, hesitant to let him in.

"Who is there?" a man's voice came from behind the girl, echoing throughout the house.

"A man ... Nick," the girl responded, never taking her eyes off him.

"Who?" the voice changed, sounded angry, and Nick instinctively took a step backward. Nick heard heavy footsteps pounding rapidly behind the door, then found himself suddenly face to face with Adam. The girl disappeared as she stepped back behind him.

"Who are you?" Adam demanded, his deep, blue eyes bloodshot and rimmed with red, his hair disheveled. Nick could smell the alcohol oozing from his pores and, for a quick moment, Nick felt overwhelming sympathy for him.

"I'm Nick," he replied, trying to keep the shakiness out of his voice. "I'm an old friend..."

Adam cut him off. "I know exactly who you are and you need to leave."

Nick knew that he should've been more prepared to face Adam and was immediately defensive. "No. I'm here to see Brynn and I'm not leaving until I do."

Adam took a forceful step outside, suddenly standing within two inches of Nick. Even though Nick was tall and lean, and used to towering over most people, he was surprised with how closely they stood eye to eye. Nick had never met Adam before and realized they could match each other physically. He could feel Adam's contempt and, without thinking about it, he realized that his fist had balled up, ready to defend himself. He hadn't been in a fight since high school, but Nick was confident, the adrenaline pumping through him.

"I said that you need to leave," Adam repeated. The only thing Nick could smell was bourbon, and Nick realized that Adam was drunk.

"I need to see Brynn," Nick said stubbornly. "Listen, I know this isn't what you want to hear, but we were going to be together. Brynn ... wanted to be with me, man. What we had was special and we were ..."

Suddenly Nick's jaw exploded with pain. He struggled to stay upright, stunned that he never saw the punch coming. Anger coursed through him and he tackled Adam to the ground, both of them rolling around on the porch until Nick realized that they were falling down the front stairs. They landed on the ground, Nick's back absorbing the brunt of their fall as he struggled to push Adam off him.

"This isn't helping anyone!" Nick yelled the best he could, winded from the fall as he blocked Adam's punches. Despite being drunk, Adam's blows were coming at him surprisingly fast.

"It's helping me," Adam snarled angrily. "Brynn is my wife. You need to leave her alone."

"You divorced her," Nick said catching Adam off-guard with a right hook to the eye. Adam fell to the ground, howling.

"Daddeeeeeee!" Both men had completely forgotten about the little dark-haired girl who had been watching fearfully from behind the screen door. She ran out to Adam, hovering over him protectively as she stared up at Nick with anger and fear on her face. "Leave my daddy alone!"

"I'm okay, Eva. I'm okay," Adam said, slowly standing up. His hand covered his eye and a thick trail of blood trickled down the side of his face and on to his shirt.

"I'm sorry," Nick said seeing the blood and feeling guilty. He lifted his hand and fingered his jaw. It still radiated with pain. "I ... man, I just..."

"I know," Adam said staring Nick directly in the eyes. "I know what you want. But you can't ... you can't have her. She's *my* wife and she's everything to me. You can't ... you can't ..."

Both men stared at one another, nursing their wounds and wondering helplessly which man Brynn had loved more.

"Please, man. I just want to see her. I've come so far ... so many times. I just ... I just ... want to see her." Nick heard himself begging but he didn't care.

Adam stared at him for a long time, his dirty, bloody face watching the other man with a mixture of anger and pity. They had never met, but Kelly had slipped one night and told Adam about Nick. For months, Adam had seethed in anger at the thought of Brynn with another man. Brynn had tried to tell Adam about Nick, but he didn't believe. her, guessing that she was making it up to make him angry. He couldn't imagine his girl ever loving anyone else but him.

As much as he hated to admit it to himself, he recognized the sadness and desperation on Nick's face because he saw it every day when he looked in the mirror. He could see in his eyes that Nick had truly loved Brynn and wondered hopelessly if she had felt the same for him.

Adam looked down at Eva and knew that he didn't want her to see the ugliness and possessiveness that he was feeling inside.

After glaring at Nick for a few more moments, he sighed in resignation. He gestured toward the house without saying a word and waited for Nick to follow him. Unable to believe his luck, Nick dusted the dirt from his clothes and slowly followed him through the foyer and up a long flight of stairs. They reached a wing of the house that felt like a mausoleum, quiet and cold, and Nick shivered without realizing it. Adam opened the door slowly and waited for Nick to step in.

Nick was in shock, first from Adam's attack, now because he hadn't expected Adam to let him see Brynn. As soon as he entered the room he realized why Adam was allowing it.

He knew immediately that Brynn would have no idea that he was there, and he felt a sharp pain in his chest as he looked around the room and surveyed his surroundings.

He took a deep breath, surprised at the quietness of the room, and shocked by the machines that Brynn was hooked up to. The whooshing sound of one machine and the occasional hiss of another was the only noise. He rolled up the crusty sleeves of his once soft gray sweater, now filthy and stained, and sat in the chair next to the bed, choking back a sob at what he was seeing.

The woman in the bed barely held any resemblance to the woman he had fallen in love with nearly a decade before. He was angry with himself for taking so long to knock on the door, but he had been avoiding the truth. He thought about his bad marriages and realized this was a trait he had been fighting his entire life. As he looked at the sparse shell of the woman who haunted his dreams, he knew that ten years had been too long as the pit in his stomach became larger and his chest became tighter.

"Dammit, Brynn," he cried as he took her hand and put it immediately to his lips. When he looked at her he remembered her only as she had been the morning he left her all those years before. He thought about the last time he had kissed her lips and promised her that he would return. He kissed her hand, cold and lifeless, putting each finger to his lips one by one, remembering what it was like to have them linger on his back and his face as she had kissed him deeply. He had replayed her kisses in his mind for many years, and touching her brought them back to reality, even in her slumber.

"I'm sorry ... I'm so sorry that I ever left you and then never came back to you like I promised. I'm so sorry that I wasn't here to save you and be here for you. God, Brynn, I'm sorry for everything. Maybe if I hadn't left, this never would've happened, but I had to leave, I had to go home and take care of things and wrap up my life. I swear to you that I was planning to come back for you. I promise you." Nick held her hand, sobbing against it as he kissed her fingers over and over.

Nick waited and hoped for a miracle, his heart breaking in his chest as he stared at Brynn. She lie there, the only movement the rise and fall of her chest. He knew that if she opened her eyes at that moment, he would never go home again, even if that meant he had to figure out how to be a father to his daughter from a great distance. He knew that if he had a second chance, he would never walk away from Brynn ever again. He already knew the pain of living without her and without the promise of a life with her. Nick sat staring at her in silence, the image of her beautiful brown eyes staring deeply into him, locked in his mind.

He didn't see the small figure that had crept up behind him, staring at the tall man who had tears running down his face.

"How do you know my mommy?" Eva's small voice startled Nick who was lost in his own grief. He jumped as he wiped his face with the back of his hand and looked down at Eva who handed him a tissue without taking her blue eyes off him.

"We ... uh ... we were friends a long time ago," Nick said, shifting in his chair.

"How long ago?" Eva asked, unblinking.

"Um ... before you were born," Nick cleared his throat uncomfortably.

"Did you like her?"

"Of course ... of course I liked your mom." Nick was surprised by the question. "There's nothing not to like about your mom. Your mom was ... is ... a wonderful and amazing woman."

Eva looked at Nick, curious about the connection between the mother she didn't know and the stranger who sat next to the bed. It was the first outsider she had met who knew her mom and she desperately wanted to know more about him. She searched his face for anything familiar, never breaking her stare as he pretended not to notice. He watched her out of the corner of his eye, fascinated and amused by her curiosity. *Is this my daughter? Does she bear any resemblance to me at all?*

Even though she had Brynn's beautifully shaped face, sweet button shaped nose and large eyes, the eyes were blue like the color of the ocean. Nick thought about Brynn's beautiful coffee colored eyes and his hazel ones that he found to be far less captivating. *Can brown eyes and hazel eyes even make blue eyes?* He searched for pieces of himself in the girl, but couldn't produce anything that reminded him of himself.

Just as he was about to give up, he saw it. His breath caught. *My birthmark!*

On her right wrist, just above the bone, he could make out the faintest freckle. He stared at it, amazed, his eyes then drawn immediately to the same freckle on his own wrist. He sighed, his hazel eyes filling with tears. He had a nearly uncontrollable urge to grab Eva and hug her as hard as he could, but he knew that such a gesture would be strange and alarming. *Keep it together, Nick. Keep it together until you can figure out what to do.*

He smiled at Eva, his lip quivering.

He looked at Brynn and silently cursed. *Did Brynn know that Eva was mine? Why didn't she tell me that we had a child? Why would she hide that from me?*

But Nick knew. He remembered with embarrassment that he hadn't told Brynn that he was married. Melanie had answered the phone once when Brynn had called. Even though he had tried to explain to her that his marriage had been over for years and that his wife was a hopeless alcoholic, Brynn had been furious. He had broken her trust and she hadn't forgiven him easily. It wasn't until she had finally agreed to meet with him did he see a spark of hope. She'd never made it. She'd been on her way to meet him when the accident occurred.

Tears flowed down Nick's face at the memories. He tried to control himself, knowing that Eva was watching him closely. His tears were a mixture of regret and sadness for a life and a daughter that he had never known, and he wondered how he could ever be the same again knowing that Eva was his. Suddenly, he felt her small hand on his arm and he smiled at her effort to comfort him. She smiled back a sweet, innocent smile and Nick's heart ached because all he could see was Brynn.

There was a buzzing sound in the quiet room that hadn't been there before, breaking through the peacefulness like an unwelcome visitor. The sound was loud and insistent. Nick looked around as he searched the room for the source and realized that it was coming from him.

He fumbled with his phone as he tried to pull it out of his pocket. His heart dropped like a rock as he read the message.

Come home as soon as you can.
Mandy's in the ICU.
Accident. Please come, we need you, honey.

Nick stood up abruptly, startling Eva who had continued to watch him intently.

"I'm sorry, there's an … emergency. I have to go right now." He looked down at the bed, torn, his heart ripping into a thousand pieces.

He leaned over the bed and put his lips close to Brynn's ear, careful not to let his words be heard by anyone else.

"I don't know if you can hear me. I don't know if you're still in there, but I'll come back for you, as soon as I can. I'll come for you and Eva. I promise."

He kissed her gently, first on the forehead, then on the cheek. He knew in his heart what he needed to do and he tried to ignore the pounding of his heart and his head.

"Tell your ... dad ... that I have to leave ... but I'll be back. I promise."

"Why are you leaving?" Eva asked, surprised by the suddenness of his departure.

"I just have to get home right away. There's been an accident." Nick turned the doorknob and gave Eva a long look, an expression on his face that Eva had never seen on another human being. "I'll come back as soon as I can."

Eva thought that it sounded like a promise and she wondered why this stranger was making such a promise to her.

As he turned and raced down the stairs, he hoped that he wouldn't run into Adam again. He made it out of the house unseen and sped toward his car, a heavy sense of dread falling over him as he picked up the phone and dialed.

"Honey!" Fiona's frantic voice on the other end made Nick's skin feel like there were a thousand pins ready to prick him. "Where are you? Come home, soon."

"What happened? Is Mandy okay? Why is she in the ICU?"

"There's been a terrible accident and I don't know if she's going to make it. She needs her daddy. You need to get home soon."

"What's wrong, Fiona? What happened to her?"

The silence on the other end of the line made him begin to panic.

"Just come home, Honey ... Mandy needs her daddy."

Nick hung up the phone, barely able to steady the wheel of the car. He drove away from The Harper House and headed toward the airport. A sinking feeling deep within his stomach told him that it would be the last pilgrimage he would ever take down this road.

9

A Miracle
July 15th, 2016

Kelly sat next to Adam in the waiting room, both of them silent, wrapped up in their own thoughts and memories. The reception had been ruined, and Eva and Chris had cancelled their honeymoon. The ambulance came and all the guests had filtered out quickly and respectfully. Eva had begged to come to the hospital, but Adam had refused. He didn't want his baby girl in the hospital on her wedding day.

"Daddy, please!" Eva's eyes were full of tears as she held on tight to his tuxedo shirt, makeup running down her beautiful face.

"Eva, no! This is your wedding day and your mom would not want you to spend it in the hospital. I promise you, I will call you or send for you as soon as I know anything. You've already cancelled your honeymoon. Please." Something in Adam's voice made Eva stop fighting. She adored her dad and knew everything he had sacrificed for her. She could never defy or hurt him, no matter how strongly she felt.

"Okay, Daddy." She said, her voice losing its fight. "I'll wait for you to call."

Adam was always surprised at how easily she gave in. In that way, she was more like him than like Brynn. He always expected her to fight him tooth and nail, like her mother always had, but Eva had been raised in a safe and comfortable environment and didn't know what it meant to truly have to fight for what she wanted. As much as he admired her tenderness, he always found himself a little disappointed that she wasn't more like Brynn.

Adam had kissed her tenderly on the forehead, and then jumped into Kelly's waiting car.

As they sat in the hard chairs in the waiting room of the hospital, Adam pushed every bit of hope down as far as he could. He had been disappointed before and as he got older, he found that it became more difficult to get over. He gasped audibly as he wiped a single tear from the corner of his eye. *God, I wish I could have just one drink*, he thought, wishing desperately the day would come when he no longer had that thought.

He felt Kelly reach over and grasp his hand. Her long, cool fingers immediately comforted him. As he looked over at his friend, she smiled at him reassuringly and he remembered a time, many years ago when she had been more than a friend. There had been a time when he had found Kelly in his bed. He had allowed her to comfort him for a short time, with her smooth, soft skin and kind heart while Brynn lay down the hallway barely clinging to life. Kelly was a beautiful woman with crystal blue eyes. Her naturally blonde hair complimented her delicate features, and she had an ever-present smile. She had been a comfort to him, but eventually, the guilt had overtaken him, and they decided to end it amicably, both of them finding the comfort they needed in one another. As she sat next to him, their minds preoccupied with other things, he knew the connection from many years ago had died and he felt silly for even resurrecting it in his mind. He smiled at her, holding her gaze for a little longer than me meant to, hoping she couldn't read anything in his eyes.

Both of them jumped as a phone on the wall that neither had noticed before began to ring.

Kelly hesitated for a moment and when Adam didn't stand up to get it, she raced over to it, anxiously.

"Yes, we are Brynn Michaels' family. Yes. Yes. Okay."

She turned to Adam, her face serious. "They want us to come back to the room. They want to talk with us."

Adam took a deep breath. The doors buzzed and opened, allowing them access into the locked wing. He followed Kelly down the hallway to the ICU, their steps in sync. As they got closer, Kelly put her hand on Adam's back and tucked her hair back behind her ears, a gesture she often made when she was nervous. "It's going to be okay," she said, softly.

Adam nodded, unable to respond. His heart was beating wildly in his chest as they approached the room that Brynn was in. He imagined her sitting up and awake, waiting for him. "Where have you been? I've been waiting for you," he imagined her saying, her tone matter-of-fact and disconnected as she had often been during their marriage. Adam felt a pang of guilt. He knew that imagining her in a negative way was a coping mechanism. At least that's what the shrink had told him.

This is not what he found as they approached the room and walked in. He saw the ventilator first, and then saw that Brynn was in the same state she had been in for the last twenty-five years.

"Why isn't she awake?" Adam demanded to everyone but no one in particular.

Kelly put her hand on his arm to calm him. He looked at her angrily. "She's supposed to be awake! Where is she? Why isn't she awake?"

"Please! Stop yelling. Are you Mr. Michaels?" A young nurse that didn't even look old enough to be out of high school approached him and put a calming hand on his arm.

Adam jerked away from her, angrily. "She was awake when I brought her in here! Why isn't she awake now?"

"Please … I mean, I don't know," the young nurse stuttered, taken aback.

"Get me your supervisor!" he said, spitting as he spoke. "Now!"

The young nurse scurried off, terrified.

As she ran out of the room, Eva ran into the room, nearly running the nurse over. Her long, thick, dark hair still tightly bound in her up-do, long wisps just beginning to escape.

"Eva … Dammit! I told you not to come!" Adam looked at her, his mind racing and his words jumbled.

"What is going on with Mom?" Eva asked, ignoring him and grabbing Adam's arm. "What did you do to that nurse?"

Eva could tell by the expression on the nurse's face that Adam must've done something to upset her. She had seen that expression on many nurse's faces before when he wasn't being told what he wanted to hear.

"She … just … nevermind. Dammit! You know how it is!" Adam was frustrated. He pulled on his collar even though the top three buttons were open on his tuxedo shirt. "Why aren't you at the house with Chris like I told you?"

"Daddy, how could you try and make me stay away?" The determined look on Eva's face reminded Adam of Brynn and he was pleasantly surprised to see it.

Adam put his head in his hands and cried. "Your wedding day. Oh God. I'm so sorry, honey."

"Daddy, stop! You always over-react. Just calm down. You would think by now you would know how to act in the hospital!" Eva's tone surprised Adam and for a moment he caught a glimpse of Brynn, strong and commanding, taking control of the situation like she used to. He always admired that about his wife, running her own business and taking care of those around her all while hiding her own secret battle.

Adam sat down in the chair next to the hospital bed and grabbed Brynn's hand, stroking it gently, carefully. Eva stood next to Kelly, their arms around each other's waists as they all settled in, waiting.

Adam looked up suddenly as though he had a thought. "Where is

Chris?" he asked, suddenly realizing that Eva's new husband wasn't here.

Eva hesitated.

"What is it, Sweetheart?" Kelly said, noting Eva's pause.

"I was going to wait to tell you, but ... we've decided to move into The Harper House. We want to be close to you. *All* of you." Eva's voice was low and barely audible.

Kelly smiled and paused, trying to hide behind her own blue eyes. She always wondered if Eva knew what happened between her and Adam. She felt the old guilt resurfacing anytime Eva seemed to refer to them as a family. Kelly had once longed for a day when Adam could openly sweep her off her feet and declare his love for her, but she knew that it would never happen. His true devotion always belonged to Brynn. Kelly had long since given up on Adam. She'd stayed married to her husband, the time she spent with Adam a beautiful distraction from her young marriage. And when the children came, she spent the years raising them, splitting time between her family and Harper House. Still, she had never fully devoted her heart to her marriage. Finally, when the children went to college, her marriage became one of convenience only, and Kelly moved in almost full-time at The Harper House, telling herself that her marriage didn't matter to her any longer. She only went home when the children were in town on break.

Kelly knew deep down that it never would've worked between her and Adam. Her own love for Brynn would never have allowed her and Adam to be any more than the faint memory of two lovers who had once buried their pain in one another, hoping to forget.

Adam was speechless. "But ... I thought ..."

"We changed our minds, Daddy. We've decided that it's just time to move in. We knew we would end up in The Harper House eventually, so we thought we should do it now." Eva was careful with her words, not wanting to give anything away. She knew how sensitive and volatile Adam could be, and she didn't want to upset him anymore than he already was. Purposefully, she peered at him through her long lashes, unwilling to let him see directly into her eyes. She knew he could read her just as clearly as she could read him, and she wasn't ready to face him with the news quite yet. He looked beaten up and broken and her heart cracked for him. She wished for the day that he could be as young and carefree as he had been in the pictures taken of him and Brynn years earlier. Eva thought it strange that her mother never looked quite as carefree as Adam did, but Eva had heard bits and pieces of Brynn's life from eavesdropping as a child. She knew that from a young age, Brynn's life had been full of sadness and pain.

"I'm happy to hear that, Eva. I just want you to be happy. When I asked you before, you said Chris wanted the two of you to live on your own, so I didn't think you'd be moving into The Harper House so soon." Adam tried to hide his relief. He never wanted Eva to leave The Harper House, but knew that it would be wrong to pressure her. Eva needed to make her own choices, as difficult as it was to admit it. While he liked his new son-in-law, Eva had been his one constant and he wasn't sure he was ready to let her go yet. Adam was comforted knowing that Eva would remain under the same roof, and he suddenly realized how much he had relied on her throughout the years.

"Thanks, Daddy. I'm excited! Chris left to get a few of his things to move in. He thought he should do it while everyone was out so he wouldn't be in the way." Eva reached over and hugged Adam tight. The Harper House had been all she had ever known and she wasn't ready to leave. Chris understood that, and she adored him for it.

Eva's phone beeped and she jumped up, excitedly. "It's Chris," she said, bouncing out the door, forgetting for a moment where she was.

Kelly smiled at Adam. "Young love."

"Yes," Adam nodded. "Brynn and I were like that once. Or were we? I don't remember."

"I'm sure you were, Adam. She loved you very much," Kelly said, patting his hand. She wasn't sure she telling him the truth. She had only known Brynn, and then Adam, separately, never together. She had loved Brynn and they had become fast friends, but, like most people in Brynn's life, Kelly was never allowed completely in. After the accident, Kelly learned more about her friend than she had ever known when Brynn had been awake. Brynn was always guarded with the deep contents of her heart and her past and Kelly's heart had broken for her friend who had endured such painful solitude her entire life. Kelly never truly knew if Brynn still loved Adam at the time of her accident, though she knew from Jane there had been a time when she had loved him as completely as she knew how.

Just then, an older man with salt and pepper hair and a matching moustache entered the room. His black-rimmed glasses were perched on the end of his nose, his thick hair jutting out wildly, almost as though he hadn't combed it. Despite his frazzled appearance, Kelly thought he looked respectable enough, though she doubted that Adam would think so.

Adam and Kelly stood up as the doctor entered the room and walked directly over to Brynn. Without looking at either of them, he picked up her hand and felt for her pulse, his eyes squinted tightly in concentration. He let her wrist fall gently onto the bed. He then opened her eyes, one at a time as he peered into them intently, searching as he flashed a little light into them that he pulled from an unseen pocket.

"Hmm," he uttered to himself. He shook his head and looked confused.

"What?" Adam said, his voice loud, unable to contain himself any longer.

"You said that she was staring at you?" the doctor asked, staring directly into Adam's eyes. His gaze was so intense that Adam immediately began to fidget uncomfortably.

"Y-y-y-es," Adam said, melting awkwardly under the doctor's gaze.

"I've seen her scans, sir," the doctor said, moving over to a mini computer station and logging in with a few clicks. He paused and cleared his throat as his eyes flicked back and forth, searching for something on the screen. "I've seen her scans ..."

"Yes?" Kelly asked, frustrated with his fumbling.

"And for her to wake up at this point after her body and brain have been atrophying for as long as they have ... well, it was more than likely just a ..." the doctor paused, looking at Adam and Kelly who held onto his every word.

"For her to wake up, what?" Adam cut him off angrily, pulling on the collar of his shirt again.

"With the brain activity on the reports, for her to wake again ... and I hate to be the bearer of bad news, but it would truly require nothing short of a miracle."

Adam stared at the doctor blankly.

"I don't think you have any idea what you are talking about!" Adam's voice rose with each syllable.

"Adam!" Kelly grabbed his arm.

"No! He doesn't know her, Kelly! He doesn't know us! He has no idea about Brynn and what she's been through in life. She's a fighter and a survivor. You don't get it. She can get through this and she can wake up! She *will* wake up! She has to!"

Adam's body fell against hers and Kelly reached over to hold him up. She looked at the doctor apologetically.

The doctor had a small, sad smile on his face as he walked out of the room. Kelly thought she hear him mumble, "I'm sorry" on the way out.

She felt the weight of Adam's head on her shoulder as she tried to ease him back into his chair. "Adam ... maybe it's time you just come to terms with the fact that she's gone. Maybe you should just let her go. Would she want to live like this? Would she want *you* to live this way, waiting for something that's never going to happen?"

"But you saw her, Kelly. You saw her eyes open. You saw her! You know she's in there! I could tell when we were at the house that you thought she was there." Adam pleaded with her, desperate for any sign that she might believe him.

"We've been through this before, Adam. She's just ... she's gone. She's been gone for a long time. Don't you want to live ... truly live?" She raised her hand to his cheek and placed her palm against it, gently. She wanted so much to caress it, but she had been down that path before and knew that it would only bring her misery.

"I bet you're sick of me, aren't you?" Adam mumbled, his voice barely audible as he buried his face against her shoulder.

"No, of course not. I ..." Kelly stopped herself, trying to disguise the sadness in her voice. She pulled him close and felt his body fall against her as it had so many times before.

As she stared at Adam, weeping against her, she fought the emotion that welled up inside of her like an enormous rolling wave, tossing her heart back and forth. She had been adept at keeping her feelings in control for many years, but as time went on, she knew that it would take a miracle to keep her from walking away from him.

The same kind of miracle that would bring Brynn back to him.

10

Adam
~Brynn

I can see Adam down on one knee with the ring in his hand and that hopeful smile on his face. I can still see his beautiful, youthful face and hear the tremble in his voice.

"Adam, we're only seventeen ..." I protested, knowing that I was creating excuses because I was terrified.

"Well, will you?" he asked, his expression hovering between fear and hope, unsure of which it would land on. He wasn't sure if I would say 'yes', and neither was I. I loved him and he knew that, but I wasn't sure that I was ready to give the rest of my life to anyone yet.

I just didn't know.

"Do you believe in marriage?" he asked me early in our relationship when I thought we were way too young to even consider it.

"No ... I mean ... I don't know. I want to ..." I thought about Thomas and Rose and how theirs had been the only marriage I'd truly ever seen from the inside out and it made my stomach turn. "You know, I didn't exactly have the best role models ... like you did."

Adam flushed. He knew that his parents were the opposite of

mine, who were the worst parents possible. He'd expressed guilt for having such great parents, which I always dismissed. It wasn't his fault he'd won the lottery with parents and I hadn't. All I had known of marriage was hatred and pain, abuse and anger, withdrawal and cruelty. That's all I'd ever experienced. I didn't know if I could imagine being married. I knew that I couldn't imagine having a baby, but that didn't seem to concern him in the least. He was convinced that I would change my mind. He thought that his love, our love, was enough to change everything.

Well ... are you going to leave me down here all night?" I realized that Adam was still on one knee.

"I ... I ... I'm sorry, I just don't ..."

Adam stood up, kissing me unexpectedly on the lips, his mouth soft and tender against mine.

"It's okay." He said, closing the box with a sharp click, the pretty little ring tucked away safely inside. "You will. You know that I'll ask again and again and again until you say *yes*."

Slowly, this vision of Adam fades away from me and I can see him again, only younger and cute, barely out of his awkward stage, passing me notes in class.

He'd been watching me, his eyes bright and mischievous. I pretended not to notice as I watched him out of the corner of my eye. I don't know why I can see it all so clearly, so well. Those moments seemed to have disappeared from my mind like long forgotten photographs, tattered and torn at the edges, the color faded with time. I remember seeing him, so young and beautiful and strong, but I don't remember what he would have seen in me. I don't understand why he chose me when he could've had his pick of any of the other girls. He surprised everybody when he chose me. Nobody understood why he would choose the quiet, bookish girl who kept to herself and had only one friend. Stacy. They never understood what Adam saw in me and neither did I.

My clothes were plain, my hair was long and un-styled, and I had never had a boyfriend, or even had a boy who liked me. Adam seemed too good to be true, and for a while, I thought he was making fun of me. Boys like him just didn't like girls like me. Boys like him liked girls like Tricia Ross who were blonde, blue eyed, and pretty. Tricia Ross was the head cheerleader, the class president, and one of the richest girls in town. Her father owned the mall in the town over, and being with Tricia meant the best of everything. Boys like Adam didn't like plain, lonely girls like me, who had an alcoholic, abusive father and a needy mother.

Boys like Adam Michaels liked girls like Tricia Ross, not broken, worthless girls like me.

But after some time passed, I could see that he did love me. He was kind and patient, and he saw the real me even though I tried desperately to hide it from him. He looked inside to see into my heart no matter how hard I pushed him away. The night that I finally decided to open up to him and give him all of me, he saw the scars on my body, left there by the blade I used to lose myself. I had tried so hard to hide the scars from him for so many years and I knew that showing him might mean losing him forever. It was then that I had no choice but to let him know me in my entirety. For the briefest moment, he knew me completely, and I was painfully vulnerable to him in every way, which terrified me more than anything in the world.

He asked me to marry him again after high school graduation and then again two years later.

When he asked two years later, lying in bed, his hands tracing the scars from the cuts inflicted years before, I finally said yes. When the cuts were no longer tender to the touch and I realized that I no longer flinched when his fingers found the scars, I knew that I no longer had an excuse to say 'No.' He pulled the ring out of his nightstand and held it in front of him, his blue eyes imploring, boring into mine. For once, I didn't want to look away and I kept my eyes on his. It was the first moment when I felt that saying *yes* was the right thing to do. When I said it, his eyes became wide and more beautiful as they turned bright with his tears. His fingers were tender as he wiped the tears from my own cheeks and we fell together in a moment of complete oneness.

The vision disappears and he reappears in front of me, and is

SAVING EVA

replaced by an Adam that I never imagined, his eyes glazed over and barely recognizable, his speech slurred.

"You let our Sophie die ... You didn' wan' to be a mom and now sshhhee's gone because of you. It's all your fault. You've ruin-t us-s-s." His words sliced deep into my heart unlike any pain I'd ever felt before. Thomas had slapped and kicked me hundreds of times, but none of that compared to the pain of Adam's words as they echoed in my ears long after they left his lips. I knew it was the alcohol speaking but it was happening more often, his frequent apologies repeating hollowly in my ears until I could no longer hear them. His infrequent touch, empty and awkward, repulsive and apologetic became unwelcome. "You killed her, you let our baby die ..." His cruel drunken words echoed in my mind long after he had passed out, repeatedly cutting me deep down inside in the place I'd let only Adam see.

The moment is gone in my mind and suddenly replaced by Adam, his face worn and tired as he sat across from me in our lawyers' office surrounded by large, overly expensive furniture. His eyes are still as blue, but they are completely devoid of any promise or hope.

"You wanted this, Adam," I remind him. He looks at me, helpless and lost. "When Sophie died, you no longer had any hope. You chose this!"

He slumped in his chair, all the beauty drained completely from his face as he avoided my gaze and signed the papers, his hand moving slowly, his letters large and scrawling unlike his usual precise signature. I didn't want it to end this way and I didn't want to lose him like this after everything we had been through. He had been the one person I could count on, the only person I could truly call "family." He was everything to me, but then he chose his alcohol instead of me, and I knew that we no longer had any promise or possibility. He knew by taking that path that he was choosing the end of us. He was slapping me in the face because I allowed our baby girl to die, and nothing I could say or do would ever convince him that it wasn't my fault. I want to. Deep down, I knew that if I had wanted to be a mother more she might've lived, and I blamed myself, too. He had said it time and time again. He blamed me, and I blamed myself, for Sophie's death.

Even though she was only hours from the womb I loved her deeply. The doctor told us that there was nothing that either of us could've done to keep her here with us. I wanted to believe her, but I couldn't, and neither could Adam.

Adam stared blankly, all expression erased from his face as he refused to look at me, his voice low and trembling every time he talked. He served me with paperwork at my restaurant because he wanted out, and he didn't want to do anything more to preserve it. He had moved out once and then back in, and had promised he would never leave again. But then he did.

Then I allowed him to come back for only one night and we allowed the familiarity of our bodies to attempt to heal one another. When he wanted to stay for good I refused. There had been a sense of finality to our last night in each other's arms, and I was ready for the door to close on what felt was a lifetime of pain. This man that I had finally allowed to love me had betrayed me, and I was gutted.

I didn't think that I would ever know love again until Nick unexpectedly came along. Nick's beautiful hazel eyes with gold flecks that changed in the light, and his chestnut hair were burned into my brain, and I loved that he was completely different from Adam. Nick made me feel like I was worthy of love for the first time in a long time.

Then my car was rammed head-on while my belly was full with Nick's child, though Adam was sure that the baby was his. Adam had wanted us to have a baby so badly after Sophie died, but having another baby would never heal our pain. He loved the idea of having a family, but he could never forgive me.

Then Eva came.

I know that it must have been torture for him to watch me love Eva and spend time with her but, I must. I need to be with her and nothing seems right unless I am.

Even though it doesn't feel like real life, I will take every moment I have with Eva, as long as she will let me.

11

Baby

June 1st, 2016

"I told you, I can't stay," he said, his voice getting that edge to it that Nora liked so much. Hearing his voice like that gave her the urge to pull him down against her naked body again and have her way with him, like she had so many other times. As she started to reach for him he jumped away quickly, out of her grasp. "No!"

"But, I want you. Now!" she purred, her green eyes beckoning, her long lashes fluttering at him the way he liked. Very few had ever been able to resist her when she had looked at them this way, and he was no exception.

"I said *No*. She'll be waiting for me and I don't have a lot of time." He buttoned up the shirt that had once been crisp and white, but was now hopelessly wrinkled from laying on the floor in a crinkled mess. He frowned to himself and wondered if anyone would notice.

"Why do you care? She's so stupid she'll never know where you've been. She's never suspected anything and she's not going to now, Baby." Nora was angry, her bottom lip pushed out, her green eyes flashing dangerously. She was used to getting her way and he wasn't cooperating. She tried to entice him by grabbing his body with her long muscular legs and pulling him toward her, but he resisted.

"What part of *No* do you not understand? You're being ridiculous!" He wrestled himself away from her, his hazel eyes turning dark and hard. "We're not messing this up. She is our *one* chance to have what we want for as long as we want it! You have to get a hold of yourself if we are going to make this work."

Nora sat up letting the thin sheet fall from her body, revealing her beautiful, pale breasts that she knew he loved and could barely resist suckling.

"Fine. Have it your way," she said, standing up slowly and deliberately, letting him get a good long glance at her complete perfection. She walked lazily over to the bathroom and slowly closed the door making sure that his eyes stayed on her. Even after all these years she could still mesmerize him by a simple move. She smiled as she thought of how uncomfortable he must be in his pants now.

"Baby, I'm sorry." Almost immediately his muffled voice came through the door as she waited on the other side. "Please, Baby, open up. I'm sorry. I can stay for a little while longer."

Nora smiled to herself as she waited to respond. Power. She had it and she liked to use it to tease him. It still gave her a tremendous amount of pleasure, making him squirm uncomfortably, both sexually and emotionally.

She had been teasing men all her life, for as long as she could remember, and by the time she met *him* she was already an expert. Nora's momma had taught her well, and Nora had paid attention to what she did until it was her turn. The moment she saw Chris at school, she knew that she would need him one day, though she was not sure exactly how or why. He was hot and confident and she wanted him badly. She had been drawn to him with his thick, unruly hair and beautiful hazel eyes that turned dark when he was angry or passionate. She had spent a lot of time observing how he dated and discarded girls, easily and without much care or concern. She watched how cruelly and carelessly he treated those who fell for him, and she found herself uncontrollably attracted to him even though she knew that she needed to be careful.

She watched him, knowing that he hadn't even noticed her—because she hadn't wanted him to notice her. Not yet. She had been patient, taking her time, studying him like a specimen until she decided what she wanted to do with him.

She toyed and played with *him* until he fell in love with her, and then she tested him. She always tested the boys to see how loyal they would be. Most failed, but she knew that *he* would be different. Unlike the other boys she had been with who were innocent and pliable, she knew *he* had a mean streak and would be a challenge. The thought of it excited her more than anything ever had and she found him irresistible.

Having someone to challenge her made her almost giddy, but she reminded herself that she was the one who always needed to end up in control. She pushed herself farther than ever before, even allowing herself to fall in love with him, though careful not give herself over completely.

Their first months together had been seamless as she satisfied him without asking for too much in return., Carefully and intentionally she left him wanting so much more. She had lured him in, making him want her over and over, and two years later she still knew how to entice him to do whatever she wanted.

She never admitted it, not even to herself, but she needed him. Somehow along the way, he had become the reason she woke up in the morning. She'd watched how love destroyed her momma, and there was no way she was ever going to let that happen to her. So, Nora kept her walking shoes on at all times, making sure to take many lovers on the side so she didn't become too attached. She vowed early and often that she would never let anyone ever destroy her because she knew there was always an end to everything, and she was going to be ready.

"Baby, let me in or you come out. I'm sorry." His voice came through the door and Nora waited, patiently, until she pictured him sitting on the floor, completely miserable. Slowly, she opened the door and he nearly fell, all his weight completely against it.

"Baby, get up, "she ordered, pulling him up, careful to push her nakedness against him so he could feel her flesh. She liked being pressed against him, and she could tell from the tightness of his pants that he liked it, too.

"I'm sorry, Baby," he said, pulling on her long auburn locks. "It's just … I don't want to ruin this for us. It makes me nervous … and I don't want to lose you. "

"I know, Baby, but if I tell you that I need you, then I *need* you. Now. And you can't make me wait!" Nora put out her bottom lip and looked up at him, enjoying their little game. "I can't stand the thought of you being with her … and now there is no choice. You *have* to be with her. I hate it because you're mine."

"Yes, Baby. I'm yours. But this is what you wanted me to do. *This* is what we talked about me doing so you don't get to be mad about it. This is what *you* wanted me to do!" He held her body tight up against him as he struggled out of his clothes once again and buried his face in her long, thick hair.

"Do you like it? Do you like *being* with her? Do you like touching her?" Nora stroked his back with her long fingernails, sending chills up his spine.

"Baby, stop … don't ask things like that." Chris squirmed at the thought of answering her.

"Do you? Do you like it as much as you like being with me?" Nora pulled him hard against her as she licked his neck.

"Stop! You know that could never happen!"

Nora stepped away from him, her tone changing abruptly.

"Good. Don't forget it. Don't forget that in the end you're *mine* and when I call you, you're going to have to make an excuse. You're going to need to figure out how to get away. But you're going to have to do it carefully because you can't ruin this. You can't ruin any of it. Do you understand?" She grasped his thick hair in her hands and pulled on it tightly, making him moan.

"Yes, I understand," Chris said, losing himself in her touch.

"Do you understand? Are you listening?" Nora's voice had risen in an alarming way. Suddenly she reached out and slapped Chris as hard as she could, leaving a red mark on his cheek, catching him off-guard.

"What the …" Chris was angry and he resisted the urge to slap her back. "Don't slap me, Nora! You know that I don't like that."

"I'm sorry. Please, just don't leave yet. I want you to stay just a little bit longer. I'm so sorry I slapped you, Baby." Her voice was husky and her lips were red from biting down on them and trying to squelch the fire that was burning for him, deep down in her belly.

He bent over and covered her lips with his, unable to resist any longer.

"Of course, Baby. I'll stay, but then I have to go back and I have to work the plan like we agreed." He panted as he pulled away from her for a moment, his eyes wild with desire.

"Yes, Baby. You'll have to do whatever you need to do, but then you're coming back to me. Do you understand?" She pulled back and looked at him, her green eyes searching his. "You're mine, *Christopher*. You understand this, don't you?"

"Yes, Nora." Chris crushed his lips against her as she moaned against him, pressing his chest against her soft breasts, then finally filling her up as she surrendered to him. "Always."

12

Home

July 20th, 2016

After days of observation in the hospital, they moved Brynn back home and settled her into the beautiful, lavish room that had been hers since the accident. A comfortable, plush couch positioned by the large bay window was where Kelly often sat for countless hours as she read to Brynn or watched T.V with her.

The night nurse, Anne, was more formal, refusing to sit in a comfortable chair or sleep or eat while she was on duty. Even though Adam and Kelly tried to convince her to get settled in and relax, Anne refused. She was old-school and felt it was her duty to be more professional.

For the first few days, Kelly, Adam, and Eva took turns sitting by Brynn's side as they looked for any sign that she would wake up again. Chris came and went, bringing them food on their shifts, doting on and rubbing Eva's back, sore neck, and shoulders. Kelly watched them with a twinge of jealousy, wishing briefly that she hadn't alienated her husband so much. She had pushed him away so often that he would never consider rubbing her neck now. Her husband was rarely home anymore, always travelling for work, or taking little trips to who-knew-where by himself. Kelly slept alone at The Harper House most of the time, and she had convinced herself that it was what she wanted. Still, as she watched Chris and Eva with a sad smile on her face, she wished that her life had turned out differently.

The familiar sound of the breathing machine filled the room as they sat and waited for something to happen. As they settled into the mundane routine of the previous two decades, they nearly forgot that Brynn had opened her eyes and stared at them. Even Adam, who was beyond the point of exhaustion, gave up hope that Brynn would ever awaken.

"I'm tired. Really tired, Kel," he said, stumbling toward the door when Kelly walked in to care for Brynn on the fourth day. "I need sleep. A lot of sleep."

Kelly nodded, understandingly. "Get as much sleep as you want, Adam. I don't know that anything is ever going to happen here, as much as we would like it to." Kelly had been caught up in Adam's enthusiasm and the disappointment of knowing that Brynn wasn't really in there was depressing.

Kelly took a deep breath and ran her fingers through her thick, blonde hair. She didn't need to look in the mirror to know that she had bags under her bloodshot eyes. She had barely been sleeping herself, unable to get Brynn out of her mind. Even when she lay down to sleep, she couldn't escape from her thoughts. The doctor had given her tranquilizers for occasional use, to calm her nerves, but she was using them more often than she thought she ever would.

Kelly sat in the chair next to Brynn's bed. Her heart felt like the weight of the entire world sat on her chest, and she tried breathing as normally as possible. With Adam out of the room, she felt the intensity begin to dissipate as she settled into her well-worn chair next to Brynn's bed. She had been sitting with Brynn for so many years that she couldn't imagine doing anything else. She had read countless books, magazines and on-line articles, often reclassifying her recipes and keeping herself occupied as best as she could.

She looked over at Brynn and sighed.

"Brynn, I don't understand why you don't wake up. I know you're in there. I didn't believe Adam, at first. But now we sense it and feel you. We've seen you, for God's sake! Yet, you won't wake up which is so frustrating! It just doesn't make sense."

Brynn lie completely still; the only movement the rising and falling of her chest as the machine pushed air in and out of her lungs. Kelly's eyes filled with tears and she shamelessly allowed them to fall, the exhaustion flooding over her.

She sat next to Brynn's bed and grabbed her hand. Brynn's early life had been difficult. She never allowed anyone to see the pain she held close unless her guard was down and it accidentally spilled out. Kelly was amazed by the transformation that Brynn made when she was with her and Jane, seemingly more vulnerable and innocent when it was only the three of them together.

Since those early years, Jane had moved with her daughters and husband to the West Coast, closer to her ailing mother. Brynn's successful restaurants were sold and turned over several times since then, much to Kelly's dismay. She knew that Brynn would've been disappointed. Jane had been the backbone of the operation since Brynn had turned it over to her and it had broken Jane's heart to leave, but with her mother's failing health, she had no choice but to move.

Kelly stroked Brynn's hand, talking to her friend as she had so many times throughout the years.

"I want you to wake up, Brynn. You were my only friend, the only one who really understood me. I've been so lonely without you."

She paused, waiting for a response and was greeted with nothing but silence.

She continued. "When Philip started to take his trips, you understood. You urged me to divorce him, but you knew that I stayed for the kids because they loved their father so much. You told me that he would only continue hurting me, and you were right. Then I realized that when he was gone, it was a blessing more than it was a curse because I was able to stay here, with you. I rarely saw him and when I did I was indifferent because he didn't care about me either, and I realized that I was fine with that."

She looked at Brynn's face, waiting for a response or a reaction of any kind.

"You were the only person I was ever able to talk to about that. You were the only person who understood and listened. You had been through so much more than I ever had and you comforted me. I loved you for it. You were my only true friend and that's why I've sat by your side year after year. But now, we're convinced that you're in there and you just won't come out. I've seen it … I've seen your eyes open and I need you to open them again. Please Brynn, open your eyes again. Please."

Kelly put her head down, holding onto Brynn's hand tightly, refusing to let go.

She placed Brynn's hand on her own forehead, relaxing against the coolness of Brynn's palm as she closed her eyes. She sighed and let herself melt against Brynn's flesh.

She felt the tears welling up in her eyes as she had so many times throughout the years during times like these.

"You always told me I could do better and that I deserved better and I never believed you. When I finally did, it was too late. It was too late."

She cried freely, the tears wetting the sheets, running down her hand that was intertwined with Brynn's.

She sobbed, her body heaving up and down, oblivious to the big brown eyes that had opened and were staring down at her.

13

Momma

~Brynn

I watch as they bring Eva to me, tiny and pink, howling as they lay her on my chest.

It's as though my life swims around her without reason, or even a natural timeline, and while I know that it must be the damage in my brain, I am thankful for anything that reminds me that I'm alive.

When I get to hold her for the first time, I remember what it's truly like to be a mother. I let Sophie go. I promise that will never happen to Eva.

I was alone as a young child and all I yearned for in life was a mother. After my birth mother, Ellie, abandoned me on the side of the road, my leg mangled and broken, Rose adopted me. Though she thought she loved me, she simply used me as the balm for her own loneliness. She saw my abandonment as the perfect recipe for healing her own pain. As a child, I had been thankful for anything other than lying on the side of the road. That was until the beatings came.

I realized much later that Rose had done the best that she could, but I was still angry with her for not protecting me better from the physical and emotional scars that never go away. I wore the physical scars collected from years of cutting myself in an attempt to take away the pain. Those were hidden from everyone but Adam, and later, my lover, Nick. The emotional scars were disguised from the world, nobody every truly understanding my secret pain.

I watched Rose die and then found out later that she had poisoned her husband to defend me. Unfortunately, it had been too late. The horror was woven into the fabric of my being and into my dreams.

But holding Eva allows me to forget.

I look down at my beautiful baby and the world shrinks to every tiny part of her face and I am in love. I spend hours counting her long, beautiful eyelashes one by one and when I lose count, like I always do, I start all over again. I gently touch her tiny fingers and toes, marveling at their perfection, and giggling when she reflexively pulls one away. Every breath she takes makes me hold my own, and as she lays her head on my shoulder, her face only inches from mine, I am intoxicated by her beauty. In all my life I never imagined that love could be this simple and complex all at once.

I know that I could stay this way forever as I run my fingers gently over the top of her head and try and remember a time when I have ever touched anything so soft. I can't. With each sigh and gentle sleepy smile, I am drunk with love for this little person who has consumed every thought and every breath.

She is beautiful in every way and she never cries. She never requires anything more than to be held, and even when she is awake, all she does is stare at me with wonder and fascination at the very sound of my voice.

I know that nothing in my life will ever make sense more than the baby in my arms. She has given my existence a purpose.

14

Nora

June 1st, 2016

Nora showered slowly, reveling in the feel of the water on her naked skin.

She thought about Chris and how she loved having him wrapped around her little finger. She could make him do anything she wanted him to do, even when he didn't want to. She languished in the power she had, smiling as she thought about how easy he was to manipulate, though it hadn't always been that way. She had to fight to break him down and when she finally did, she wondered if she would get bored with him. It had been two years and he still kept her interest, even though she hadn't given up other men completely and had become an expert at hiding it from him.

She got out of the shower and towel-dried her long, wet hair. She decided she would let it air dry as she wrapped up in her favorite satin, pink robe and sauntered onto her bedroom patio. Lighting a cigarette, she selected the familiar contact on her phone and settled into the lounge chair for a good long talk.

"Hi Mother, it's me," she said, her voice low and sweet. She knew that starting conversations with her mother on a positive note were always best.

"Hi, 'me'," the voice on the other end sparkled with amusement. Her mother always enjoyed her daughter and her antics more than she enjoyed most. "How are you?"

"Things couldn't be better." Nora wanted to tell her everything, but she knew that she needed to take it slow. Her mother had always been unpredictable and if she wasn't in a good mood, then Nora knew the conversation wouldn't go the way she wanted it to.

"Do you still have that boy turned inside out, doing everything you want him to?" Nora could hear the tinkling of the ice in her mother's glass and wondered how many drinks she'd already had. From the sound of her voice, she hadn't had more than two.

"Yes, Mother. So far, he's still doing everything I want." Nora leaned back in her chair, waiting.

"I don't know what you're trying to do, but I've always told you that men can't be trusted. You know this." Mother's voice changed and Nora frowned. She knew the direction the conversation was going and it wasn't going to be the conversation she wanted.

"Really, Mother, everything is just fine."

"Be careful, Peanut. You don't want him to catch you playing with him. He's a good-looking one, but not too bright. I would be worried if I were you! The stupid ones usually like to hit because they're not smart enough to do much else."

"I'm *always* very careful so that he doesn't suspect anything. He has no idea that he's my puppet and that I'm pulling the strings."

"It's important that he doesn't suspect. I know you're careful, but just when you think you've done it right, double-check. Don't forget, I know *you*, and even though you don't mean it, you always mess things up. If you're playing with this boy, you better not screw it up. You know I love you, Peanut, but if I don't tell you these things then nobody will."

"I know," Nora was getting annoyed. She knew what she needed to do and didn't need to be reminded. She had been begging for approval from her mother for years and for the first time she felt like she might be earning it. She definitely wasn't going to mess that up!

They continued to chat for another hour, until Nora set the receiver down, finally exhausted. Phone conversations with her mother usually invigorated her and then drained her, but they always kept her on track. Her mother reminded Nora that Chris was just a distraction and that the real prize would be in the end. As she thought about his body and how he much he pleased her, she knew that eventually, she would be forced to let him go.

She walked slowly to the mini-bar in her room and poured two fingers of scotch. She let the peaty flavor wash over her tongue as she slowly felt the tension leaving her. She knew she had to limit herself to only one because anything after that would cause her to lose judgment and inhibitions. Alcoholism ran rampant in her family and she had experienced enough blackouts to know that losing control could be detrimental to her mission. She had awoken in many strange houses and beds over the years and had finally disciplined herself to only one drink at a time. She relished it. She took her time sipping and letting it slide down her throat, almost sensually, until her glass was empty.

As she stared into the bottom of the glass she felt a pit in the bottom of her stomach. In the end, Nora knew she was going to end up alone. She always had been, ever since she was a child, yearning for a mother that could be attentive and loving and for a father who never existed.

She fought the urge to pour another drink, though she desperately wanted to. She tipped the bottle toward her glass and at the last second, changed her mind. She stepped onto the balcony and lit the joint she had rolled earlier, enjoying its earthy smell. Pot always mellowed her out when she needed her mind to slow down and her body to give in to sleep. She had been so tightly wound ever since seeing Chris that nothing relaxed her. She knew that she had to play him tight and close, but not too close. She knew what the consequences of falling for him were and she wasn't going to let herself become a victim of love, no matter how much she was tempted to. She had seen first-hand the power that love had to obliterate, and she promised herself at a young age that she would never let herself fall in love with anyone.

She took a deep drag and allowed the smoke to fill her lungs. She held her breath as long as she could and then blew the smoke out slowly. She took a few more drags until she began to feel numb and heady. She knew she was moving in slow motion as she picked up her phone and dialed the familiar number.

"Hey darling, what are you doing? Come over. I want you now." She hung up the phone, smiling to herself. She knew the doorbell would be ringing within the hour and she would be able to get lost in the distraction of one of her many men who made themselves available whenever she called. She was a skilled lover, and had perfected the art of pleasure by using her body in every way necessary.

She'd made a game of teasing and torturing her lovers until they were begging for more. She loved how she could make them do anything to and for her until she had her fill of them. Then she sent them home, always willing to come back to her soft, welcome bed. She especially loved the one she had just called with his hard body and affinity for hair pulling and slapping. He was just the distraction she needed from the emptiness that threatened to consume her.

She laid back and waited, anticipating the next few hours that would remind her that she was in control of her own life, and that she didn't need anyone to love her.

15

Firsts

~Brynn

I try and think about all of Eva's firsts and I smile at the memories, happy to be there for all of them.

I can almost see her first birthday with the smash cake and how she cried when she realized that it was all over her, frosting everywhere; in her hair, her diaper, and all over me. I remember the first tooth that was loose. She wiggled it over and over, sticking her tongue through it until it finally came out, the blood making her throw up. I remember the triumph on her face when she held it up victoriously.

Everything that was a first for Eva was also a first for me.

This time she comes to me with another first.

"I'm pregnant, Momma," she says, her eyes downcast, avoiding mine.

She's afraid that I'll judge her and that I'll be angry with her for getting pregnant before she got married, but I'm not. I'm not angry with her in the very least. I just want her to be happy and when she tells me about the baby, I can tell that she is, even though she doesn't want to admit it right away.

"Are you happy, Love?" I ask her gently.

Eva hesitates and in an instant I can still see her as a tiny girl, venturing out into a world that seems far too big for her.

"Are you?" I prod, careful not to push too hard.

"I'm scared," Eva says, honestly. "I don't know how to do this."

I see her standing in the doorway of the classroom, frozen with fear on her first day of kindergarten. I see me kneeling down next to her and encouraging her to go in with the other children, and how she slowly walks into the room, looking behind her with terror in her soft, beautiful eyes. But then after a week, she couldn't wait to go to school. It was as though she had always been there.

"You do this like you do everything else. You do it with your entire heart and everything you have within you. You're going to be a wonderful mother."

I realized that I didn't know who the father was.

"You don't know him," Eva said as though reading my mind.

"How can I not know him?" I ask, alarmed that the gaps in my mind were growing larger and wider with every day. It seemed as though the medications could knock me out for days and it terrified me how much more frequently it felt that way. I feel as though I come and go so often that when I awaken I'm disoriented and it takes a long time to regain my footing.

"It's okay, Momma. He's a good man and I love him very much. I ... just ... need you for this because I can't do it without you. I need my mother."

My heart shatters into a thousand sharp pieces inside my chest as Eva's eyes shine with tears that refuse to fall. The look on her face is so desperate and sad and all I want to do is take her pain away.

"But I'm here, Love. I'm not going anywhere, and I'll be here for you and your baby. I promise." I hold her hand tightly, suddenly trying to convince her with my whole heart because I feel as though she doesn't believe me.

"I see you, Momma. But I need ... I need ..." Eva turns away, unable to speak, and the exhaustion hits me like a truck. I hate this medication and what it does to me! I hate that I can't be here for Eva like she needs me to be here. I struggle against it, my eyelids growing heavy, unable to hold my arms up any longer. I surrender against the cool pillows, no longer able to fight against the exhaustion any longer.

"I'm sorry, Love," I sigh as I close my eyes and allow the darkness to consume me. "I'm sorry."

As I fade into sleep I think I hear Eva say "It's okay, Momma. It's okay."

16

Husband

September 2ⁿᵈ, 2016

After weeks of settling back into normal life and realizing that Brynn was not going to wake up again, Chris convinced Eva to take a small honeymoon, though she refused to go too far from home.

Chris knew that she needed to get away to give Eva a break. As soon as they returned Eva began the task of getting the third floor of The Harper House renovated so that she and Chris could live there permanently.

They had already moved back in to her rooms after the wedding, but she knew that with the baby on the way, they would need a much larger space of their own. She hired an interior designer and had the many rooms, including the kitchen area, painted, updated, and restored.

Their space in The Harper House had once been her grandmother, Ellie's, where Ellie and Brynn had lived for the first two years of Brynn's life. The rooms were large and had been converted into a comfortable living space many years before. Adam had given Eva permission to make it hers and told her to spare no expense, even though she had never been comfortable with extravagance. She smiled at the beautiful simplicity of the rooms and how they reflected her classic taste. She thoughtfully chose comfortable items that she knew Chris would enjoy. She wanted him to be happy living in the house that had belonged to her family, even though that hadn't been the original plan.

She had convinced him to move in, especially when she found out that she was expecting. He had been resistant at first, worried about her and wondering if that was truly what she wanted.

"Eva, are you sure you want to do this?" he had asked, concerned. "I thought you wanted us to live on our own. I thought you wanted independence? I mean ... I'll do whatever you want, but ..."

"I *did* want us to be independent, but now, I just want our baby to grow up in the house that my mother should've grown up in," Eva said, pulling him close and breathing in his warm, masculine scent.

"Are you sure you won't feel too ... stifled?" Chris asked, stroking her long, thick hair and trailing his fingers down her back.

"I don't think so," Eva paused, wondering if she was being honest. "I mean ... I did want us to venture into the world on our own, but if our baby can grow up here, then I don't want to deprive it of that. I think Daddy understands and will give us our space. One day, I promise, we'll move out ..."

"But you've felt so suffocated and lonely growing up in The Harper House," Chris reminded her. Eva appreciated that he always listened and realized that she had fallen in love with him because of it.

He knew the sadness that weighed on her and the massive loneliness of the house often made it difficult for her to breathe. She had told him about the many days and nights throughout her childhood when she wandered around the floors and rooms of the large house by herself, often not talking to a single soul for hours. Adam was busy grieving and trying not to drink while Kelly was taking care of Uncle Noah, and then Brynn. Everyone else who worked in The Harper House had a job to do, and while they doted on her, they were too busy to help fend off her loneliness for too long. For as long as she could remember, she had been left on her own to care for herself, finding her escape in the books that nobody read that lined the massive library walls once belonging to her grandfather.

Nearly three months after the start of the renovation, Eva looked around their new quarters, taking great care to put everything in its place. She thought about the first time she met Chris.

When Eva was finally old enough to drive, she often went into town. She would sit in a corner booth at the local coffee shop for hours, reading and drinking one cup of tea after another. The staff wasn't sure what to make of this rich girl who regularly left them fifty-dollar tips. They took her name from her credit card and did some research, learning who she was and from which family to belonged. She would return faithfully, day after day, week after week, and the employees were happy not only for the generous gratuity, but for her kind manner. They took pity on the beautiful girl who seemed so sad and alone. They were protective of her, though no one ever bothered her. That is until one day when Chris walked into the diner, sat down at her table without her permission, and wound up stealing her heart.

He came into her life on a day when she was especially lost in her misery, unable to wrestle her thoughts away from her father, who she was sure had been drinking first thing that morning, and the shell of her mother who lay in the bed unmoving. Reading distracted her, but on the more difficult days, she struggled to concentrate on the words on the page, no matter how hard she tried. The day she met Chris had been the worst and she'd been staring at her book, unable to turn the page for over an hour.

Chris was handsome and confident, instantly taking Eva's breath away. She was drawn to him immediately and realized right away that he was everything she wasn't.

She was suffering over her inability to focus on her book when he walked over to her table.

"Hi." The voice came unexpectedly from above her head and Eva looked up to find she was staring into the most beautiful hazel eyes she had ever seen. She looked around the near empty room, wondering if he had mistaken her for someone else.

"Hi," she said, her voice barely audible.

"Do you mind if I sit down?" Chris sat without waiting for her to say 'yes.'

They stared at one another for a moment and Eva could feel her cheeks getting warm.

"What are you reading?" Chris asked, trying to catch a peek at the cover of her book.

"Um … Maya Angelou," Eva said, showing him the cover.

"Who's that? I've never heard of her," Chris said turning the empty cup in front of him over. The waitress materialized with a hot pot of coffee and glared at him suspiciously, which was lost on Eva but not on him. He gave her a charming smile, pulled a ten-dollar bill from his pocket and placed it gently in her hand. She took the bill and put it in her pocket without smiling, and looked over at Eva, protectively.

"Miss?" the waitress said, looking down at Eva's empty cup.

"No thank you," Eva said kindly. "I'll have some more tea in a little bit, but not quite yet."

The waitress smiled, walked away slowly, and Eva turned her attention back to Chris.

"So … who is this Maya … what's her last name?" Chris said, resuming their conversation.

"H-h-h-ow do you not know who she is? I mean … she was amazing … how … do you live under a rock?" Eva asked, her voice going up an octave before she could stop herself.

Chris' eyes grew wide and then he laughed at her out-burst as Eva's cheeks grew even redder than they had already been. "I'm sorry, Angel, I just don't know who she is. Educate me then. Why don't you read it to me?"

"Angel? Why are you calling me Angel?" Eva was taken aback. Nobody had ever called her anything like that before.

"You look like an angel to me. Is it okay if I call you that?" Chris' eyes never left her face and Eva shifted uncomfortably in her seat.

"Um … I guess …" Eva stuttered.

"So, are you going to read to me?" His voice was seductive and it made Eva's cheeks burn. Nobody had ever talked to her the way he did and she realized that she liked it.

Eva stared at him, hesitant. "You want me ... to read it ... to you?" Eva's eyes were wide.

"Please." Chris stared deep at her, not blinking, and suddenly Eva felt completely exposed. Nobody had ever taken such a deep interest in her before and she felt naked.

"Please. Read to me," Chris urged.

Eva paused and took a deep breath. She looked at him once more before she began to read in a low, quiet cadence as Chris listened intently and sipped his coffee.

From that moment on, they were inseparable, and after spending a few weeks together, Chris quickly became her refuge. She fell hard and fast, allowing him to sweep her away. He was handsome and funny, and he moved with the ease of someone who felt completely comfortable in his own skin something she did not. He always seemed to know the right thing to say, knowing her better than she seemed to know herself and she wondered how it was possible.

They had only been together for seven months, but Eva knew that Chris loved her. She hadn't hesitated to give him her heart and her body, the familiar emptiness disappearing with his touch.

She looked around the renovated space and was pleased with the choices she had made. She was confident that Chris would love it as much as she did. She made him stay in her old bedroom during the renovation, making him swear he wouldn't sneak a peek. She wanted so much to do something for him that he would love in order to give him a small taste of the happiness that he had given her. He told her that he hadn't grown up with much and she knew that the small extravagances, like the largest screen T.V. and all the updated technological touches she had added, were going to blow him away. The "Man Cave" she had created would make him so happy, and she glowed at the thought of what his face would look like when he saw it for the first time.

She couldn't believe how much she loved him. When he proposed to her, he gave her his mother's engagement ring. He had loved his mother so much and was careful to preserve his memories of her from his young childhood. Chris told her that she had passed away when he was ten, his face falling every time he mentioned it. They had that in common, the loss of their mothers, bonding them close. Eva was thankful to have someone that truly understood what it felt like to be alone. He was the first person she could open up to about how painful it was to be without her mom growing up. Even though her own mother was only a few rooms away at all times, the absence remained real and painful.

Eva walked slowly through the rooms one by one, running her fingers along the smooth wood of the doorways and pausing to make sure that every detail was in place. She paused in the doorway of the nursery, her favorite room. She had decorated it in bears and clouds, unsure if the life growing inside of her was a boy or a girl. She sighed happily as she imagined herself holding and rocking her baby with Chris by her side.

Suddenly she froze. The sound of a low wailing filled her ears. She looked around, frantically searching for the source of the sound. As suddenly as it began, it disappeared.

"Eva! Eva!" her dad's voice came shouting down the hall. "Eva! Come quickly!"

Eva ran from the nursery following the sound of Adam's voice.

"What is it?" Eva said nearly running into him, both of them breathless. She wrinkled her nose when she smelled the alcohol on his breath. Eva wondered why he still attempted to hide his drinking, and as time went on, he tried to hide it less and less.

"It's your mom … Eva. Your mom … she's awake! This time it's real, Eva! She's really awake."

17

Awake

~Brynn

I open my eyes and everything is different.

I've opened my eyes a thousand times, but this time when I do it, I am struck immediately with a cacophony of light and sound, unlike anything I can ever remember experiencing. I feel as though I am choking from the inside out. I am starting to panic and I know without a doubt that I am suffocating.

Suddenly, there is a woman looking at me. She begins to yell for help, her blue eyes wide, her pretty face wearing an expression of shock and happiness. I know her, but I can't remember her name. It's the first time I've seen anyone but Eva in a very long time and something tells me that something ... possibly everything ... has changed.

"Brynn, just calm down and don't panic. There's a tube down your throat to help you breathe. Just relax, relax. We need to get you to the hospital."

I try desperately to calm down like she says, but my body doesn't want to cooperate. After a few long moments, I am able to calm myself down, but the feeling that I am choking sits on the edge, threatening to overtake me. I know that I am so close to losing control. I don't understand how I got here to this room and why things are suddenly so different. I look around, but I can barely move my head. I desperately search for any sign of Eva and I realize that she isn't there. Nothing about the room speaks to me of her. I've never been awake without her and I can't be without her now.

The room is alive and loud and I can't mute the sounds that are violating my senses, making me want to explode. I try and put my hands over my ears to quiet the sound, but something is wrong with my hands and arms and they feel as though they are weighted down. No effort can move them, not even a little.

The woman continues to tell me to breathe as tears run down her face. She lifts her fingers from where they'd been resting on my chest and speaks into something small she has cradled in her hands

"Adam! Come quickly! She's awake." She drops the small thing on the bed and stares into my eyes. Everything is so bright and I cringe. I hear footsteps rapidly approach the room and I flinch as the sound echoes painfully in my ears. All the commotion is hurting my head and I realize that this is far different than the peace and quiet that I'm used to. I don't know what has happened, but I want this woman to stop screaming so loudly.

"Oh Mom! Mom!" Eva's voice is a welcome sound and I strain toward it. I try and move my hands again, but nothing happens. It's in that instant I realize I have no command over any part my body. The only thing I can do is to blink, and even doing that takes a great deal of effort. "Mom!"

There is a beautiful girl's face suddenly inches from mine. I can feel that my cheeks are growing wet, but I can't tell if they are her tears or mine. I recognize her immediately, but she is not the Eva I know. She is not the delicate young girl I've made sandcastles with, or spent endless days at the park with. This girl is different. She is desperately beautiful, but fragile. I recognize the brokenness in her because it's the same brokenness that has consumed me my entire life. She reminds me of *me* as a young woman. Her eyes are deep, dark, blue, but the resemblance to me is uncanny and I see the connection between us immediately. While I had never thought of myself as beautiful, when I looked at the woman standing in front of me, it strikes me for the first time that maybe I had been pretty after all.

Eva's brows are perfect, just like the rest of her. Her face is oval-shaped and delicate. I can feel the soft strands tickling my face as she leans over me, her warm lips kissing my cheeks over and over. She buries her head in my chest, her small body heaving over mine, and I know she is trying hard not to crush or hurt me. Her voice is muffled as she cries into me with everything she has, though I don't understand a word she is saying.

I can hear the faint sound of sirens and for a moment, it becomes the only thing I can focus on. I fight hard to keep my eyes open, the sleep threatening to overtake me and steal me away once again. I'm afraid that if I go to sleep, I won't wake up. I'm terrified to lose this beautiful woman-child in front of me, afraid that if I go to sleep again, the Technicolor will disappear and Eva and I will be left with a gray landscape once again.

Without warning, Eva is gone and Adam's face is in front of me. I recognize him immediately though his face has aged tremendously. His eyes are still the beautiful blue that entranced me as a girl, but the lines around them are cut deep and they betray his youthfulness. His thick hair remains, but the darkness had been replaced by white and he is in desperate need of a haircut. The pungent smell of bourbon oozes from his breath as he speaks to me. I blink my eyes rapidly, wishing the smell away. He immediately backs away as though he knows what I'm doing.

"I'm sorry, Brynn," he whispers, his eyes sad and ashamed. "I-I-I've missed you so much. I just … I've never been able to live without you. I've tried to stop, even after everything I've done to you … but I can't. I've tried to …" He buries his face in his hands, his body shaking uncontrollably.

There is a loud sound in the hallway as the paramedics and police walk into the room with their heavy boots.

I close my eyes and allow myself to drift off to sleep, unsure if I will wake back up, but too exhausted to stop. The noise disappears slowly in the thickness of my slumber. The last sound in my ears is the sound of Adam's sobs and a woman's voice saying, "It'll be okay, Adam. It'll be okay."

I awaken in what appears to be a hospital room, so much more quiet and sterile than the room that I woke up in before. I realize that I'm alone and am thankful for the blessed silence. There is no crying or sadness consuming the people around me. I am alone with only the blipping and whooshing sounds of machines.

I try wiggling my fingers.

Nothing.

I will them to move, but my fingers remain stubbornly still on the stiff sheet of the hospital bed. I struggle within, imagining that they are one-hundred pound weights, but no matter how hard I try, they defy me, and I find myself getting angry.

I want desperately to move my finger.

I want to move my damn finger.

I want to move my fucking finger.

I want to … suddenly my finger twitches ever so slightly and I am elated.

Nothing else on my body will move and I feel like I'm buried deep inside a cocoon, but the tip of my finger twitches just by sheer will.

My will.

I don't understand what is happening to me and why everything has suddenly changed. The world around me has become so much louder and more confusing than anything I've ever imagined or experienced.

A tired but upbeat nurse breezes into the room.

"Hi Brynn," she says smiling, cheerful. "Do you remember me? I've been taking care of you here in the hospital for a few weeks now. I'm Lil."

Weeks? I've been here for weeks? I just woke up … how has it been weeks? Time seems to move slowly but fly by at the same time and I feel dizzy.

She checks the machines that I'm hooked up to, then carefully picks up my wrist to feel my pulse. I realize with horror that I can't feel her touching me. "Good." She taps on the keyboard and smiles at me, a beautiful toothy smile. "You're doing well, Brynn."

She says this in a way that makes me feel as though I should be proud of myself, but I'm not. I feel hopeless. Helpless.

I don't want her to think that I am ungrateful and try to blink at her.

Thanks.

My throat hurts and I swallow. There is nothing stopping me from doing so and I suddenly realize that I am breathing on my own. I feel a moment of panic as I wonder if I can do this. *Breathe in and out. In and Out. In and Out. In and Out.* I swallow hard again, my mouth feeling very dry and chapped.

"Is your mouth dry again?" Lil comes closer with a little sponge on a stick.

She opens my mouth and I feel some welcome relief as the liquid soothes me. I try to suck on the sponge, but there is nothing left. She dips it in the cup again and again until my mouth is less parched. "You're a miracle, you know that?" She shakes her pretty head at me and smiles. She seems genuinely happy that I'm awake. "The doctors are still trying to figure out what's happened to you and how you're awake like this. None of them have ever seen anything like it."

I listen carefully, still grateful that the horrible tube is out of my throat.

How long? How long has it been since I woke up?

"You're really doing so well. Even though it's only been a month, you're breathing on your own and staying awake longer. We're so happy for you! You even have your own Facebook page and there are a lot of people supporting you! The next step, young lady, is to be able to get rid of the feeding tube. Then home."

What is Facebook? Home. All I want to do is go home.

"You've been through so much. We all want you to get better so you can go back to your beautiful home and be with your family." Lil hadn't stopped smiling since she came into the room. As much as I want to dislike her because she's keeping me prisoner, I find that I can't

Where is my family? Where is Eva? Where is Adam?

I can hear Eva's voice from down the hall, beautiful and musical, mingling with a deeper voice, one I don't recognize. I'm sure that I would recognize Eva voice anywhere. It's the one voice aside from Adam's that is imbedded in my brain. Even as she's grown and the tone and timber of it has changed, I've always known it, feeling it in my heart first before it reaches my ears.

"Mom, you're awake," Eva floats into the room, her beautiful face glowing. She sounds excited.

I blink, still unable to move my head though I try with everything I can.

"Hi Mom," the handsome young man who is with her tells me as he leans over and kisses me, his lips harder than they look. I don't like the feel of them, quick and obligatory on my cheek.

I look at him, questioning.

"This is Chris, Mom. You've met Chris many times, both at our house and here. *He's my husband.*" Eva holds his arm tight, her face beaming.

He looks at me, his eyes warm, but something about him unsettles me. Eva repeats hopefully, "You've met Chris a lot of times."

Why can't I remember?

"It seems normal that she won't remember everything," Lil says, squeezing Eva's arm, reading the frustration in my eyes. I realized that Lil and Eva seem to be about the same age and there is an unspoken understanding between them. "She's getting better day by day, which is a very good thing. You have to take it one day at a time."

Eva smiles a small smile that doesn't reach her eyes completely, but when she turns her face toward me, it is bright and hopeful.

"Don't you remember, Mom? Chris read to you the last time we were here. He read Dickens to you, which is one of my favorites." Eva's voice is hopeful and she seems almost desperate for me to remember him.

I blink, hoping she will decipher that to mean that I remember.

She smiles, seemingly relieved. *She does.*

The entire time Chris stands too close to my bed and I watch him

84

out of the corner of my eye. I don't like the helplessness that I feel, and I realize that I haven't felt this way since I was a young child, cowering at the feet of my adopted father as he hit me. Something about Chris reminds me of Thomas, though I can't put my finger on it, When he is close to me I feel afraid.

At least when I was asleep, I didn't realize how vulnerable I was, but now that I am awake, it frightens me that I am unable to move, sit up, or stand on my own. Eva grabs Chris' arm and pulls him away from me as though she knows that I am uncomfortable. It's as though she can read me although I have yet been able to speak a single word. It occurs to me that she has never heard my voice and the thought makes my heart feel heavy.

Eva gasped, pointing to my hand, her eyes dancing happily. "Mom, you're moving your fingers! You're moving them on your own!"

I look down and am startled to see that my fingers are moving without me having to give much effort. I have been trying to move them for so long and had forgotten that I was still trying. Chris is looking at me, smiling a small smile.

I close my eyes, anxious for him to leave. My head has begun to pound slightly. I hope he will take this as a cue to leave, though I want Eva to stay. Almost immediately, I find myself sinking into a deep sleep, and the dreams still come even after all these years.

Thomas always haunts me at night. He always has throughout my entire adulthood; during my marriage to Adam, and even in my dreams now. For a long time, the dreams seemed to disappear, only resurfacing occasionally. They've come back again, this time more frequently. Lately, though, Thomas' face is replaced by Chris', and the fear I feel is no longer for me, but instead for my baby girl.

I realize with horror that I'm not afraid of Chris for my sake.

The fear I feel is for Eva.

18

Eva's Momma
September 18th , 2016

Chris had gone out hiking for the day. Eva knew he would be out of cell-phone range for a while and come back a sweaty and disgusting mess, exhausted from his excursions but she didn't mind. She loved that he enjoyed nature and being so active. She was so proud of him and made sure to tell him so as much as she could.

With him being gone for the day, it gave her time to spend with Brynn in the hospital. It has been almost two months since Brynn had awoken, but she was still confused and slept most of the time, her body trying to regain its strength. Eva was fearful every time that Brynn went to sleep, watching her intently when she was there to make sure that she didn't stop breathing. She was terrified that she wouldn't wake up, although the doctors assured Eva that she was well out of the danger zone and was being monitored heavily.

Brynn was slowly getting stronger every day, still visited by doctors who were amazed at her progress, and that she had been able to wake up at all. They called her a medical miracle.

Eva continued to talk to Brynn during every visit just as she had been doing her entire life, but now she knew that Brynn heard her, and Eva was thankful to no longer wonder if she was listening. Although Brynn couldn't speak yet, her dark expressive eyes told Eva that she was in there, taking in everything she said. For the first time in her life Eva no longer felt alone in the world, and her heart felt unusually light and happy.

Eva was excited to spend the day with Brynn. When she got to the hospital, even though Brynn was asleep, she took her place in the chair next to her bedside and settled in for a long visit.

"Momma, I know you're getting stronger, but you'll need to hurry because you're going to be a grandma very soon. I'm going to need you to help me with this little one!" Eva said, as she put her hand on her belly and smiled at Brynn, looking for her to make eye contact. "I've been waiting for you to wake up for so long, and now that you're finally here, there will never be a day that goes by that I won't see you or be with you. I just ... I've ... I've missed you so much." Eva spoke convinced Brynn could hear her. Eva held it in her heart that when she told her that she was pregnant it had helped Brynn wake up.

Eva had tried hard not to cry since the first night that Brynn woke up. She was filled with as much happiness as she could possibly imagine and she knew that she no longer had any reason to be so empty. But there were still times when her heart reminded her of all she had missed during her childhood and the sadness came over her like a sudden darkness, unexpectedly.

She watched Brynn as she slept, her chest heaving up and down, gently, her face slack with sleep. The scars on Brynn's face were still slightly visible though Kelly had diligently put cream on them, twice a day, as part of her daily care. Brynn had been very self-conscious about the scars on her arms and stomach from when she cut herself to forget the abuse from her adoptive father, and Kelly knew that she wouldn't like the scars on her face. Even though shards of glass from the accident had pierced her cheeks and forehead, Eva marveled that they didn't diminish her mother's beauty.

The only scar that still stood out was the one that ran down the right side of her face from her temple to the bottom of her cheek, deep and fairly straight. Eva ran her thumb down the scar, gently, as she had so many times when she was a child. Brynn amazed everyone by surviving the crash and now amazed everyone by waking up. Eva knew that it was nothing short of a miracle to have Brynn with her. But she often thought guiltily about the many times when she had prayed for closure and the opportunity to grieve the mother she never had. It had been difficult missing her mother, especially when she was right in front of her. She couldn't help wanting her, expecting her, to sit up at any moment, so she could ask her to braid her hair or read a story.

Eva shook her head, a single tear running down her face, angry with herself for even thinking about such things.

Suddenly she realized there was a hand lying gently on hers. As she looked down, she saw Brynn's hand on top her own. She gasped and looked at Brynn who still remained asleep but had somehow found Eva's hand during her slumber. Eva sat still, refusing to move and barely breathing. In Eva's entire life, Brynn had never reached for her, and Eva was both startled and thrilled, afraid that if anything in the room changed, that the moment would disappear.

She looked up just as Kelly entered the room, Eva's big eyes shining with tears. Kelly's eyes immediately went to Brynn's hand resting gently on top of Eva's, and she stared in stunned silence.

"Did she do that?" Kelly whispered pointing to Brynn's hands.

Eva nodded, unable to contain her happiness. Kelly pulled out her phone, took a picture, and sent it immediately to Adam.

Kelly smiled at Eva, happiness and relief flooding through her.

"That's so good, Eva! So good!" Kelly sat next to Eva and put her arm around her. "I told you not to lose hope. We have to take it one moment at a time!"

Eva leaned against her, careful not to disturb Brynn's hand.

"Thank you," Eva said, happy that Kelly was able to witness her beautiful moment.

"Why are you thanking me?" Kelly said, kissing the top of Eva's head.

"Because you've always been there for me. You've been … like a mom to me … and I don't know what I would've ever done without you. I just … I'm just so happy that you are in my life." Eva spoke softly but deliberately, as though she had rehearsed the words so many times before. "I never told you how much you mean to me because I was afraid it would betray the love I have for my mom, but now I know that she would be happy you were there for me. I don't know why I know, but I do."

She could feel Kelly nod above her. "Your mom was … is … a good woman. She would never want you to be alone."

Kelly thought about her own children, her youngest daughter at college, her middle son married and living across the country, and her oldest son overseas in the army. She wondered for the thousandth time if they would've stayed close if her marriage had been better, but she thought sadly that there was nothing she could do about that now. She had been openly more in love with The Harper House and the Michaels family than she had ever been with her husband, and he knew it even before she did. Now his absences were so long and so often that she knew the day would come when he wouldn't come home at all. She often wondered why he never divorced her, and no matter how hard she tried, she couldn't think of a good reason. Since she practically lived in The Harper House, she realized she wouldn't even know if he stopped coming home. Strangely, she knew that it wouldn't make a difference if he did.

"I wasn't alone." Eva looked up at Kelly, her eyes suddenly dark and serious. "I had you and your kids. I had both of my moms with me my entire life and I never realized how lucky I was until now."

Kelly's breath caught in her throat as she pulled Eva toward her and held her close. She had thought of Eva as her own daughter so often throughout the years, but never felt she could say so. She thought about the numerous shopping trips with her own children and Eva, the first time she took her to get her ears pierced, and the talk about the 'birds and the bees'. The first trip to the gynecologist and the daily ritual of brushing and braiding Eva's hair first thing in the morning when she would arrive at The Harper House, were all the moments that Kelly had spent mothering Eva. But Kelly never felt as though there had been a choice.

Jane, Brynn's closest friend would've helped, but when she expanded the restaurant which had been Brynn's dream, and then had to move away to care for her own ailing mother, Kelly knew she couldn't let Eva down.

Kelly hugged Eva close. They sat in silence for a long time, both of them wrapped up in their own thoughts as they sat quietly with Brynn. All of a sudden Brynn's hand started to tremble and she began to moan as though she was in pain.

Before they could grab the call button for the nurse, Brynn turned her head toward Kelly and Eva, her coffee colored eyes opened wide.

She opened her mouth and Kelly and Eva held their breath.

"Save me," Brynn said, staring straight through them, her voice low and gravelly. "Don't let him get me ... please. I'm begging you."

"Who? Don't let who get you?" Eva cried, grabbing Brynn's hand and holding it tight.

"Him ... don't let him hurt me again." Brynn's fear was palpable and Kelly could feel her heart beating faster.

"Don't let who hurt you?" Eva asked, feeling helpless. "There is nobody here to hurt you. You're safe!"

"Adam. Keep him away. Where is Maxie? Please, just don't let Adam hurt me!" Brynn cried out desperately before she fell back onto the bed and into a deep sleep.

19

Broken Plans

September 18th, Previous Year

"It's so strange, Baby. It's almost as though she *knows*." Chris was shaken up. Brynn had stared right through him during his last visit with Eva, her brown eyes dark and strange, and he felt as though she was looking deep into his soul. He shuddered at the memory as though a ghost had passed right through him and he couldn't get the feeling out of his mind.

"She couldn't possibly know," Nora scoffed, flicking a long ash from her cigarette and directly onto the balcony where they sat enjoying an after-dinner cocktail. "You're imagining things."

"No, Baby, you don't understand. She can barely fucking move, but she stares directly *through* me, as though she can see *inside* of me. It's so damned unnerving." Chris puffed hard on his cigarette.

"Relax, Baby. Just relax." Nora knew exactly what to do to help Chris relax as she straddled him and kissed him long and hard on the lips. She could feel Chris fight her at first, but then he gave into her like she knew he would. They weren't meeting as frequently as they had, careful not to arouse suspicion. She had missed him more than she realized she would and had been anxious and excited for him to arrive. She knew they had to be careful, especially now that Eva was pregnant. They couldn't get caught or it would ruin everything they had been working for.

"I've missed you," Chris moaned against her, their clothes coming off easily and naturally as though they had rehearsed it a thousand times. His hands grabbed her tight and positioned her firmly against him until there was no longer any space between them. Their bodies moved in complete sync with one another, each knowing exactly what to do to please the other.

"Me too, Baby. I've missed you, too," Nora was surprised at how much she had missed him. Ever since high school, they hadn't spent more than a few nights apart and she had convinced herself that she didn't need him to sleep next to her at all. But now that he was no longer in her bed, she had to find others to sleep next to her or she could barely sleep at all. Even when the others were there, she still lay awake staring at the ceiling, missing the feel of Chris beside her.

For the first time, Chris could tell that she missed him by the way she grabbed him so hungrily the moment he walked in the door. She had never held him before with such abandon. Until now, he hadn't been sure if she loved him as much as he loved her. Since they'd spent time apart, he could see the misery in her eyes when he had to leave and could feel the intensity of her touch when she was near him. Chris had always been the one to give into her completely, but now he felt the desire shifting between them, and it made him feel strangely euphoric.

He had missed her desperately, but he tried not to think about it when he was with Eva. He didn't want Eva to see through him, and he realized that he didn't hate his new life with Eva as much as he thought he would. He wasn't as anxious to get away from her and back to Nora as he had in the beginning. Eva was kind to him and he had grown accustomed to spending time in the "Man Cave" that she had made for him. He knew that his time with her could be much worse and he fought the pleasure that he felt when he was with her.

She was hard not to love, and he knew that he could never let Nora see that side of him.

Still, Nora felt like coming home and, while he reveled in his love for her, every time he got to see her he understood why the separation was necessary. He realized that as Eva's pregnancy progressed that he would see less and less of Nora, and that it had to be that way or they risked exposure.

After they'd had their fill of one another, they sat in opposite chairs on the balcony, their fingers entwined, sweat still slick on their skin, and their clothes strewn on the balcony around them. They could feel the clock ticking as they pretended that their time together wasn't coming to an end.

"When am I going to see you again, Baby?" Chris asked as he stood to dress. He was reluctant to hear the answer.

"We should probably keep it to once a week," Nora said, her voice catching in her throat as she looked around for her discarded slip. "We don't want to get caught and ruin everything. It would've been easier if you weren't staying at that big goddamn house with all those people, but since you are, you can't be gone for too long or they'll wonder where you are. You know those rich people have a way of holding onto what's theirs ..." Nora's voice trailed off as though she had something else to say but didn't want to say it.

They sat in silence for a few moments, the air between them thick with dread.

"I don't know if I can go for an entire week without touching you. How am I going to survive without seeing my baby?" Chris asked, pulling her close to him again. "A week is just too long."

Nora pushed him away gently and settled back into her chair. "I know, but once this is all over, we'll be together again. And it'll all have been worth it! I promise you."

"I hope so ... it's just that ..." Chris paused, running his hands through his hair, unsure of how to continue.

"What?" Nora said, practically purring. "What is it, Baby?"

"It's just ... I want to change the plan a little. I mean ... I don't want to hurt … I mean, I want Eva to be safe … she hasn't done anything and …"

Nora bolted up, practically exploding out of the chair. "What? What do you mean? What are you asking? We've talked it all out and planned this for a long time! We aren't going to change it now because you knocked her up and now you feel bad for her. You weren't even supposed to touch her, but then you convinced me that you needed to in order to gain her trust! I told you to fucking be careful, but obviously you weren't and … Jesus, are you in love with her? Are you changing your mind? You promised that you wouldn't go soft on me. Is that it? You're a fucking sissy now?" Nora was angrier than she had ever been with him.

"No … I mean … No … I just …"

"You just what? You love her? You want to actually stay married to her? Is that what you're saying to me? You don't love me?" Nora broke down in tears, falling to the floor. "I knew this would happen. I knew you couldn't handle it! If you think that I'm just going to be your bitch on the side while you play house, then you're out of your mind!"

"No! That's not what I want, Baby! I *can* handle it … it's fine. Stop it! I just … I don't know that we should go through with the entire plan. I just don't want to … hurt her. There are other alternatives …" Chris got down on his knees and tried to hold her but she shoved him away violently.

"I get it, Christopher. You don't love me anymore. You love her instead. I knew that would happen. I knew you would fall for her. God! I hate you!"

Chris took a deep breath and continued. "That's not true, Nora, and you know it. I don't love her! I love *you*. But you wanted me to seduce her and I did that! I didn't mean to get her pregnant, but now she's carrying my baby inside of her and that's a game-changer. I didn't expect that, but you should've known that it would change everything for me. Nora, please, she's a really good girl, and we should reconsider the original plan. That's all I'm saying!"

Nora stared at him, her green eyes icy. "I thought you were stronger than that, Christopher. I thought you were more focused and less emotional than that. I thought you would be able to stick to the plan, but clearly I was wrong."

"No … No … Listen, Baby, we can work this out. We can fix this and make it so that nobody gets … hurt. We can make it so that …"

"You should leave now."

"No … stop. I don't want to leave like this." Chris was desperate, alarmed by the look in Nora's eyes. He had never seen her so angry and never with him. As she stared at him, he felt himself shrinking in front of her.

"It doesn't matter *how* you leave. You just need to leave. Now." Nora was angry with herself for getting so upset in front of him. She knew when she devised the plan that she would have to allow herself to be okay with him sleeping with Eva. In her mind, she had envisioned it a hundred times, even when she was in her own bed naked with the others.

She pictured her momma sitting her down when she was eight. "Nora," she had said, the bright green eyes so much like her own, as serious as she had ever seen them. "Never, ever, ever, fall in love with one man, Peanut. All they do is break your heart when they don't love you back. And believe me, they'll never love you back the way you'll love them." Even as a young girl, Nora had nodded as her mother spoke, knowing her words to be true. She had watched her mother fawn over every man she had ever been with since Nora was a little girl, and they had all ended up leaving. None of them had loved her mother enough to stay, and Nora knew that had torn her up inside. "Never ever fall in love with one man, Peanut," her mother had said over and over.

Nora loved her mother with all her heart, and it pained her that she hadn't listened and had accidentally fallen for Chris. Nora had tried to protect herself by filling her life with others, both men and women, whichever she could sleep with or order around. But none of them stayed very long, often growing impatient with her demands and put off by her inability to commit to anything longer than one night at a time. While some of them understood they were just a pawn in her game, others fell hard for her and wanted much more. Nora refused to commit, even to Chris, though he was the closest that she ever came.

Nora never lied to Chris about her many lovers, but Chris had loved her so much and for so long, he allowed the assortment of people who filed in and out of Nora's bed believing she would change her mind one day. She never flaunted it and tried to be as discreet as she could, but Chris still knew.

"Never, ever fall in love with one man, Peanut," Nora's mother's voice rang in her ears as Nora looked at Chris with disgust.

"You need to leave. I don't even want to look at you right now." Nora's voice was colder than he had ever heard it and he was stunned by her sudden hardness. He had seen her turn quickly before, but never like this.

"Baby, no. I don't want to leave like this," Chris said, his voice shaky. "We're not going to see each other for a long time, and we can't just walk away like this and not talk for a week. I won't be able to stand it."

"It may be longer than a week, *Christopher*," Nora said, emphasizing every syllable of his name as she said it. "In fact, we may not see each other ever again now that you've made it clear to me that you care so much about that little bitch."

She turned away from him, angrily.

"Leave. Now."

"No … please," Chris said, trying to sound strong and failing miserably. "You can't be serious, Baby."

"Don't beg. It's pathetic," Nora said, her voice flat and barely audible. "You're pathetic."

Chris slowly stood up and walked away, feeling as though he had just been run over by a truck. He knew there was no point in fighting with her any longer. Her mind was made up and he knew that he would need to give her space. He hadn't been without Nora for longer than a few days in many years. He wasn't sure if he could do it.

Eva flashed before his eyes and he pushed the image aside angrily. *If I lose Nora because of Eva, I don't know what I'll do.*

He waited for her to stop him, but when he finally closed the apartment door behind him and got onto the elevator, he realized that she was letting him go. He paced the elevator like a caged animal, wondering where he should go. He knew that he couldn't go back to Eva without cleaning himself up. He could still smell Nora's scent on him and he closed his eyes, breathing her in.

He stepped off the elevator, walked into the lobby and then onto the street. He looked around trying to remember which direction to go. When he figured it out, he took off anxiously. He knew there was nothing more that he wanted to do than drink until he could no longer feel the knife plunged deep into his heart, tearing it into a thousand pieces.

20

The Stranger
September 19th, 2016

The loud banging woke him and he jumped up, disoriented.

He stood up clumsily, confused by the constant pounding in his head as he tried to figure out where he was and why he was on the floor. The surroundings were familiar, but no matter how hard he tried he couldn't place where he was. His eyes were fuzzy and his head hazy from too much alcohol. There was a sharp, stabbing pain directly behind his right eye that made it impossible for him to think.

It took him a few minutes to get his bearings as he stared at the red, sticky liquid that covered the floor and his clothes. It took him several long minutes to realize that the red liquid was blood. He couldn't believe how much there was, the smell of it nauseating him.

"Open up, right now! Police!"

Chris realized that the pounding wasn't just in his head, but was coming from the direction of the door. His heart began to thump faster in his chest. He stood unsteadily, willing his feet to move, but they felt cemented to the ground. The pounding continued until he heard the sound of wood splitting, then a loud explosion, and the sound of heavy feet entering the room.

"Get down now! get down!" A loud voice yelled at him and he obeyed.

As he slid back down to the floor, his hands instinctively went up in the air. He had done this before, but this time he knew it was different. As he lay down, trying to keep his face out of the blood, he felt a foot on the back of his neck. He didn't need to look up to know that he had several guns being pointed down at him. "Don't fucking move or I'll shoot you!"

He could tell from the intensity of the voices swirling above him that he dare not move even an inch. He barely allowed himself to breathe, the fear coursing through every cell in his body.

"Fuck, look at all this blood!" one of the officers noted, shock in his voice.

"Don't move, don't touch anything!" another voice shouted. Chris wasn't sure if he was shouting at him or at someone else, and he tried to stay as still as possible.

"Jesus, what did this asshole do? Look at 'em, he's completely covered in blood."

"Oh God, look at this shit!"

Chris lay still, trying not to breathe as more and more voices entered the room, shouting all at once. The voices kept yelling and he wondered what was going on and what they were seeing. He knew the room was a mess, but he'd barely had time to see anything, and was now keeping his eyes squeezed closed out of confusion and fear. The contents of his stomach kept threatening to come up as the smell of the blood continued to assault his nose.

"What are you doing down there?" The voice above him was agitated. "I told you not to fucking move, why are you moving?"

"I'm going to puke ... I can't help it." He was retching and trying not to vomit, but it was coming up in waves and there was nothing he could do about it.

The puke exploded out of his mouth and onto the floor, splashing up on his cheek. The smell hit him, and he opened his mouth again, unable to stop it from coming out. He had never felt more disgusted with himself in his entire life, and he hoped for a split second that the cop would just shoot him and put him out of his misery.

"Fuck! Stop it, dammit!"

It was the last thing he remembered before he passed out, and when he woke up, he was no longer covered in blood or his own puke, but was wearing a bright orange pair of overalls. His mouth felt as though it was full of cotton as he stared helplessly at the walls of the small cell. He sat on the cot, his head in his hands, and wondered what he was doing in jail. His memory was mostly blank. He knew he had fought ... with Nora. It had been an ugly one and she had kicked him out. Instead of going back to The Harper House like he should have, where he felt like a prisoner, he went to a bar ... multiple bars.

The flashes were hazy and he tried to lick his lips, but his tongue was dry and thick. He desperately wanted water, the taste of ashes and old whiskey coating his teeth and his tongue. He fought the urge to throw up again, but he knew there was probably nothing left in his stomach. He hated the thought of dry heaving and he pushed it down as deep as he could.

Chris tried to think about where he had been and what he had done to end up in a jail cell. *Oh God ... Nora. Nora! I was in her apartment, but where the fuck was she? I didn't see her anywhere. I hope she's okay! Whose blood was that?*

He thought about her beautiful face and how angry she had been when he'd seen her last. She had been completely furious with him for wanting to change the plan, but Chris just didn't feel right about what Nora wanted to do to Eva. Chris shook his head at the memory, but he had seen her like that many times before and knew it would pass. But why was he in jail ... *I haven't made my phone call! I need to make my phone call.*

Suddenly, a door opened and light flooded into the dim cell. Two officers and a man dressed in a button-down shirt, jeans, and a gun holstered against his ribs stood outside of his cell staring at him. The man with the button-down shirt looked pissed, and Chris felt himself tense up as the man stared at him with hard, steely eyes.

"Connor Michael Martin?" the man in the button down looked at him, his voice hard and raspy from smoking too many cigarettes. "I'm Detective Lyons, and we have some talking to do."

"No … you have the wrong man. I'm Christopher Brian Garrett." Chris said, looking at him evenly.

"Who are you saying you are now?" the detective asked, his right eyebrow cocked slightly.

"I'm Christopher. Brian. Garrett." Chris said slowly, as though mocking the detective.

"No. You're Connor Michael Martin. There is nobody named 'Christopher Brian Garrett', even though your license says that's who are you are. We know it's a fake because we ran your prints. You're in the system quite a bit Mr. Martin, so cut the shit. You know exactly how this works."

Chris looked at the man, his eyes growing dark and angry, slowly transforming him into someone dark and sinister.

"You need to come with us. We have some questions to ask you."

"I need a lawyer and I need you to call my wife." Chris knew that Eva would help him, especially when he hadn't done anything wrong. He just needed to see her so that he could explain it to her.

"Of course you do," the detective said, sneering. "But your wife isn't going to want to come near you with a ten-foot pole after what you've done."

"I didn't do anything! I don't even know what happened. Is Nora … the girl who lives in that apartment … is she okay?" Chris asked, his voice angrier than he intended it to be.

"Are you kidding me?" the detective stared at him in disbelief. "Is that the angle you're going to play? Are you going to act like you don't know anything?"

"I don't, I swear!" Chris' eyes widened. "All I want to know is whether the girl is okay!"

"I'm not telling you anything," the detective said with contempt. "If you're going to pretend that you don't know what you did, then I'm not going to play your game."

The detective stood up abruptly and walked out of the room, slamming the door behind him.

The next hour felt like days as Chris waited for the detective to come back.

When he returned, Chris was panicked and agitated. "Did you call my wife? Did you call my lawyer?"

"You'll get to call both, when we say."

They led him to an interrogation room and he sat down on the uncomfortable chair, hating the shackles on his wrists.

"Okay, Mr. Martin … do you want to tell me why you did it?" Detective Lyons asked, never breaking eye contact.

"You get right to the point, don't you Detective?" Chris asked sounding amused.

"Does that bother you?" the detective looked at Chris and fought the urge to break eye contact. He knew that he was being toyed with and he didn't like it.

Michael Lyons had been a detective for twenty-five years and had been in the interrogation room with psychopaths like this one hundreds of times. He had moved from Chicago to a smaller town five years ago, to get away from crimes like this because he no longer had the stomach for it. When he got word about the crime scene, he couldn't believe it, and sitting across from Connor Martin was more unnerving than he'd anticipated.

He tried to shake it off, trying to convince himself that it was just the pictures of the dead girl that were throwing him off. Whoever had stabbed the girl was pissed at her and wanted to see her suffer. The stab wounds all over her body had been deep and vicious and the detective had never seen anything like it.

"No, it doesn't bother me at all," Chris said, smirking. "But I'm wondering what you think I've done."

"That's what I'm waiting to hear from you, Connor. I can piece together what you did, but you'd make it so much easier on yourself, and on us, if you'd just tell us what happened and why you did it. You know we'll figure it out anyway."

Chris stared coldly through the detective, his hazel eyes dead and giving nothing away.

"I have no idea what you're talking about. I woke up and I was lying on the floor, but I didn't do anything to anybody. You're not going to get anything out of me, because there's nothing to tell," Chris said, his voice flat and low.

The detective flipped over a picture and Chris' voice caught in his throat. Long strands of red hair were mixed with blood, the face bruised beyond recognition.

Chris took a deep breath and looked the detective in the eye.

"I'm not saying anything to you unless I have a lawyer present," Chris said, his voice hard.

As Detective Lyons stood up, he flipped over another picture, and then left the room.

Chris looked at the picture and tried to stop the sob that erupted from his chest.

"Nora," he whispered, recognizing the delicate bracelet that he had given her for her birthday wrapped around the dead woman's blood-soaked wrist.

21

Sobering

September 20th, 2016

Adam sat in the cold, uncomfortable, folding chair in the old church hall two towns over from his own. He tried to shrink down in his seat as much as he could, tugging on his ball cap and hoping that nobody would recognize him. Married into the deeply affluent and public Harper family, he had been in the paper and on the news more than he ever wanted to be. He rarely went out in public, but when he did, he was always careful to disguise his identity. He had made a drunken spectacle of himself in the past, the sting of it difficult to forget.

That last thing he wanted was to be in the news going to an AA meeting, especially when it failed him, which it always did. Adam had attended meetings like this before, but had never gone to more than a few. He had tried rehab in the posh country club setting, and he had even been to jail and done court-ordered rehab, but nothing worked. He had finally learned over the years to stop driving after he had been drinking, but it had been a difficult lesson.

It took Adam many years to realize and finally face the reason that caused him to drink.

Nothing that Adam did, either sober or drunk, could make him numb or make him forget the moments he got to hold his daughter, Sophie, in his arms before she died. She hadn't even lived for an entire day, and letting her go was the most difficult thing he had ever done. What had made it even more difficult was that he had to convince Brynn to let her go. She had been paralyzed and completely unable to help make any of the difficult decisions. Instead, it was left up to Adam and the resentment he harbored grew like a slow dark poison, coursing through his veins. Even still, when he closed his eyes at night, he envisioned Sophie, soft and sweet, so innocent in his arms. She had been terribly fragile, her labored breathing torturing him with every shallow breath, and he couldn't stop thinking about those last moments when he'd been able to hold her just before she died. She had spent most of her short, painful life filled with tubes and electrodes. Letting her go had been the right thing to do, but he hated himself for it. He hated Brynn for not being there for him, and he was sure to punish her for it.

He had become a man that he no longer recognized, and he loathed looking at his face in the mirror, hating the weakness in his eyes that he couldn't hide from. They were so blue once, but now they reflected nothing more than failure, no matter how many times he tried to convince himself that he had done the best he could.

He had been a terrible husband and a horrible father to Eva. He knew that she'd deserved more from him, but he hadn't given it.

Adam was a broken man, unable and unwilling to stop drinking permanently, no matter how many meetings or therapy sessions he had been to. Nothing he had done since Sophie died could inspire him to stop drinking completely. Not even Eva's birth.

Adam hated himself, the pain so deep that he lay in bed for hours in the fetal position holding his legs close and tight so that he wouldn't cry out in the middle of the night. He was terrified of waking up the entire household and having them catch him this way. He had been struggling for years, and had recently given into the pain and the fear, sneaking sips of vodka until the sips no longer sustained him and he needed so much more. Adam knew that with Brynn waking up, he would need to get sober and clear-headed, but deep down, he was afraid that she wouldn't recognize him after all these years. He knew that he had changed, his handsome features dulled by the poisonous liquor. He was anxious about spending time with her, unsure if she would even remember him and afraid she wouldn't forgive him for divorcing her, though she didn't know they were technically still married.

He thought back to when their marriage had crumbled, the animosity still held cautiously at bay until the day he began drinking. It had been so long ago that the nearly twenty-year-old memories had been remembered and forgotten a thousand times, faded like a long-forgotten love letter.

Adam replayed one of the worst nights of his life over in his mind. They had been at their beloved Victorian house, the one that he bought for Brynn, and he had been drunk and in his usual state. He was so drunk that he could barely look at her, a mess of a man, and a poor reflection of the boy who had once loved her so much.

"What has become of you?" Brynn had whispered angrily, her brown eyes hard and rimmed with red. "I don't even recognize you anymore. I've tried so hard to forgive who you've become because you're not the Adam I fell in love with. You're not anything like him. What have you done with him? I want *him* back!"

Despite her anger, she spoke slowly and deliberately, her voice raw from crying. "Why have you done this to us?"

Adam's eyes were glazed over and when he finally looked up and tried to meet her gaze, he couldn't find her, his blue eyes wandering and unable to stay focused. "I-I-I-I don' know what happened to him ... he's gone ... dead ... dead like Sophie ... dead like our baby. Dead like you and our love."

"But I'm not dead, Adam. I'm right here."

"You're a liar," Adam slurred. "You weren' there when I needed you ... you were selfish ... only caring about yourself and your selfish bitch mottther ... you didn' care about me more'n you cared about yourself ... You didn' care about Sophie ... It's your fault she's gone. Your damn selfishhhhness killed our baby."

Brynn sucked in her breath, her stomach suddenly hollow as though he had punched her. She stared at him, his face still handsome but unshaven, his hair longer than she had ever seen it before. His eyes, the beautiful blue she had fallen into as a teenager, belonged to a stranger, someone she had met but didn't want to know any longer.

She knelt down and hugged Maxie, her beautiful dog who stood close to her, protecting her like he always did.

"I want you to go," Brynn said, her voice low.

"Go? You wan' me to go? Go where? Where am I going?" Adam took a step toward her, swaying.

Brynn involuntarily flinched and took a step back. Her reaction automatic, unable to stop herself even after so many years had gone by and Thomas was dead in his grave.

"Dammit Brynn ... why do you always step back? Why are you always so afraid? I've never hit you ... never even touched you." Adam's eyes were suddenly wide, and he spit as he talked to her. "I never hurt you. I never wan' to hurt you."

He grabbed her arms and held them tight as Brynn let out a tiny squeal. Brynn felt herself beginning to panic as she looked up at him. Thomas' face flashed before her eyes and she could feel her heart beating wildly in her chest. Adam had never grabbed her so intensely, her arms beginning to hurt as he squeezed her.

"Stop looking so afraid! Stop it! Stop! You never trust me, you never ever trusted me be your husband." Adam was angry, his hands shaking as he stepped back and tried to regain control of himself. He had been frustrated with Brynn before, but he had always maintained his distance, always careful not to upset her, knowing that she would be fearful. Maxie stepped firmly in front of Brynn, his growl so low at first that neither Brynn nor Adam heard it. Adam's legs buckled, taking him off balance., He fell toward Brynn and suddenly Maxie jumped on him, toppling him over. Maxie latched on tight to Adam's arm, his teeth sinking into his skin refusing to let go. Adam cried out and Brynn screamed as she saw blood oozing from his arm. No matter what she did, Maxie refused to let go until Brynn gave up and fumbled helplessly for the phone.

Adam barely remembered it as she called 911 and he lay on the floor, blood oozing from his arm, Maxie still growling as he stood fiercely in front of Brynn, all loyalty to Adam gone.

Brynn approached Adam cautiously, trying to get past Maxie who was blocking her from getting to him and still looking at Adam threateningly. "How bad is it?" she asked, staring at the blood dripping all over the carpet on their bedroom floor.

"Bad, that stupid fucking dog." Maxie growled louder. Adam glared at him, angrily. "It's bad ... Brynn, it's bad. God ... Look what you made that damn dog do to me."

Brynn knelt down beside him and picked his arm up gently and carefully, tears running down her cheeks uncontrollably. The taste of salt burned her lips as she tried to lick the tears away.

She jumped up and grabbed a towel from the bathroom and held it tightly against the wound.

"I'm sorry Brynn, I didn' mean to yell at you. You know I would never hurt you ... ah Hell, what am I saying? I'm always hurting you, I just don' know why. I don' hate you, I mean, I don' think I hate you. I don' 'know ... I don' know." Adam cried out and Brynn wasn't sure if it was from the pain of his wound or the pain in his heart that he refused to let go of.

Brynn nodded, unable to speak. Brynn blamed herself for Sophie's death too, and Adam only reinforced that. She knew that nothing they did could get them past Sophie's death. Sophie was supposed to bring them together, but losing her was tearing them apart and any love between them had been buried with her.

He remembered how Brynn had held her hand on his forehead to comfort him as they waited for the ambulance while he faded in and out of consciousness. The only evidence remaining from that night was the long scar on his arm and the unsigned divorce papers that were still tucked in the bottom drawer of his desk. After all that had passed between them, the trust and love had disappeared and he thought guiltily about how he *had* wanted to shake her and hurt her, even though he told himself that he never would. Maxie knew that he wanted to hurt her, and he wasn't going to let him. Adam regretted that Maxie never let him get close again and never trusted him near Brynn. Adam's eyes began to burn at the memory.

He had loved that damn dog so much.

Then Adam had moved out and met Jessie. After that, Brynn had the accident that nearly killed both her and Eva, and Adam's heart ached at the memory.

He absently rubbed his scar as he thought about the past. After a while, he forced himself back to the present where he was no longer a young man. He sat in the folding chair and reminded himself that because of his drinking, he had hurt the ones he loved the most.

Adam knew in the end that divorcing Brynn had been the only way to protect her. The anger and rage he felt toward her was something he couldn't control when he was drinking. He'd never wanted to shake her or hurt her before that night. The fear in her eyes had been enough for him. He had tried to stop drinking intermittently throughout the years, but he always came back to it, needing it as much as the air that he breathed. Adam thought sadly that if it hadn't been for the accident, he would've lost Brynn forever, and was struck once again by the irony of it all.

Adam sat in the chair, his butt already hurting, his back uncomfortable, and listened as the "Welcome" began to start. He remembered that the meetings always started on time, and he was grateful for the entire hour that he would be around people like him, who struggled so much. He needed to hear from others who fought their demons much in the same way he did. Some fought and failed, while others were successful warriors, able to help others. Strangely, Adam found comfort in hearing from both.

Adam listened to the stories. After ten years of sobriety, Paul, had gotten drunk at work and lost his job after he found his wife cheating on him. Jamie had gotten so drunk she passed out for five hours, leaving her child at school without anyone to pick him up, and Sara had cheated on her husband and gotten pregnant by his best friend. As Adam listened, he was disgusted by them and with himself. Alcohol had turned him into a man he never imagined he'd be, full of anger and sadness that he couldn't control. He listened intently to each story, a painful reminder that he had his own terrible story to tell, and fought the urge to walk out of the meeting. But as he sat and contemplated the sadness of everyone's life in the room, a nagging feeling came over him. He felt that someone was watching him. He turned around and looked throughout the room, but wasn't able to see anyone staring at him. Still, the hairs on the back of his neck continued to stand on end.

The hour went by swiftly and when it was finished, Adam stood up quickly to leave. He never liked to talk to anyone, or about himself, at these meetings, and didn't want to mingle with any of the attendees. He had taken as much as he could from it, the urge to drink not diminished in any way.

"Excuse me," a light tap on the shoulder from behind startled him.

He turned around and looked into the most beautiful pair of emerald green eyes he had ever seen. They were almost glittering as they looked up at him, and he had the sudden and distinct feeling he had seen those eyes before.

"Yes?" he said, mesmerized.

"I know you," the woman said, tucking a long strand of red hair behind her ear.

Adam stared at her blankly for a moment until his eyes widened in recognition. It had been over two decades since he had seen her last and she had left without so much as a good-bye. While part of him had loved her, she had only been a temporary salve, a futile attempt to try and heal from his divorce.

"J-J-J-Jessie?" Adam was stunned. This was the last place he would've expected to see her. "What are you doing here?"

"So … you remember me? I thought you would've forgotten all about me by now." Jessie said, her voice soft and her eyes sparkling, just as he remembered her.

"Of course I remember you," Adam said warmly, feeling a familiar tug inside of him as he hugged her. He was surprised at how tightly she squeezed him after how she had left. For a small woman, she was stronger than she looked, and he remembered how strong she had been, often holding him through an entire night as he cried and sobbed. "Um … I guess we can't go for a drink like we used to. Would you like to get some coffee … I mean, would that be okay?"

Jessie looked up at him and smiled brightly. He suddenly remembered how her smile was the only thing able to get him through some of his darkest days. He was surprised at how much his heart suddenly ached for what might have been between them, if she hadn't disappeared so abruptly. "I would absolutely love to, Adam Michaels. I was hoping this moment would come one day."

22

The Guardian
September 20th, 2016

John "Jack" Palmer III was exactly like his grandfather in many ways.

He was diligent in his duties as CEO of Harper Enterprises and careful to honor the family name in everything he did. He was also committed to his care of the Michaels family, who his family owed everything to. James Harper, Brynn's grandfather, had been a good friend and mentor to John Palmer I. Jack knew that he could delegate the family's affairs to someone else while he attended to other important matters, but he knew that his grandfather would be disappointed in him. John made it his personal mission to take care of the family, like his grandfather before him, but he was forced to do so from afar. While he had initially tried to form a closer bond with the family, Adam had been resistant in allowing him to get too close. So, he did the best he could. He knew that he owed it to his grandfather.

Jack's grandfather had never forgiven himself for allowing Brynn's grandparents to be kidnapped, which resulted in the murder of James Harper and the kidnapping of his beloved wife, Amy. Even though

John found Amy many years after her kidnapping and reunited her with her family, he felt personally responsible for allowing James to be murdered. The fact that there was nothing he could have done to prevent it didn't make it any easier on him.

Unlike his grandfather who had been a family man, Jack was a bachelor. He had watched his own father struggle to be there for his family. He refused to put any children through the long absences and indifference that his own father had shown him. John Palmer Jr. had been a disappointment to his father and to his own family. He wasn't kind or thoughtful like his father had been, and he was lazy. When given the opportunity to take the reins of Harper Enterprises, John Jr. had been quite a disappointment in every way. He frustrated his father who had put his heart and soul into the company in honor of his mentor and friend.

John became more of a father and mentor to young Jack than his father had ever been, recognizing his thoughtful brilliance at an early age. Jack and his grandfather bonded very early in his life, and he only cared about what his grandfather thought. He worked hard and excelled in everything he did; school, sports, and even in the arts, playing piano and guitar as a respite from the intensity in his life.

"Jack," his grandfather had said to him repeatedly throughout his young life, "Work hard and make me proud of you. I've put my heart and soul into Harper Enterprises, and I'm not going to watch it go down the drain. James would be so disappointed in me and I can't … I won't allow it. I want you to do well and take it over when you're old enough."

"I won't let you down, Grandpa, I promise," Jack had been earnest in everything he did and was more dynamic than anyone had ever expected. He was the only child and his mother adored him as much as his father ignored him.

Jack was true to his word. He took the company from his father very early in his career, which was a unanimous decision from the board. For the first time in many years, the company began to thrive and become the powerhouse it had once been under James Harper's direction.

Even though Jack could afford to live lavishly, he chose a modest house down the street from his mother. He knew that as she got older she would need him more often. Aside from his grandfather, she was the only other person he'd ever loved, his grandmother passing away when he was only four years old.

When he received the call that Brynn Michaels had, by some miracle, awakened from her coma, he was stunned. His grandfather had talked about Brynn often, admiring her strength and character. Jack managed the details of The Harper House from afar since his last encounter with Adam, but knew he must go there now in order to determine their needs. His grandfather would've expected it, and he knew that he couldn't possibly stay away.

He got into his car, refusing the request of his assistant to have a driver take him, and set his GPS for The Harper House. The drive from the city was pleasant, and forty-five minutes later, he pulled up to the massive gate of the house. The voice on the intercom was crisp as it asked him to identify himself. After a few moments, the gate opened slowly and he drove up the long, winding driveway to the massive house that James Harper had dubbed "The Harper House." The house had been designed and built to James' specifications. He had constructed it for his family envisioning an active, lively home, but was disappointed when his daughter, Ellie, had not embraced her life in it as he had hoped. With two massive wings, twenty-six rooms, an Olympic-sized pool, tennis courts, and a large gym, James had built The Harper House as a part of his legacy to pass down to this family, generation after generation.

Jack walked up to the front door, imagining his grandfather walking up the very same steps, and feeling more than a little nostalgic for him. He hesitated and rang the bell, wishing he had changed into jeans and a button-down shirt instead of still wearing the suit he had worn to the office that morning.

The door opened and a small woman with dark hair and the most amazing eyes he had ever seen came flying out, nearly toppling them both down the front steps.

"Oh, my gosh. I'm so sorry!" she breathed, as he reached out to catch her from falling. "I just … I'm so sorry … I wasn't looking where I was going."

"Oh, that's okay," Jack said feeling a little unsettled, which was unusual for him. He couldn't stop himself from staring into her eyes. They were large and blue, and as deep and glittering as sapphires. For a moment he forgot where he was and what he was supposed to be doing. The woman was about a decade younger than he was, and was so small that his 6'2" frame towered over her. Something about her made his stomach begin to churn unexpectedly. *What is wrong with me?*

"I'm sorry, I'm Eva … Eva Harper Michaels," she held out a dainty hand for him to shake.

Jack's eyes opened wide in recognition.

"Of course! I thought you might be. I'm John Palmer III, but you can call me Jack." Jack shook her hand and felt a surge of electricity pass through his fingers. He pulled his hand back, alarmed. He had known many beautiful women in his life, many of whom viewed his bachelor status as a challenge and were determined to tie him down. Jack never stayed with one woman for more than a couple of months, easily bored by their lack of imagination, and always annoyed with their desperation. He didn't mind being alone, and he had never met anyone who he thought was worth committing to.

With Eva standing right in front of him, it crossed his mind that she was different. He didn't know why he felt that way, but something about the way her eyes sparkled made him curious about her. Her smile was unguarded, and when she aimed it toward him, his stomach fluttered though he tried to convince himself it was just hunger pangs.

"Hi … Jack," Eva said, holding his deep brown eyes a moment longer than she meant to. His sandy hair had been ruffled when she ran into him and she thought about how handsome he was, almost boyish, even though he was clearly much older than she was. Jack was one of the best-looking men she had ever seen, and Eva looked away from him, feeling guilty for even letting the thought creep into her mind.

"I'm sorry I haven't been out. Until recently, it was always my grandfather who called on the family. He had a special bond with you all as I'm sure you know … and after … well, I tried to come and call on you but … your father wanted … privacy …" his voice trailed off sadly.

"I know. I'm so sorry about your grandfather," Eva touched his arm instinctively. "We donated to the hospital in his name. He was truly such a wonderful man."

"Thank you," Jack said, gratefully. The service had been closed and private, his grandfather not wanting a huge fuss made over him. Jack knew that he deserved more. He had been a generous man who was well-loved, and many had honored his wishes by donating to the children's hospital. Enough so that they were able to renovate an entire wing, just like his grandfather had hoped.

Jack's father hadn't even bothered to show up for the service, which was half-expected. After Jack took over his position, his father had virtually disappeared, leaving his mother without a word.

"Where are you going in such a hurry?" Jack asked, curious.

"I'm going to the hospital to see my mom. Kelly texted and said that it's a good day and she's awake a lot, so I want to get there to see her."

"Would you like me to take you?" Jack gestured to his car that was right in front. "I've been meaning to go and visit and this would give us some time to catch up."

"Oh, no. I couldn't ask you to take me," Eva took a step back, shaking her head.

"I don't mind at all. I'd love to meet Brynn. My grandfather loved her and always spoke so well of her. He even told me that I'd met her before, though I was too young to remember." Eva enjoyed the sound of Jack's voice and how warm it sounded when he talked about his grandfather. Eva realized that she had never heard Chris' voice warm up quite like that when he talked about anything, and for a brief moment she wondered why.

"Um … well, if you really don't mind, then I would love a ride."

"Great!" Jack exclaimed guiding her to his car. He held the door open for her and closed it gently once she settled in. As he walked around to the other side, he realized that he was happier to be giving her a ride to the hospital than he should be.

As they drove, they talked non-stop and Jack was surprised at how easy it was to converse with her. He wasn't used to speaking to women so easily and casually, and he realized that he was enjoying their conversation tremendously. She wasn't interested in impressing him and spoke freely. When she stared at him with her large, beautiful eyes, it was as though there was nothing in the world she would rather be doing than listening to him.

When she mentioned her husband, he bristled. He was surprised by how disappointed he was at the reminder that she was married, even though he already knew it. He didn't make it a habit to become interested in married women, and he told himself that his interest in her was strictly professional. The pounding of his heart told him something different.

When Jack had initially been told that Eva was dating, he had his people do a complete background check on Christopher Brian Garrett. Everything had come back clean. It was common practice to check out everybody who came in contact with the family, and Jack was glad that for once there would be some happiness at The Harper House. He had been unable to attend the wedding because he had been out of the country on business, but had his assistant send a beautiful and expensive gift.

"We've met before, you know," Jack said, smiling.

"Yes, I remember," Eva said, her face flushing a little.

"You do?" Jack seemed amused.

"Yes, it was one of the most embarrassing moments of my child-hood." Eva turned and looked out of the window, her hand going directly to her lips.

"You kissed me," Jack smiled.

"I know! I know! That is so embarrassing! I was hoping you would forget that … I was so young and so silly. I just had the biggest crush on you and I couldn't help it. I was eight, and you were …"

"Much older," Jack grinned at the memory. "You asked if you could hug me and instead, you kissed me on the cheek."

"Yes, it was a very strange moment for me. I was a pretty quiet, shy child, but for some reason I took a chance …" Eva's face was bright red with embarrassment.

It had been one of the few times when he had accompanied his grandfather to The Harper House. Jack was always welcome to go with him to the office, but that time he had taken him to visit some of his favorite people. Noah had still been alive and Amy had barely been holding on at that time. It was Eva who caught Jack's attention, though. She had been a bright and beautiful child, but Jack had been surprised at how dismissive Adam had been of her, and he was saddened by how lonely she seemed. During their short visit she had followed Jack everywhere he went. Jack, who was much older than she was, had been flattered by the obvious crush she had on him.

He grinned at her, amused by her embarrassment.

"I can't believe you remembered that," Eva said, not meeting his gaze, "It was so long ago and so unlike me."

"It was a memorable kiss," Jack teased. It wasn't his nature to be so light-hearted, but Eva brought it out in him. He couldn't believe he was teasing her. He couldn't remember the last time he had teased anyone.

They drove in silence for a few moments, both of them smiling at the memory. As they got nearer to the hospital Eva's phone rang.

"Hello? This is Eva," Eva said, not recognizing the phone number. "Yes. Yes, of course I'll accept the charges."

Jack looked over at Eva, her voice immediately alarming him.

"Chris!" Eva said, her voice high and sharp. "Are you okay? Where are you? What's going on?"

Jack could barely hear the voice on the other end of the line, other than a few words.

Eva hung up the phone, her eyes wide and glistening, her breath coming in short, panicked gulps. "Please, turn around. Please. I have to go to the county jail."

"The county jail?" Jack asked, confused. "Why?"

"It's … m-m-my husband. He's been arrested. I need to go help him right away!" Eva was breathing hard, her chest heaving uncontrollably.

"Wait ... what you do you mean he was arrested? What was he arrested for?" Jack asked, immediately alarmed.

"I don't know. I don't know. But ... Oh God ... he sounded like it might be really bad." Eva's eyes were wide with panic, her hand holding her stomach tightly. Jack was concerned for Eva as he looked for their new destination in his GPS and changed direction. Eva's face was gray and she looked as though she might throw up.

"Oh God," Eva repeated, her hands rubbing her stomach anxiously. "This is really bad, really bad."

Jack started to console her and at the last second, closed his mouth and didn't say anything. Instead he reached over and put his hand on top of hers, a gesture that seemed too intimate, but felt like the only thing to do.

He was startled as he felt her tiny stomach protrude. He looked down and saw the tiniest outline of what looked like a baby bump and wondered how he could have missed it as it suddenly sunk in. He kicked himself mentally as he realized for the first time that Eva was pregnant.

23

Going Home
September 20th, 2016

Kelly sat with Brynn and waited patiently for Eva.

She hadn't wanted to tell her the good news on the phone, but the doctors finally felt comfortable with letting Brynn go home, as long as she was under close observation and had constant care. After daily trips to physical therapy, she'd gained more movement and the strength in her limbs had progressively gotten better. She'd been reminded, though, that it would continue to be a long journey, and there was no way they could estimate what level of control or movement she would be able to get back, if any.

Brynn was frustrated when she couldn't walk as well as she wanted, and when her hands still knocked things over as she tried to grasp things. Kelly reassured her that she was doing far more than anyone had ever expected her to. She had never been expected to wake at all.

"We are still in uncharted territory with our little miracle," said Kelly's favorite doctor, a beautiful Indian woman whose soft spoken voice was both comforting and pleasant to listen to. "Mrs. Michaels is an unprecedented case at this hospital, and we will need to see her regularly in order to monitor her progress. We are pleased with how far she's come in the last two months, and feel she will possibly recover better at home."

Kelly had been pleased to hear the news and was anxious to see how Brynn would react

"Brynn, you're going home," she said, smoothing Brynn's dark hair across her forehead. She smiled at her friend and Brynn smiled back, but Kelly sensed there was something wrong.

"E-va?" Brynn said her voice hoarse and her words slow.

"She should be here soon," Kelly said, checking her phone for the time. "I called her two hours ago, and she said she was on the way. Did you hear me tell you that you're going home?"

"Ad-am?" Brynn asked almost cautiously.

"Adam isn't here, Brynn. I don't know where he is or when he'll show up. I don't know … I … wouldn't worry about him if I were you. The only thing you should think about right now is that you get to go home."

Adam's visits to the hospital hadn't been as regular as Kelly had expected. While he was happy that she was awake, his visits were intermittent and inconsistent, and nobody ever knew where he was. After years of waiting for Brynn to wake up, Kelly thought he would be there by her side every single day. Instead, Kelly sat at Brynn's side just as she had at The Harper House.

Brynn's shoulders relaxed when Kelly said she hadn't heard from him, almost as though she was relieved. The air between Adam and Brynn seemed to be thick with tension during his visits, which Kelly couldn't understand. She had watched her friend cry over Brynn's motionless body for nearly two decades, and wondered if the ugliness of the past was resurfacing to haunt them. When Adam visited, he was careful to do it only when Kelly or Eva were there, and he and Brynn never spoke too much. It was almost as though they had a mutual agreement.

Kelly wondered if Brynn remembered that she had been on her way to see Nick when the accident occurred. Actually, she was curious if Brynn remembered anything at all. Brynn still struggled with her speech, so Kelly was careful not to ask her too much. She decided she would wait to ask her about Nick until the time was right.

"Do you want me to try and get Adam for you so he can take you home? Do you need him?" Kelly asked, pulling out her phone.

Brynn shook her head back and forth a few times and Kelly wondered what she was thinking. Her friend's face was a dark, silent cloud.

"No? Okay, let me know what you need. Hopefully we can get you talking … I miss our talks." Kelly smiled at her, patting her hand.

Brynn attempted a small smile and, for a brief moment, Kelly could see a glimpse of her old friend, beautiful and unscarred, as she had been before the accident.

"If we don't hear from Eva soon, we'll just call Bill, the driver, and have him come get us and take us back to home," Kelly said trying to disguise her concern for Eva.

Brynn nodded. *Where is Eva? Wouldn't she want to take me home? I hope that she's okay and that nothing has happened to her. Nothing can happen to my baby girl. Now that I'm awake I don't know what I would do. We have so much to catch up on and I need her.*

Kelly texted Eva and got no answer. She stared at her phone, willing Eva to pick up. Eva usually answered immediately and Kelly was getting more anxious.

"E-va?" Brynn asked, her face showing worry.

Kelly tried not to appear afraid as she smiled at Brynn. "I'm sure she's just … busy, or maybe she fell asleep or something."

She called the house to confirm whether Eva was there and Rachel, the head housekeeper, told her that she was gone but her car was still there. This alarmed Kelly even more. She asked her to have Bill come and get them. She hung up and began to pace the hospital room, worry overcoming her.

Her phone beeped and Kelly jumped a mile as she stared down at her phone. The text had come from Eva.

"*Sorry. I'm at the police station with Jack. I'll call in a bit.*"

"*Jack? Who is Jack? Why are you at the police station? Are you okay?*"

Kelly typed furiously, her mind racing as she tried to figure out who Jack was.

"*Jack Palmer. Long story. Chris is in jail.*"

Kelly gasped as she read Eva's text.

Brynn looked at her questioningly and Kelly shook her head. She wasn't sure if Brynn could completely understand everything yet and she was hesitant to worry her needlessly until she knew more.

"*Do you need your dad?*" Kelly typed.

"*Tried. He isn't answering. Probably passed out.*"

Kelly's heart ached and for a moment she flashed back to when Eva was a small child and couldn't understand why her daddy fell asleep so early all the time and couldn't play with her like she wanted him to.

"*Let me know what you need me to do.*" Kelly typed.

"*Jack will help me out here. I'm in good hands. XO*"

Kelly sighed, grateful that Eva was safe. *Why would Chris be in jail? What could he have done?* Kelly was stunned but tried not to show it. She had never disliked Chris, but she had never completely trusted him, either. There was something about him that she couldn't and never tried to explain to Eva. She had dismissed it knowing how happy she was. She and Adam had discussed it privately, but neither one of them ever said anything out loud. Eva's happiness was all that mattered, but Kelly had her reservations until the background check came back clean. When the background check showed that he hadn't even had as much as a speeding ticket, she and Adam had sighed in relief and convinced themselves that they were just being overly protective.

"E-va ...?" Brynn's large brown eyes were questioning as she tried to control her arm well enough to reach out and grab Kelly's hand.

Kelly grabbed her friend and held it tight. "Yes, she'll be okay. She's with Jack Palmer, John Palmer's grandson."

Brynn's brows furrowed in concentration, her brown eyes lighting up after a few long moments, much to Kelly's delight. "John!"

"Yes! You remember John! You were very good friends. He was your grandfather's protégé and he took care of the family. Now his grandson, Jack, looks after everything for you." Kelly was thankful that Brynn remembered him. Her memory was still unpredictable, though it seemed to get better as the days passed.

After the nurse came to give them instructions, they wheeled Brynn down to the lobby. Brynn's eyes grew large when she saw the big, black car that was waiting for her. Bill had been with the family for many years and had never known Brynn before the accident, but he approached her with a warmth that surprised even Kelly.

"Hello, Miss Brynn. I've come to take you home," Bill said, tipping his hat to her and smiling with his eyes.

Brynn nodded and smiled back. "Thank … you," she said, her voice husky and low.

He helped her get into the car and gave Kelly a quick hug. "She looks good, doesn't she?" Kelly said, wiping a tear away.

"Yes ma'am, she looks great!" Bill said, smiling at her. "You're a good friend, Miss Kelly."

"So are you, Bill." Kelly hugged him again, appreciative of the compliment.

They drove the forty-five minutes to The Harper House mostly in silence, Brynn staring out the window, her eyes big and full of excitement as though she were seeing things for the very first time.

"Does this look familiar?" Kelly asked as Brynn nodded, happily.

Brynn's eyes were full of wonder, and Kelly marveled at her child-like pleasure. Kelly realized that this was the first time Brynn had been awake on any of her rides back home. Kelly wondered how much Brynn remembered of the house that she had taken care of and renovated years before when she had first inherited it. The house remained exactly as Brynn had left it, with the exception of the floor Adam had given Eva for her new family.

Kelly stared at Brynn and wondered what she was thinking as she watched the expression on her face change from excitement to sadness and back to excitement again.

As they pulled up to the massive house, Brynn's eyes grew even wider and Kelly reminded herself that it had been years since Brynn had been awake in the home.

"Home?" Brynn asked, pointing awkwardly to the house, her mind desperate to grasp any memory that tied her to it.

"Yes," Kelly said smiling. "This is The Harper House, which was your grandparents house and they passed it down to you. This is your home. You lived here for a while. Do you remember it?"

Brynn closed her eyes as though trying to evoke a memory of any kind. When she opened them again, she smiled.

"Yes," Brynn said, her face warm and happy. "I do."

24

The Stranger
August 19, 2016

The loud banging woke him and he jumped up, disoriented. He stood up clumsily, confused by the constant pounding in his head as he tried to figure out where he was and why he was on the floor. The surroundings were familiar, but no matter how hard he tried he couldn't place where he was. His eyes were fuzzy and his head hazy from too much alcohol. There was a sharp, stabbing pain directly behind his right eye that made it impossible for him to think.

It took him a few minutes to get his bearings as he stared at the red, sticky liquid that covered the floor and his clothes. It took him several long minutes to realize that the red liquid was blood. He couldn't believe how much there was, the smell of it nauseating him.

"Open up, right now! Police!"

Chris realized that the pounding wasn't just in his head, but was coming from the direction of the door. His heart began to thump faster in his chest. He stood unsteadily, willing his feet to move, but they felt cemented to the ground. The pounding continued until he heard the sound of wood splitting, then a loud explosion, and the sound of heavy feet entering the room.

"Get down now! get down!" A loud voice yelled at him and he obeyed.

As he slid back down to the floor, his hands instinctively went up in the air. He had done this before, but this time he knew it was different. As he lay down, trying to keep his face out of the blood, he felt a foot on the back of his neck. He didn't need to look up to know that he had several guns being pointed down at him. "Don't fucking move or I'll shoot you!"

He could tell from the intensity of the voices swirling above him that he dare not move even an inch. He barely allowed himself to breathe, the fear coursing through every cell in his body.

"Fuck, look at all this blood!" one of the officers noted, shock in his voice.

"Don't move, don't touch anything!" another voice shouted. Chris wasn't sure if he was shouting at him or at someone else, and he tried to stay as still as possible.

"Jesus, what did this asshole do? Look at 'em, he's completely covered in blood."

"Oh God, look at this shit!"

Chris lay still, trying not to breathe as more and more voices entered the room, shouting all at once. The voices kept yelling and he wondered what was going on and what they were seeing. He knew the room was a mess, but he'd barely had time to see anything, and was now keeping his eyes squeezed closed out of confusion and fear. The contents of his stomach kept threatening to come up as the smell of the blood continued to assault his nose.

"What are you doing down there?" The voice above him was agitated. "I told you not to fucking move, why are you moving?"

"I'm going to puke ... I can't help it." He was retching and trying not to vomit, but it was coming up in waves and there was nothing he could do about it.

The puke exploded out of his mouth and onto the floor, splashing up on his cheek. The smell hit him, and he opened his mouth again, unable to stop it from coming out. He had never felt more disgusted with himself in his entire life, and he hoped for a split second that the cop would just shoot him and put him out of his misery.

"Fuck! Stop it, dammit!"

It was the last thing he remembered before he passed out, and when he woke up, he was no longer covered in blood or his own puke, but was wearing a bright orange pair of overalls. His mouth felt as though it was full of cotton as he stared helplessly at the walls of the small cell. He sat on the cot, his head in his hands, and wondered what he was doing in jail. His memory was mostly blank. He knew he had fought ... with Nora. It had been an ugly one and she had kicked him out. Instead of going back to The Harper House like he should have, where he felt like a prisoner, he went to a bar ... multiple bars.

The flashes were hazy and he tried to lick his lips, but his tongue was dry and thick. He desperately wanted water, the taste of ashes and old whiskey coating his teeth and his tongue. He fought the urge to throw up again, but he knew there was probably nothing left in his stomach. He hated the thought of dry heaving and he pushed it down as deep as he could.

Chris tried to think about where he had been and what he had done to end up in a jail cell. *Oh God ... Nora. Nora! I was in her apartment, but where the fuck was she? I didn't see her anywhere. I hope she's okay! Whose blood was that?*

He thought about her beautiful face and how angry she had been when he'd seen her last. She had been completely furious with him for wanting to change the plan, but Chris just didn't feel right about what Nora wanted to do to Eva. Chris shook his head at the memory, but he had seen her like that many times before and knew it would pass. But why was he in jail ... *I haven't made my phone call! I need to make my phone call.*

Suddenly, a door opened and light flooded into the dim cell. Two officers and a man dressed in a button-down shirt, jeans, and a gun holstered against his ribs stood outside of his cell staring at him. The man with the button-down shirt looked pissed, and Chris felt himself tense up as the man stared at him with hard, steely eyes.

"Connor Michael Martin?" the man in the button down looked at him, his voice hard and raspy from smoking too many cigarettes. "I'm Detective Lyons, and we have some talking to do."

"No … you have the wrong man. I'm Christopher Brian Garrett." Chris said, looking at him evenly.

"Who are you saying you are now?" the detective asked, his right eyebrow cocked slightly.

"I'm Christopher. Brian. Garrett." Chris said slowly, as though mocking the detective.

"No. You're Connor Michael Martin. There is nobody named 'Christopher Brian Garrett', even though your license says that's who are you are. We know it's a fake because we ran your prints. You're in the system quite a bit Mr. Martin, so cut the shit. You know exactly how this works."

Chris looked at the man, his eyes growing dark and angry, slowly transforming him into someone dark and sinister.

"You need to come with us. We have some questions to ask you."

"I need a lawyer and I need you to call my wife." Chris knew that Eva would help him, especially when he hadn't done anything wrong. He just needed to see her so that he could explain it to her.

"Of course you do," the detective said, sneering. "But your wife isn't going to want to come near you with a ten-foot pole after what you've done."

"I didn't do anything! I don't even know what happened. Is Nora … the girl who lives in that apartment … is she okay?" Chris asked, his voice angrier than he intended it to be.

"Are you kidding me?" the detective stared at him in disbelief. "Is that the angle you're going to play? Are you going to act like you don't know anything?"

"I don't, I swear!" Chris' eyes widened. "All I want to know is whether the girl is okay!"

"I'm not telling you anything," the detective said with contempt. "If you're going to pretend that you don't know what you did, then I'm not going to play your game."

The detective stood up abruptly and walked out of the room, slamming the door behind him.

The next hour felt like days as Chris waited for the detective to come back.

When he returned, Chris was panicked and agitated. "Did you call my wife? Did you call my lawyer?"

"You'll get to call both, when we say."

They led him to an interrogation room and he sat down on the uncomfortable chair, hating the shackles on his wrists.

"Okay, Mr. Martin … do you want to tell me why you did it?" Detective Lyons asked, never breaking eye contact.

"You get right to the point, don't you Detective?" Chris asked sounding amused.

"Does that bother you?" the detective looked at Chris and fought the urge to break eye contact. He knew that he was being toyed with and he didn't like it.

Michael Lyons had been a detective for twenty-five years and had been in the interrogation room with psychopaths like this one hundreds of times. He had moved from Chicago to a smaller town five years ago, to get away from crimes like this because he no longer had the stomach for it. When he got word about the crime scene, he couldn't believe it, and sitting across from Connor Martin was more unnerving than he'd anticipated.

He tried to shake it off, trying to convince himself that it was just the pictures of the dead girl that were throwing him off. Whoever had stabbed the girl was pissed at her and wanted to see her suffer. The stab wounds all over her body had been deep and vicious and the detective had never seen anything like it.

"No, it doesn't bother me at all," Chris said, smirking. "But I'm wondering what you think I've done."

"That's what I'm waiting to hear from you, Connor. I can piece together what you did, but you'd make it so much easier on yourself, and on us, if you'd just tell us what happened and why you did it. You know we'll figure it out anyway."

Chris stared coldly through the detective, his hazel eyes dead and giving nothing away.

"I have no idea what you're talking about. I woke up and I was lying on the floor, but I didn't do anything to anybody. You're not going to get anything out of me, because there's nothing to tell," Chris said, his voice flat and low.

The detective flipped over a picture and Chris' voice caught in his throat. Long strands of red hair were mixed with blood, the face bruised beyond recognition.

Chris took a deep breath and looked the detective in the eye.

"I'm not saying anything to you unless I have a lawyer present," Chris said, his voice hard.

As Detective Lyons stood up, he flipped over another picture, and then left the room.

Chris looked at the picture and tried to stop the sob that erupted from his chest.

"Nora," he whispered, recognizing the delicate bracelet that he had given her for her birthday wrapped around the dead woman's blood-soaked wrist.

25

Old Friends
September 20th, 2016

As Adam slowly awoke, he realized how hot and cottony his mouth felt. It was an old familiar feeling, like putting on his favorite sweater or a comfortable pair of shoes. The moment he realized what it was, he felt an overwhelming sense of self-loathing that reminded him of how weak and pathetic he had become.

He was afraid to open his eyes, suddenly aware from the tightness of the sheets against his naked body and the weight in the bed next to him that he wasn't alone.

Jessie!

Flashes of her creamy-white, naked flesh and her bright, beautiful smile exploded in his mind and he fought the urge to groan out loud for fear he would awaken her. *Oh shit. What have I done? What time is it?*

The pit in the middle his stomach told him that he hadn't been in contact with Kelly or Eva for a long time. He had left the hospital to go to a meeting, but his internal clock told him that it had been much longer than it should've been since he had checked in. *Brynn ... why did I leave? I have to get out of here!*

Brynn had been awake but wouldn't speak, and the weight of her dark eyes staring at him had been unnerving. He had cried against her when she had awoken, but for months, no matter how hard he tried, he couldn't bring himself to get close to her or spend time alone with her. He had convinced himself that her eyes were warning him to *Stay Away*, and he had. He had no excuse to give when Eva and Kelly asked him why he visited the hospital less and less, knowing that he would sound like a coward. Deep down in his gut he told himself that Brynn didn't want him there, and it was ripping him apart from the inside out, shredding him slowly and painfully. After spending two decades begging her to wake up, his heart was shattered by the depth of her eyes, and he had no idea what to do next.

He decided that getting sober was his first step since he hadn't been able to do that in years.

Running into Jessie at the AA meeting had been sheer luck. He recognized her immediately, his heart leaping toward her before he could stop it. She had smiled at him with that amazingly toothy smile that had comforted him so long ago. The years that had separated them were gone in an instant.

"Why did you leave me without saying good-bye?" he vaguely remembered asking her after countless shots of tequila. Her answer had been deep and soulful as she grabbed at his unruly hair in the depths of their passion.

"I left because I loved you too much," she responded breathlessly, her long red hair silky and soft against his face. It had been so long since he had been close to a woman, and he realized for the first time just how much he missed it. "It hurt me too much to be with you."

"You shouldn't have left me," he said, trying his best not to slur.

"You didn't love me," she said, licking his ear.

"I would have ... I could have," he said, grabbing her tight, pulling her as close against him as he possibly could. "I did."

"But you didn't love me like I loved you," Jessie said, sobbing against him.

"I'm sorry," Adam remembered saying, holding her tight and kissing her tears.

As he lie there next to her, he tried to ignore the pounding in his head and the panic growing in his chest.

He tried to pull his arm out from under Jessie, without waking her.

"Mmmmm," she moaned, and Adam froze until he realized she was still sleeping.

"Sorry," he whispered, as he successfully pulled free. He fumbled around for his pants, the cool air against his naked skin making him feel exposed.

Shit ... where am I? He looked around the room trying to find a door, but it was too dark.

He heard a buzzing and desperately strained toward it, nearly knocking himself out on the doorknob. He followed the noise into the living room where he vaguely remembered tossing his pants. When he finally located them, he fumbled clumsily as he tried to pull his phone out of the pocket to see who was calling. He sucked in his breath when he saw that he had missed six phone calls.

Kelly had left him ten messages and Adam felt the pit in his stomach growing.

4:00 pm *"Adam, we are leaving the hospital today. Where have you been?"*

4:26 pm *"We are leaving in an hour."*

5:02 pm *"Are you coming to the hospital? Where are you? We can't find you or Eva."*

Eva? Fuck! Where is Eva?

5:17pm *"I called for a driver from the house. I'm taking Brynn home."*

6:07pm *"We are on the way to the house. I don't know where you are, but I'm worried and pissed. WTH?"*

6:39pm *"Eva's at the police station. Chris is in jail. It's bad. Where are you?"*

9:17pm *"Where in the hell are you? Brynn is home. She's sleeping. Things with Chris are bad. Call me!"*

10:45pm *"I hope you have a really good explanation for where you are."*

11:50pm *"Damn you, Adam. Call me as soon as you can."*

1:15am *"I'm calling the police in the morning if I don't have a text when I wake up."*

Adam looked at the time on his phone. *5:00 am. Shit!*

"Who is it?" The voice startled him, and Adam dropped his phone, swearing as it bounced off the floor, unharmed.

A light flicked on and Adam turned to see Jessie, covered in nothing but a sheet, her eyes narrowed.

"Oh ... it's uh ... Kelly. A friend," Adam stuttered, unsure if he wanted to tell Jessie what had been going on. His head was splitting from the impending hangover and he licked his lips, trying to find some relief from the dryness that had overtaken him from the inside out.

Without a word, Jessie walked over to the kitchen and poured a tall glass of water. She reached into the cabinet above the sink and grabbed a white plastic bottle out of it. As she did so, the sheet fell away, but Jessie didn't seem to notice as she walked toward Adam and handed him four little red pills and the glass of water.

Seeing her naked in the light, Adam's mind travelled back to the time when she had lived with him. They had spent days locked away in his apartment, naked and together, saving one other from their collective loneliness and filling each another's emptiness. He had loved her in his own way, but he knew it would never be enough.

"Do you love her?" Jessie asked, picking up her sheet and wrapping it around herself as she moved closer to Adam.

"Who? Kelly? Do I love Kelly?" Adam asked, confused.

"No. Brynn. Do you still love Brynn?" Jessie asked, her voice tinged with jealousy.

"Jessie ... I don't know that we should talk about this right now. It's not the right time ... I need to go ..." Adam suddenly felt cornered.

"How can you just leave? We just found one another ... I thought we could ... spend some time together." Jessie's tried to keep her voice steady.

"It's just ... It's not the right time, Jessie. I'm sorry ... I just," Adam fumbled with his pants as he tried to pull them on, Jessie's eyes burning into him.

The silence between them was deafening as Adam searched for the rest of his clothes that were strewn all over the floor and the furniture.

"I know, Adam. One of us always has to go," Jessie's voice was low and sad, her green eyes filling with tears. "I didn't expect you to stay. I just hoped that you would want to."

"No … It's not that I don't *want* to stay. I just … I can't. Not tonight … I mean … I don't know what to say. I shouldn't have come here …" Adam dressed slowly, his clothes refusing to cooperate. He looked around blindly trying to find his sock, realizing that it was right on the floor next to him but only a few inches from Jessie. He reached over and grabbed it quickly, as though she might take it from him, his eyes avoiding hers at all costs.

"I don't know who you're trying to fool by going to AA, but I can tell. From one drunk to another, you always drink, and tonight wasn't anything special." Jessie's smile had a hard edge to it and Adam cringed, wondering how she could see through him so well.

"I loved seeing you tonight, I really did. But things are … complicated …" Adam stumbled, finally meeting Jessie's gaze.

"How?" she said, inching closer to him.

"They just are. I can't explain it to you right now because you won't like it, and I know that I shouldn't have come here. I'm sorry. I shouldn't have done this …" Adam stepped closer to the door.

"I don't understand why you can't talk to me or open your heart up. After everything we were to each other and all that we meant, you can't even stay for a little while. I don't understand it. No matter what, you've never been able to love me," Jessie said, her voice rising.

"I'm sorry. This isn't going to work right now. There's too much going on … I'm sorry, Jessie. I … I can't do this right now, I have to go." Adam was sweating, the pounding in his head subsiding slightly, but not enough.

Fuck, I don't even know if I drove here. He fumbled around in his pockets and was relieved to feel the familiar jaggedness of the keys he had shoved in his pocket.

"But I don't want you to go. I don't want you to leave me, just yet."

Jessie said, pleading desperately. "Please, stay with me until the morning."

"I can't, Jessie," Adam said, getting closer to the door. "Please, I'll call you."

Jessie stared at him wordlessly as Adam opened the door and walked out.

He didn't look behind him as he walked down the two flights of stairs as quickly as he could. As the door opened to the outside and the blast of cool air smacked him in the face, he looked around frantically for his car. As he spotted it and sunk down into the driver's seat, he leaned his head back for a moment onto the headrest and breathed a huge sigh of relief.

As he drove away, he realized for the first time that he had never taken Jessie's phone number.

26

Connor Martin
September 20th, 2016

"Who?" Eva looked at the detective, her blue eyes as large as they had ever been, confusion etched all over her beautiful face as she strained to understand what he was saying.

"Connor Martin, Miss." Detective Lyons spoke slowly and tried to be as patient with the girl as he could. Connor had clearly done a number on her, and, after taking note of the ring on her finger and the baby that was growing in her tiny belly, the detective almost felt sorry for her.

"No sir, you've got it wrong. His name isn't Connor. It's Christopher. Christopher Brian Garrett." Eva looked at the detective with a mix of confusion and annoyance on her face. She stared at him stubbornly. She didn't want to be defiant and anger him. It was obvious by the look on his face that there was a lot at stake.

"I'm sorry, Miss, I don't know what he's told you about himself, but I've got fingerprints and numerous records to prove that he is Connor Martin. I can't go into detail, but he's in a lot of trouble."

Against his better judgment, Detective Lyons' voice softened as he spoke to her. She reminded him of his own daughter, and he tried to keep his emotions in check as he thought about his little girl getting mixed up with someone as terrible as Connor Martin.

"Detective, I had my own people do a background check on him. I don't understand how this could've happened." Jack was angry with himself because he knew that his grandfather would never have allowed this to happen to Eva. His grandfather never would've been so careless, and Jack was ashamed of the position he had put Eva in.

"It happens all the time with career criminals like our friend, Mr. Martin. This is what they do," Detective Lyons said to Jack, trying to be patient. "I'm sorry, I didn't catch who you are or what your position is here."

"I'm Jack Palmer, the CEO of Harper Enterprises. I oversee the Harper Estate and take care of the family. I'm here to look out for Eva." Jack squared his shoulders and stood in front of the detective as he extended his hand. Detective Lyons shook his hand begrudgingly as he stared hard at him for a moment. The detective shook his head without saying anything as he turned his attention back to Eva.

"I don't know if you want to get a lawyer, Miss, but you might want to consider it. I'm going to need to question you and ... well ... my advice would be to have a lawyer present."

"Why would I need a lawyer? I haven't done anything wrong," Eva said, suddenly angry. "I don't need a lawyer for anything."

"I'm not saying you did anything wrong, Miss. I'm just looking out for you and your rights. I'm going to have to ask you some questions, and I want you to have the option of getting a lawyer in case you wanted one."

"I don't need one. You can ask me anything you'd like," Eva glared at him, suddenly transforming from a scared young girl into a strong woman, surprising the detective.

Detective Lyons paused, realizing that he had underestimated her.

"I'm married to this man, so if he's not who he says he is, I want to know and I want to know right now. I'm having his baby for God's sake." Eva stared at the detective angrily.

"Okay ... then I have to ask you some questions," the detective said, eyeing Jack. "Alone."

Eva nodded, putting her hand on Jack's arm for a quick moment when she saw him flinch out of the corner of her eye. In the short time they had spent together, she had already seen his protective side and knew that he wouldn't like the officer talking to her alone. She also knew that he wouldn't have a choice.

The next few hours were brutal and Eva felt exhausted. The detective asked her question after question until the answers were all the same. Eva refused to cry, although she wanted to desperately.

"No, I didn't know his name is Connor."

"No, I had no idea that he was capable of any type of violence."

"No, he's never hurt me or hit me."

"I've never given him money."

"He's never stolen anything that I know of."

"I've never heard of anyone named Nora Symon."

"No, he's never pushed me. No, no ... he's never been anything but kind to me."

She hadn't known what to expect when she sat down in the stark room, but it had been so much worse than what she imagined. The detective hadn't treated her poorly, but she was frustrated and tired, and she still didn't know what Chris had done.

"Please, tell me what has happened. What has he done, please ..." Eva wanted desperately to know what Chris had done in the hope that the queasiness in her stomach could finally dissipate.

The detective had been waiting as he pulled a folder out, seemingly from nowhere. He held his hand on top of it as though he was stalling, debating with himself about whether he wanted to show her the contents. His gut told him that she didn't know anything, but he had to be sure. Eva stared down at the folder as though it were a vicious animal ready to attack her.

Two hours later, when she was finally escorted back to Jack who had been anxiously waiting, the detective looked at her evenly. "Don't leave town, Miss. We'll probably have more questions for you."

Eva nodded, the tears threatening to break free, her face white, and her eyes burning from the images that were now seared into her brain. She was in a daze, her eyes wide and glazed over.

When the detective walked away, she turned toward Jack and began sobbing. He instinctively reached for her and, without thinking, she fell into his arms. His shoulder was instantly soaked from her tears. He held her tight and was both surprised and happy to have her so close. He marveled at how natural it felt to hold her even though he had only just met her again. He pulled her closer and comforted her, feeling guilty about how much he enjoyed the feeling of her tiny body against his, her arms clasped tightly against his back. They stood together and time seemed to stand still until he heard her sniffling against him. She pulled slowly away, leaving him with a sudden and strange emptiness that he could hardly stand.

The look of shock on her face quickly registered with him, and he was alarmed as he searched her eyes for a sign that the interrogation hadn't broken her.

"Are you okay?" Jack asked wiping her tears away gently with his thumbs.

Eva nodded, her face red as she tried to hide the embarrassment she felt.

"Are you hungry? Do you want some coffee?" Jack steered her toward the exit, anxious to get her out of the police station that was suffocating both of them.

Eva shook her head, her dark hair framing her face. Jack couldn't help but marvel at her beauty, even in the midst of her pain. "No. I just want to go home," Eva said, her voice a whisper.

"I've got you," Jack said, keeping his arm around her protectively.

They rode for the first ten minutes in complete silence. Jack fought the urge to put his hand on hers, watching her out of the corner of her eye as silent tears continued to course down her cheeks. She held her hands clasped tightly in her lap.

He waited for her to speak first, wanting desperately to ask about the interrogation. Jack could see the fear in her eyes and could see her looking at him. She kept opening her mouth as if to speak, but closing it again. He waited patiently, knowing that she would speak when she was ready.

Finally, her voice came out raw and raspy, as though someone else was speaking for her. "They s-s-s-said that he's a really bad person. They asked if he ever hurt me or stole from me. They asked if he ever hit me ..." Eva's voice trailed off.

"Did he?" Jack asked, trying to hold his anger in at the thought of anyone ever hurting her. His pulse quickened as he thought about what he would do to the person who ever tried.

"No ... no ... he never hurt me. Chris ... I mean, Connor ... was kind to me ... he was always very nice to me." Eva flashed back to the many times he had brought her flowers and how he comforted her when she cried about her mother. She thought about the moments when he read to her and held her close anytime she needed it without her asking him to. He had been her first and only lover, never pushing her farther or faster than she was willing to go, his hands soft and gentle on her body. His perfectly muscled body warm against her own had enticed and excited her and she blushed at the memory.

He had only ever shown her kindness and love, and her mind was reeling as she tried to imagine the monster they made him out to be.

She shuddered as she suddenly envisioned his hands around her neck, and it made her cry even harder.

"It's okay, please, Eva ..." Jack suddenly pulled the car over and awkwardly gathered her in his arms. He held as close as he could without hurting her. "You're safe, Eva. Nobody will ever hurt you as long as I'm here. I should've looked into this guy myself, and I should've protected you. I'm so sorry that I failed you, but I promise that I won't let it happen again."

Eva cried against him, her entire world was crumbling. What she'd heard at the police station had destroyed the only true happiness she had ever known. She felt the familiar pain of emptiness as she realized that without Chris, she would be alone once again. She thought about the baby growing inside of her and how it would grow up with a father that didn't care about it. *I'm so sorry, baby. I'm already the worst mother in the world. How could I have let this happen to you? How could I have let this happen to me? Why didn't I know who he was? Why did I trust him so quickly without truly knowing him?*

"Did they tell you what was going on? Did they say anything about what he might have done?" Jack had asked the officers himself during the hours that Eva was in the interrogation room, but they refused to tell him anything.

Eva nodded, taking a deep breath when the images from the pictures in the folder resurfaced without her permission. When she closed her eyes all she could see was the blood because there had been a lot of it. There was thick red blood covering floors, walls, and skin. The detective had apologized repeatedly for showing her the pictures, but Eva was smart enough to know that it was all done by design. She could tell by the way he showed them to her, slowly and deliberately, pausing long enough to burn the image into her brain, that he was trying to lure her in. It was obvious that he thought she knew more than she did. The detective had been nice enough, but Eva knew that he was trying to trick her into telling him something she knew nothing about.

The pictures had made her sick to her stomach, almost as though she could smell the blood, or feel its stickiness on her own skin. She had never seen or imagined anything like it, and she knew that it would be difficult, if not impossible, for her to sleep for a very long time. The blood was intermingled with the victim's long, red hair and skin, and as hard as she tried, she repeatedly told the detective that she didn't recognize the victim. The crime scene was brutal, and she had been thankful when the detective finally felt she'd "had enough" of the photos. She never imagined that anyone would accuse Chris of doing something so heinous, the thought of it taking her breath away, and she had asked the detective several times to pause while he was showing her the pictures so she could catch her breath.

"Did they tell you what he did?" Jack repeated, alarmed by the way Eva froze when he asked her the question the first time.

Eva sat, staring straight ahead and Jack could see her flinch, almost imperceptibly. He watched her face carefully and patiently, not yet knowing her well enough to know if he was pushing her too hard. Eva was surprised to find that she wasn't ready to tell him about the pictures yet, and she decided to keep that part to herself until she could make more sense of everything. She could tell by his protective nature that if she told him, he would never leave her alone again, and she needed to be alone in order to think.

"Yes," she said carefully. "They said ... I was very lucky. They said ... he killed his lover ... and they said ... that ... I ...was probably next."

27

Fear
~Brynn
September 20th, 2016

As we pull up to the massive home, I'm overwhelmed by its size.

While my memory continues to come and go, I know that I should recognize this place, although there is still nothing specific yet. Now that I am awake, the world remains so loud and confusing, and I struggle to make sense of it. My body still moves slowly and refuses to move the way I want it to, my limbs incredibly heavy and awkward. While the world seems to be stunned and excited by this unexpected awakening, I am still not whole and probably never will be again.

As we walk up to the house, Bill and Kelly have to hold onto me, guiding my fragile, shaky legs as they slowly make their way up the ramp and into the house. Kelly wanted to take me in the wheelchair, but I shook my head and refused, my stubbornness the likely reason I'm still alive.

I have to admit that being at home makes me afraid of something I can't explain and I hate it. Fear is a familiar enemy that has crept slowly back into my heart and settled in my bones. As the years have passed, I had hoped that it might disappear, but it returns stronger and more intense than ever and paralyzes me when I least expect it. While my memories are hazy, by a cruel twist of fate, I can still see my adoptive father, Thomas, as clearly as I saw him decades ago chasing after me with hatred in his eyes and rage in his heart. The terrifying explosion of his anger often transitions into the explosion of twisted metal and wreckage from the accident that turned me comatose and stole my life and my daughter from me.

Fear plagues me every morning when I awake, almost paralyzing me until I find the strength to fight it. As difficult as it was to be asleep for all these years, it frightens me even more to be awake. Though I've somehow managed to become this *miracle* that everyone refers to me as, I'm terrified that one day I won't wake up at all, and that I'll never have the chance to love Eva the way I've always dreamed of. I realize that it makes me weak to be so fearful, after everything I've lived through, but the fear comes from the inside out, borne in me when I was just a small girl.

Still, I am thankful for those around me who help me fight.

Kelly has proven herself to be a true friend who is patient and compassionate. As she rides with me in the elevator up to my room, she steadies me against her so that I don't fall. I can feel the strength in her limbs as she holds tightly to me.

Though I know that my presence complicates her relationship with Adam, she still loves and looks out for me. I can feel that she cares deeply for him. Her confessions of love are somehow imbedded in my mind like a hazy dream, surely from a bedside conversation I overheard while lying in a deep sleep. And while she must wonder whether I remember, I'll never let her know that I do, happy to keep her secrets hidden in my heart until she asks me to show them to her.

Something about her love for him moves me. I don't know why Adam has held on so desperately to me. I want him to let go of his love and his guilt so that he can move on with his life and be the man he was never able to be.

Lying cocooned in my body has caused me to speculate how beautiful a life without sadness and guilt could have been. When I was so young, harshly abandoned by my mother in a puddle of mud, my life was wasted on cruelty and sadness, and I never wanted that for Eva. I just wanted her to be happy and free to live and love the way I was never able to.

But I realize as I've come home that there is still much sadness here and I wonder if this house will ever see the happiness that my grandfather intended.

Still, I remain hopeful.

28

Protected

September 21st, 2016

Jack had never met a female in his entire life that had ever piqued his interest as intensely as Eva Michaels Harper.

There was something about the frailty that she wore as a cloak to carefully disguise her inner strength that intrigued him. On the outside, she appeared to be a spoiled little rich girl, but the look in her eyes had told him from the very beginning that she was much more than that. He didn't know if she even realized how surprising she was.

After she told him that her husband "Chris" was accused of killing his lover, Jack decided that she and the family would need twenty-four-hour protection. It wasn't enough to have the surveillance cameras and security gate. He wanted armed bodyguards, even though Eva scoffed at the idea.

"Chris ... I mean, Connor, is in jail now. He's not a threat any longer, Jack. I don't want to talk about this. I can't believe we need to have this conversation," Eva said, trying to disguise the sadness in her voice. "I don't want a bunch of strangers with guns here twenty-four hours a day. I don't even know what's going on with my mom right now, and I don't want the house to be disrupted any more than what it already is."

Jack looked at her evenly, his brown eyes dark and serious, telling her that it wasn't up for discussion. "Eva, I'm not taking any chances. My grandfather would be very disappointed in me for allowing this to happen to you in the first place, so you're just going to have to indulge me and allow this for you and your family. We don't know if he was in this alone, or what his motive was. We have no idea why he changed his name and went through all of this to marry you. There is much more to this and I'm not going to sleep well unless I know that you're completely safe."

Eva stared out the window as they approached The Harper House. She sighed sadly and Jack fought the urge to reach for her hand. He tried to imagine what she must be going through, knowing that her husband wasn't who he said he was. Jack realized she had closed herself off and was keeping her thoughts close, careful not to reveal too much. Her vulnerability was appealing, and he was sure from the look on her face that she was completely devastated. It was her strength he was most drawn to. As the large gate closed behind them, Eva watched it in the side view mirror. For the first time in her entire life, she wondered if she had ever truly been safe at all. She had never questioned this before, but with the baby growing inside her belly and the bloody pictures burned into her brain, she felt very exposed as she tried to hide the fear that shook her to the core.

Jack stopped the car and jogged over to open her door before she could even grab the handle. As he reached out his hand to help her, Eva felt a surge of electricity flow through her fingers. His hands were strong and warm. She admired his strength and the way he carried himself, so self-assured and confident. Something about him made her feel safe, as though nothing could hurt her, and she admitted to herself that she needed that at the moment.

She blushed involuntarily as she allowed him to guide her gently to the house, his hand cradling her elbow.

As they approached the door, it flew open and Adam raced out, engulfing Eva in a hug.

"God, Eva, I'm so sorry that I wasn't there for you," Adam cried, tears streaming down his cheeks. "I'm a terrible father and I'm so sorry."

Eva looked awkward and embarrassed, her nose wrinkling as she caught a strong whiff of him and his clothes. Jack looked away, trying not to notice the look of disgust and frustration on her face. "Okay, Dad," she said, pushing him away. "I'm fine, really."

"Eva, how can you be fine? Kelly told me a little about what is happening, but I don't understand … how could you possibly be fine? How do you think that I would believe that after all you've been through?" Adam held her face in his hands and breathed directly in her face, causing her to gag.

"Dad! Please, you need to shower right now and brush your teeth. You smell like … like … you just smell. I've been at the police station all night and feel disgusting and I need to get cleaned up, too." Eva pushed him away and opened the door to go into the house. "Dad, go in, right now. Go and get cleaned up and I'll make you some coffee, I'm really fine. Jack has been looking after me and I'm fine."

Adam looked at Jack, as though seeing him standing there for the first time. "Oh … Jack. I'm sorry. I was so upset that I didn't see you there. Thank you very much for looking out for my girl!"

Jack held out his hand reluctantly, remembering their last meeting when Adam had shunned him. He had told him that he didn't want him hovering like his grandfather had, which had stung Jack, knowing how much his grandfather had devoted of himself to the family. Jack knew it was the alcohol talking, but had followed Adam's wishes and allowed others to watch over the family's affairs from a distance. It was a decision he was beginning to regret. "You're welcome, Mr. Michaels. I'm adding security to the house, just so you know. I've already discussed it with Eva, but based on the current circumstances, I feel it would be best."

Adam looked at him, confused. After a long pause he said carefully, "You do what you feel is best to protect my family."

Jack nodded. "I plan to."

Adam and Jack stared at each other for a moment, then Adam looked at Eva and smiled weakly before turning to go into the house.

Eva lingered on the large porch for a moment, staring at the door long after he closed it.

"Is he okay?" Jack asked, nodding in the direction that Adam disappeared.

"No," Eva said sadly. "He hasn't been okay my entire life. He's broken and sad, and there's nothing that can be done about it. He has always refused to come back to the land of the living, missing my mom and missing his life. I don't know what will happen to him now that Mom is home and awake."

"Love changes people, Eva." Jack thought about his own mother and father and how his father's hardness and meanness toward his mother had nearly ruined her. But when she met and married his stepfather, she seemed to be revived in a way that changed her completely. She had blossomed and was beautiful and happy for the first time since he had known her. "Love can either make someone better, or break them completely, and I've seen it happen both ways."

"Dad has been a mess forever, and just when I think it's not possible for him to fall any further, he manages to find a way," Eva said, tears welling up in her blue eyes. "I missed my entire childhood because of it. I think I jumped into this relationship and got married to Chr-Connor because I was so lonely and desperate to have someone love me. Foolishly, I thought that he did."

Eva eyes immediately looked toward the ground, tears falling continually.

"No! You can't blame yourself for this, Eva!" Jack grabbed her hand and held it tightly. "It happens to all of us. I had a pretty shitty child-hood myself." Jack had never talked to anyone about his childhood and didn't even realize he was doing it until he heard his own words tumbling out of his mouth. "My dad was lazy and didn't love any of us more than he loved himself. He was an utter disappointment to everyone who loved him because he didn't care about any of us. At least your dad loved you even if he had a hard time showing it."

"Yes, well ... I still fell for and married a psychopath ... and now I'm going to have his baby. Oh, my God!"

Before he could stop himself, Jack pulled Eva close and held her, her tiny body trembling uncontrollably with grief. He was proud of her for even being able to stand upright, but thankful that he could be there when she needed to let go. He had grown unusually attached to her for reasons that excited and terrified him at the same time.

She cried for what felt like hours, and when she finally stepped back, exhausted, her blue eyes puffy and rimmed with red. "I'm so sorry," she said eyeing his soft, white, cotton shirt where her eye makeup had come off on both of his shoulders. "I've completely ruined your shirt."

"Oh," he said looking down and smiling back up at her. "This old thing? Don't worry about it!"

"I'm so sorry, Jack. I don't usually have meltdowns like that in front of someone I don't know that well ... I'm mortified that you've seen me this way. This isn't me ..."

"Eva," Jack said, grabbing her shoulders gently and tipping her chin up so that her eyes met his. "You've just had the worst day of your life. You can cry in front of me anytime. I hope you'll consider me a friend, so please don't worry about it. I just want to make sure that you're okay."

Eva nodded, gratefully.

"I do feel better now," Eva said, sniffling as she looked toward the door. "I should probably go in and check on my dad. Hopefully he's sobered up a little by now."

Jack nodded. "I just want you to know one thing. As long as I'm around, I'm going to make sure that you're well-protected like I should have from the very beginning."

"You can't possibly blame yourself for Connor! It wasn't your fault at all!" Eva's big blue eyes dazzled him as she spoke.

"I should've taken the time to have him checked out better. Of course it was my fault." Jack said, his handsome face full of guilt.

"The detective said that he targeted me for some reason and planned this all along," Eva said, matter-of-factly. "He was trying to get me, Jack, and he wasn't going to stop until he did. Please don't think there is anything you could have done."

"I should have been more careful," he said, his voice hard. "From now on, Eva, you'll be safe. I promise you that."

Eva nodded, suddenly conscious that the sound of his voice made her heart skip when he spoke. Her grief quickly crushed the thought as she smiled cautiously at him and made her way into the house to look for Adam.

As Jack watched her walk in, his phone buzzed and he looked down at it, irritated for being interrupted at such a moment. As he read the message from his private investigator, his jaw dropped and he turned back toward the house immediately.

"*My source at the police station is telling me that Connor may not be the killer. It smells like he's being set up, but we won't know until the forensics evidence comes back. This could mean that Eva and the family are still in danger.*"

Jack dialed the phone immediately as he paced back and forth on the porch. For the next thirty-minutes he made arrangements for twenty-four-hour protection for the home and the family. He knew that Eva wouldn't like it, but he had no other choice. He knocked on the door and was let in by the housekeeper who graciously ushered him into the kitchen to wait, offering him coffee, which he politely declined. He sat and waited impatiently until a sleek gray SUV pulled into the driveway. He met and instructed the team to set up a plan for securing The Harper House, as well as replace the outdated security system that had been put in when his grandfather took care of the family's affairs.

Jack was exhausted and thankful he had a strong VP to relinquish his duties of the company to. As he prepared to leave The Harper House for the day, he looked around for Eva. Much to his dismay she was nowhere to be found. He walked out to his car, his shoulders aching and his head pounding. He suddenly understood the loyalty and commitment his grandfather had for the Harper family and Jack felt guilty, realizing that he had not done nearly enough to watch over them.

As he walked out to his car, he felt as though someone was watching him. He looked up to the house but could see no one. He shook his head, reminding himself that there were already a dozen men and the most updated surveillance system available watching over the home while he was not there. He got into his car cautiously and drove away.

~

As Brynn stared out the window at the tail lights pulling away she thought of how much the man reminded her of an old friend she used to have, her mind muddled with memories. She slowly wheeled her way back toward her bed and waited.

When will Adam come and finally talk to me? Is he going to avoid me forever?

It had been months, and aside from the first time she awoke, Adam had been careful to avoid being alone with her.

I'm ready to hear what you have to say. I'm ready to talk to you now if you would only find it in your heart to come and sit with me.

Brynn sat down carefully on her bed, happy to be alone for a short time. She knew that it wouldn't last long, but she hoped it would last long enough for her to collect her thoughts. She enjoyed the quiet as she looked around the room and did what she had been doing for two decades.

She waited.

29

Daddy Issues
September 23rd, 2016

Jessie lay on the floor where Adam's clothes had been, unmoving, as she imagined that she could still smell him. She missed him even though he had only been with her for a few hours. She realized that in all the years after she had run away from him that she had never felt truly whole. Now the emptiness within seemed even greater than it had before, and she wondered how she would move past it this time.

She had found herself on the floor so many times before, unable to breathe or move, her heart torn open wide over and over with the knowledge that Adam didn't love her.

She had never truly gotten over him, often seeking him out online and always trying to garner as much information as she could about him. He was a part of one of the wealthiest families in the area, so it hadn't been difficult to find what she wanted. His life overall was completely unexciting. Still, occasionally she was able to get small snippets of information that satisfied her curiosity. She had learned to stalk his social media sights where he was fairly inactive, but it was enough to make her believe she was still a part of him though she had spent many years without him. She'd tried her best to forget, but she knew that she never would.

The morning after she left him, so many years before, she called her sister who she hadn't talked to since high school. Then she hopped on a Greyhound bus to visit, thankful to have family to go to. She was desperate to find quiet, to still the chaos in her head and the misery in her heart. Jessie could still recall the two-day bus trip, fighting the morning sickness, her seatmate a crazed woman who snored incessantly. She remembered how she collapsed into her sister's arms when she finally saw her, exhausted and on the verge of a nervous breakdown. It had been a long journey from Adam's small apartment to her sister's rambling farmhouse, but when she arrived, she thought she might have finally found peace.

Jessie wrote letters to Adam every night in her journal, sharing with him the details of her pregnancy. For many long months she imagined that he was with her and was excited as she about the baby. When the baby finally came and she held him in her arms, she searched his face for any sign of Adam, convinced she would see it more as he grew older.

She had put off naming him for as long as she could until she was finally forced to put a name on his birth certificate. She wanted to name him "Adam", but at the last second changed her mind, deciding the baby needed to have his own identity. She named him after her brother who had died from an overdose, using Adam's last name for the child's middle name.

She wrote the baby's name out on the birth certificate form with a shaky hand, saying it over and over in her mind. *Connor Michael Martin, Connor Michael Martin, Connor Michael Martin.*

After Connor was born, things changed at her sister's house, and when her brother-in-law tried to shove his tongue down her throat, she knew she had no choice but to leave. For a split second, she thought about leaving Connor behind, knowing it would be easier for her to fend for herself alone. At the last minute she grabbed him. She knew that she would never forgive herself if she abandoned him. She took another bus back toward Adam, but settled a town over, unable to find the courage to return to him.

She was intent on raising her son to be the type of man she had never met but saw on TV and in the movies; the good kind who loved women and knew how to treat one. She was watching her son grow up, knowing that her boy was destined to be handsome and desirable. She taught him to listen to classical music and read poetry. She coached him incessantly on how to be a good listener and how to be affectionate, and she told him repeatedly, "You're going to be someone special."

She remedied the guilt she felt over almost abandoning him by showering him with love. It tore a hole in her stomach along with the alcohol she consumed to dull the pain of the memory. Jessie became obsessed with raising Connor to treat women the way she had never been treated. She wanted him to have everything she hadn't, and she convinced him that he deserved it.

As Connor grew up, Jessie did her best to make ends meet, bartending night after night, hoping to meet the man of her dreams who would rescue her from everything. She tried repeatedly, but could never quite pick the right one, and every man she ended up with was charmed by her beautiful smile, but disappointed by her booziness. It didn't help that she never remembered to tell them about the son she had right away, either.

Even with all the men who came and went in her life, she was never able to forget about Adam. When Jessie had read in the paper about Brynn's near-fatal accident, she thought about going back to him, but she could never find the courage. She knew from the news stories that he was staying at The Harper House, and she marveled at the massive estate and imagined that she might live there with him one day. But The Harper House was too intimidating and terrifying for her to approach, and she knew she could never force herself to go there, even for him.

Jessie always hated Brynn for ruining Adam. When she heard about the accident, she knew that some greater good was shining down upon her. Brynn had destroyed the promise of a life with Adam that Jessie felt she deserved. She had lain awake at night, her brain turning over with a thousand different ways to hurt Brynn, but when she heard about the accident on the news, Jessie was convinced that something or someone had heard her cries and had taken care of things for her.

As the years went on, Jessie's life consisted only of her fantasies of Adam. She found that more often than not, reality and fantasy would to converge into one, until she was barely able to tell the difference. She often referred to Adam as "her husband" when she was talking to others, and she imagined having a life with him. Jessie knew that she needed help and she tried, for her son's sake, to follow the doctor's orders so that the delusions would stop and reality could set in. But the medications were expensive, and they interfered with her drinking, so she often refused to take them or ran out without refilling them.

As her Connor grew older, he began to see how obsessed she was with a life that never belonged to her, and he began to resent the father who had completely abandoned the both of them. Jessie had told Connor about Adam's life before them, and how he had chosen Brynn over her. She told him that she was convinced that Adam loved her more, but hadn't the courage to leave his wife once and for all.

As the years went by, Connor became a strong, handsome young man. He watched Jessie nearly kill herself in an attempt to slit her wrists. She told Connor later that she thought it might bring Adam back, though they still hadn't seen each other since the night before she walked away.

"I'm sorry," Jessie apologized to him after every episode. "I just forgot to take my meds … I forgot to pick them up … please … things will get better, Con. I promise. I swear I'll be good!"

Connor wanted nothing more than to believe his beautiful mother. She was the only thing he had in the world, and he adored her more than anything. When she was happy, their life was good, and laughter and contentment were abundant in their small apartment. Connor learned that the darkness always came without warning, and there was nothing and nobody to protect him either physically or emotionally from Jessie's cruelty and anger. He grew accustomed to the ups and the downs, and learned how to navigate the tumultuous waves of love and abuse that his mother could never control.

As soon as Connor was old enough, he began to question his own sanity and the genes that had been passed down to him from Jessie. He also became more curious about the man she claimed was his father. He watched her stability begin to deteriorate, and he wondered with pressing concern if this, too, would be his fate.

"If you know where my father is, I want to meet him," he insisted repeatedly.

"Yes, you are welcome to meet your father anytime," Jessie often told him during the times she was lucid and the world was full of excruciating reality. "But he doesn't know you exist. I never told him that I was pregnant with you."

"How do you know for sure who he is, then?" he had asked her, wanting desperately to believe her. "Are you sure it's Adam?"

Her face always fell and she looked embarrassed when Connor pushed her, and he could tell from the look on her face that she wasn't quite sure.

"I just … I just know … I knew your dad very well and I think you are just like him." Jessie was always so adamant. The thought of anyone being her son's father except for Adam seemed ridiculous to her. She had loved Adam with all her heart. He had been the only guy that she had ever been mostly faithful to, with the exception of those nights when she worked late at the bar and her friend Dean had arrived to close up with her. Dean, a lifelong friend, had often professed his drunken love for her, which Jessie found flattering. Even though he was extremely attractive and had a good job as a mechanic, she didn't love him, but he kept finding his way into her life much like she kept finding herself naked with him. Every time she'd swear it was the last. Jessie convinced herself that she only slept with Dean as a distraction to temporarily dull the pain of knowing how much Adam still loved Brynn. The memories of those long nights at the bar, her body entwined with Dean's, were fuzzy, and, after a while, she wasn't even sure if the details were real. She pushed them out of her mind and tried to forget that he even existed. She never mentioned his name to Connor, and when she talked about his father, she was talking about Adam. There were no other contenders as far as she was concerned.

Connor always pushed her for as many details about Adam as possible, knowing that her muddled mind didn't often share the most accurate information. It was then that she would tell him everything she knew, and Connor tucked it away in the recesses of his mind. He knew he would use it later, although he wasn't sure how. Without realizing it, Jessie had made her son afraid to love by hardening his heart against anything that could destroy him the way his mother had been destroyed. When he finally did fall in love with a beautiful little redhead named Nora, he shared with her what he knew about Adam and his mother.

"You don't look like him at all," Nora said, staring at a picture of Adam that she had found on the Internet. "You look a little like your mom, but you don't look like this Adam guy at all. Your nose is long and straight and his isn't. You don't resemble him in any way. Jesus, what is she thinking? This guy can't possibly be your father!"

Connor stared at the picture, amazed that Jessie could even pretend that Adam was his father. He agreed with Nora that there was nothing about Adam Michaels that even remotely resembled him. He and Nora dug through old letters and pictures, which were the remnants of Jessie's life, until they came across a single photo labeled simply "Dean". Connor knew at that moment that Adam wasn't his father. He immediately saw himself in Dean and realized that Adam being his father was a figment of his mother's imagination. It still hurt him to know that Adam had not loved her the way she needed to be loved, and an irrational hatred for Adam grew inside him until it was nearly uncontrollable.

Nora liked to feed his hatred by searching for Adam on the Internet.

"God, look how rich he is! Forget the petty stealing we've been doing to get by, this is where it's at, Baby. This could and should be all yours, and then you can take care of her and put her in one of those expensive hospitals that she needs to be in. If he hadn't hurt your mom the way he did, she would be normal and things could have been so much better for both of you." Nora's eyes had grown large as they stared at the picture of The Harper House on the Internet. "You deserve to live in a house like that with me."

Connor had stared at the house in awe and tried to imagine what it would be like to live in a place like that. He had never known more than a couple of rooms and a bathroom, and the thought of anyone living in a house so large made him angry.

"I want to hurt that selfish bastard for what he did to my mom." Connor's hazel eyes flashed in that way that excited Nora, his voice gritty and angry.

"I think that the best way to hurt him is to hurt his daughter," Nora purred, staring menacingly at the picture of Eva and her father that was frozen on the screen in front of them. She was thrilled at the dangerous edge in Connor's voice and her mind turned over, searching for a way he could use this to get her out of the mundane life she was trapped in.

"How would I do that?" Connor asked, trying to imagine physically hurting Adam Michaels the way he truly wanted to.

"It's simple, Baby. You make his daughter fall in love with you, you marry her, and then you make her have an accident so you can take all their money. If you can make it look like the father did it, then double whammy," Nora said smoothly, as though the answer was obvious.

"That's crazy!" Connor said, realizing what Nora was suggesting. He had always loved her edginess and the way she loved to take risks, but he'd never imagined she could devise a scheme like that. She had already talked him into so many things, and he had already paid the price for it with a RAP sheet and a few short stints in jail. So far, everything she had ever convinced him do had been petty, until now.

They had talked it over for weeks until he had the courage to agree.

"Nobody says you have to sleep with that little rich bitch. Just ... make her fall in love with you ... and the rest will be easy. You should be able to do that, Baby." Nora pulled him close the way he liked, and

Connor suddenly couldn't remember any reason not to do what she said.

Connor thought a lot about his mom as he moved forward with his plan to hurt the man she claimed was his father. He thought about her suffering and how Adam had caused her so much pain. It fueled his desire to take away everything Adam had ever loved. Then he met Eva, and something in him changed. He realized that he no longer wanted to hurt her as he fought his love for her, knowing how wrong it was for him to feel the way he did. Connor knew the connection was there, real or imagined, and he hid it away inside of him as best he could, afraid that Nora might discover it.

Jessie knew something inside of her son had changed, though she didn't know why. She had watched as the darkness that hovered around him lifted, and it gave her the courage to approach Adam after months of following his every move outside of The Harper House. She thought that if Connor could find happiness, she could, too, so she "accidentally" ran into Adam at the AA meeting.

Having him in her arms and in her bed once again was more than she had imagined. When he left her so abruptly, it was as though a bitter wind had blown in and the emptiness consumed her completely. While she waited for him to call like he promised, she slowly began to realize that he never would. The pain of his absence left her unable to get off her bedroom floor, the place where she last saw him. After a few days, she crawled painfully into the bathroom and ran a hot bath. She stood up only long enough to get into the tub wearing the thin slip she had been wearing when Adam left. She sank into it, ignoring the burning water on her skin. When the water stopped running, she picked up the razor blade she kept in the soap dish, testing its sharpness on her finger and happy for a moment to feel something other than emptiness. She watched as the blood pooled into the water, her green eyes mesmerized as it swirled around her slowly, until it finally disappeared.

She realized that this was what she had wanted for a long time. She had watched and waited for Adam to acknowledge her existence. She had hoped he could feel her near him just as she always felt him with her. When the moment had finally come, he had discarded her easily and thoughtlessly as though she meant nothing to him, just like she always knew he would. It happened again, just as it had all those years ago when he let her walk out the door without begging her to stay. She had forgotten that she had left him without any warning. Jessie's memories revised the past until she could no longer recognize the truth.

If he had truly cared for her, she told herself, she never would've left. In the deepest part of her, she knew that he didn't love her the way he loved Brynn, and he never would.

Now, after one final time in his arms, Jessie wanted nothing more than to disappear, because in Adam's eyes, she knew she didn't exist. She thought for a moment that she should leave a note, but realized it was too late. She didn't want to track water all over the floor, or slip and crack her head on the side of the tub. She thought that it was ironic that she would think about something so small at a time like this, but was thankful for the momentary distraction.

She held the razor blade to her right wrist and drew a long, deep line on the inside of her arm. The pain was intense, but then she no longer felt it as she put her wrist in the water and watched the blood quickly flow out. She laid her head back and closed her eyes. Briefly, she hoped that it wouldn't be Connor that found her, even though she knew he was the only one who would.

"I'm sorry for being such a shitty mother," she whispered into the steamy air. "I'm sorry. I thought I could be better, but I couldn't."

She inhaled slowly, feeling a little faint, and then marveled at how she no longer felt any pain. She wondered if Adam would ever find out what she had finally done for him and their love, preserving it in time with their last night together so that it could never be forgotten.

She held her breath as she waited for the moment she hoped would come, when she would finally and blissfully, disappear.

30

Pilgrimage
September 1st, 2016

Nick hadn't made the trip to The Harper House in over a decade. As he drove the familiar road to the house, he thought about the last trip he had made which was cut short by his daughter, Mandy's, suicide attempt.

When he had gotten home, he had joined his estranged ex-wife, Fiona, at the hospital. The next few months had been nothing but a whirlwind as they reconciled so that they could work together to help Mandy manage her schizoaffective disorder. Thoughts of Brynn all but disappeared as his life became centered on his daughter, who needed constant care and monitoring. But as Mandy became older, with the mix of the right medication, she became more stable. As it became clear to Nick and Fiona that Mandy's condition would have its constant highs and lows, they finally came to terms with their failed marriage and decided to divorce. Any love between them was only found in remnants of the past and their daughter, who had decided to go to a nearby college in order to be close to home.

Nick no longer felt guilty about keeping Brynn close to his heart. He knew that his refusal to forget her never allowed him to love anyone else. He tried to open himself up to love, but he was unable to help himself no matter how much he wanted to. He had fallen hopelessly in love with Brynn from that first moment he met her in her own restaurant. She'd been reluctant to spend time with him at first. If it hadn't been for her friend, Jane, Brynn never would have met with him, and he wouldn't have fallen for her so hard. He knew that after that, nothing he could do would ever change his love for her.

As he packed his final bag for the pilgrimage back to The Harper House, his hands shook nervously. The thought had crossed his mind that Brynn was no longer alive, a sharp pain sparking in his heart every time he considered it. If she was alive, he knew he needed to see her again, and was prepared for anything, even Adam. Nick realized that it was time for him to start living his life, just as he should have when he met Brynn and knew immediately that he loved her. He was full of regret for leaving her the first time, knowing in his heart that he intended to return. Life, it turned out, had conspired against him, and he felt as though he was swimming upstream to get to back to her.

Nick was determined this time to claim the life he had walked away from all those years ago, and he knew that meant that he might have to fight Adam. Brynn had been coming for him when she had her accident, and now it would be up to him to finally go to her. He worried that she would've forgotten all about it, but he couldn't allow himself to believe that after everything he had been through that he would have been completely erased from her memory.

He called Mandy to let her know that he would be leaving, but she didn't return his call. He and Fiona no longer talked, an unspoken agreement between them. Though they had ended their marriage amicably, Fiona's bitterness at his inability to love her had grown over the years until she could no longer communicate with him civilly. When they parted ways, they realized they would only need one another for the sake of their daughter.

Nick drove anxiously to the airport. He thought about the conversations he'd had with Brynn, many of them muddled in his mind, some of the words lost forever. The memories he had of her, though, remained strong and intense. The vision of her huge brown eyes staring up at him with love was burned deeply in his mind. The subtle smell of vanilla always brought her back to him, if even just for a moment.

"I've never been able to talk to anyone the way I talk to you," he remembered Brynn confessing, her voice husky and low as she stroked the side of his face. "I've always been so closed, even with Adam, who I've known practically my entire life. With you … it's different. I feel as though somehow … maybe … you and I were meant to be."

"I feel the same way about you." Nick remembered how he had kissed her lips over and over, enjoying their sweet saltiness. "I feel as though I've known you my entire life, almost as though I could never be whole without you."

When he closed his eyes, Nick could still feel her hands on his back and her lips on his. He could still hear her sweet, deep voice in his ear telling him to "go faster" or "go slower," her sighs setting him on fire with each one.

Their time together had been incredibly short, but it had felt like a lifetime, and Nick wanted so much more. Nick wanted what he knew was impossible because he wanted her to wake up so he could be with her. Every day. He knew that his life wouldn't be complete without her because he had already tried everything he could to forget about her, doubting that he could love someone so intensely and so completely after their time together. He had tried to find love, get married, and have a family. He had done all the things that he knew he should do in order to erase her memory from his mind. He had even been single for a short time between his two marriages, dating carefully and trying to find the woman who could heal him and make him forget Brynn. No matter what he did, whose bed he slept in, or what life he lived, nothing could make him forget. The more he tried, the more he loved her.

He sat back on the airplane and closed his eyes.

It would be a seven-hour flight and an hour to The Harper House. He sighed anxiously. In roughly eight hours, Nick would be with Brynn once again.

31

Daddy's Girl
September 23rd, 2016

Eva was having a hard time forgiving Adam for abandoning her once again. They hadn't spoken much since the night she had arrived home from the police station.

After leaving her alone when she needed him the most, he was making it difficult for her to find him so that he could properly apologize to her. She had been thankful for Jack who had taken care of her at the police station, but she had needed Adam. He had left her alone her entire life and she had never said anything about it, but after a day and a half, she couldn't wait any longer.

She searched the massive house and when she finally found him he was hiding on a soft leather couch in the library pretending to read. The library was a magnificent room with beautiful, large windows. It was adorned in rich wood with thousands of books lining the walls. It was a room that was seldom used anymore since the passing of her grandfather.

"Where have you been hiding?" she asked, her arms crossed as her blue eyes penetrated him.

"I'm sorry, Eva. I'm … ashamed." Adam refused to look into her eyes as he turned away from her.

"Turn around and look at me, Dad." Eva said, her voice low and angry. Adam thought of how much she sounded like her mother. Brynn's voice had often reverberated in anger toward him, especially toward the end of their marriage. He would've given anything to hear her voice while she had been asleep, but now he thought that it was ironic that he was avoiding Brynn, too.

"You sound just like …"

"I know. I sound like Mom. You've said it a thousand times throughout my life, yet you haven't been alone with her in a room since she's been awake. This is what you've wanted for twenty years! This is what you've begged for, dreamed about, yet you refuse to go to her! I don't understand it. I don't understand you." The words spilled out, quick and furious. Eva had watched him suffer her entire life and couldn't understand why he would behave this way now.

"Eva, please. Take it easy on your old dad." Adam looked beaten up and Eva thought he reminded her of a sad old hound dog.

"No! I'm not going to take it easy on you. I'm not going to let you off the hook. You're a coward and I'm angry with you. You've let me down my entire life and now when I've needed you the most …" Eva's voice trailed off, her words stuck in her throat as she choked back a sob.

Adam stood up and started to take a step toward her but she stepped back. He sank down on the couch, dejected.

"God, I'm so sorry that I let you down. I don't even know what's happening with Chris … please, tell me what is happening. Please, I'm sorry."

"No! I needed you more than ever. I've never ever needed you more, and you were nowhere to be found. And when you were finally found, you looked like hell and you smelled like a brewery. I just don't understand you." Eva tried not to cry as she looked at him. He looked small and pathetic. She thought about what he had looked like to her when she was a little girl and how he had seemed so big and strong. Despite his grief and many faults, he had at least always been there for her. The thought of him abandoning her was terrifying.

"Eva ..." Adam looked at her, desperate. He rubbed at the scruff on his face, his blue eyes, very much like her own, were bloodshot and tired. "I'm sorry ... I have no excuses. I'm sorry. I'm just ... I'm scared. I've wanted your mom to be awake, and now that she is, I'm terrified. I don't know what to do ... What if she hates me? What if she remembers how horrible I was to her when we were married and she kicks me out? Where will I go? Who will I have in my life if I no longer have her or you?"

Eva stared at him in disbelief.

"Do you truly think she would kick you out? You've taken care of her, you've looked out for her. Why would she hate you? Why would she not want you here?"

Adam sighed, knowing this day would come.

"There are a lot of things you don't know about your mom and I, Bitty." Adam used the nickname that she hadn't heard since she was a little girl. Eva immediately softened when said it, suddenly comforted against her will.

"I know, Dad. But you can tell me." Eva said, her voice more gentle than it had been. She sat down next to him on the couch, drawn in, her anger fading.

"You're going to hate me, too, once I tell you what I did." Adam's voice was so quiet she could barely hear him.

"No, Dad. I won't," Eva said, her heart pounding. "You can tell me anything."

Adam was silent for a long time, and when he spoke, his voice cracked. "Your mom and I ... divorced."

Eva sucked in her breath. The news was devastating, and even though she had known that her parent's life together had been tumultuous and difficult, nobody had ever mentioned that they had divorced.

"But ..." Adam continued. "I never signed the final papers that I was supposed to in order to finish everything. I hid them away. She had the accident before she was ever able to found out, but she thought it was a done deal." Adam said the words slowly, letting them sink in.

Eva was quiet for a few moments as she thought about what he had said.

"Is ... is that why you have been avoiding her?" Eva asked, finally.

"Yes." Adam admitted. "It's not that I don't want to see her. I love your mom more than anything in this world. God knows I haven't done anything that I set out to do where she was concerned. When we were young, I thought I would always take care for her and protect her, but ... I failed miserably. I didn't want to get a divorce, but I drove her away. Your mom was ..."

Adam paused, unsure if he should tell her about Thomas and her past.

"Please Daddy ... tell me the rest." Eva could tell there was more to the story and she urged him to continue.

Adam looked at his daughter, so young and beautiful, and he was amazed at how much she reminded him of Brynn when she had been Eva's age. They were practically identical in every way. The only difference between them was the color of their eyes. But even as a young child, Brynn's eyes had been so much older and full of pain reflecting a horror that Adam protected Eva from in every way.

Until now.

For the next hour, Adam gave Eva a brief history of Brynn's childhood. He shared how she had been ruthlessly abandoned by her birth parents, and then abused by her adoptive father, Thomas. He hesitantly told her about Rose, Brynn's adoptive mother and her incessant neediness and selfishness, and how as a teenager, Brynn had resorted to cutting to free herself from the pain. Adam tried to be careful as he watched Eva's eyes well up over and over as she kept repeating, "I didn't know, I didn't know." Brynn's past became more colorful and more alive than she had ever imagined.

When Adam was done, Eva was completely numb, unsure if she could possibly take anymore. Adam continued to spill the truth about how he had ruined their marriage after baby Sophie died with his drinking, and how the guilt had eaten him alive every day since.

But he stopped, careful to leave out the part where the doctor told him that if he continued to drink, he would die. He knew that he didn't have it in him to quit, and he didn't want to burden his sweet daughter with that as well. Adam had been feeling the effects on his body for quite some time, even though he hated to admit it. The doctor had been warning him that this would happen and, as his body began to fail, he knew that the pain would eventually come. Adam had purposely ignored every warning that he had been given. He knew that it was already becoming more than he could handle, and that he would need to go to the hospital soon.

Eva stared at him as he paused, trying to decide what to say to him that could make a difference.

"You need to talk to her, Daddy," Eva said, keeping her voice steady. "She'll forgive you for whatever you feel that you've done wrong. You've taken such good care of her over the years, and there's no way she could be angry with you now."

"I don't know," Adam said, fearfully. "I don't know if she will forgive me. I don't know if *I* could forgive me. I haven't been an honest man or the kind of man that I thought I would be when I fell in love with your mom. Life has passed so quickly. I think that it's just too late for us now."

"Daddy, you've been there for her nearly her entire life. It would be impossible for her to not see how much you've loved her."

Adam grabbed Eva and held her close, wishing, not for the first time, that he had been a better father. He didn't remember much of her childhood, and when she had needed him as a child, he had turned to Kelly and Jane, unsure of what to do for her. When she had been the most devastated and needed him, he was completely absent. He knew that he would have to add that to the load of regrets that he carried with him every day.

"I'm sorry that I've been such a shitty dad to you," Adam said, his voice barely a whisper. "I wanted to be a dad so much and I thought I would be a better one ... but I wasn't. I tried to stop drinking so many times ... I tried to get help and I tried to do better, but I fucked it up every single time. I just couldn't ... I couldn't ..."

Eva looked at Adam and focused on his dark hair speckled with gray, the stubble on his face making him look so much older. She closed her eyes and tried to remember back when he had been a young father and what he had looked like. She remembered how she had always been so proud of her handsome daddy. She hadn't known that he was drunk when he held her, and didn't feel his absence in quite the same way he remembered it. She had convinced herself that her childhood was only filled with emptiness and loneliness, but as she tried hard to look back, she recalled the trips to the zoo and the nights reading on the couch. She remembered when he built forts with her in the massive living room, and how he had tried to teach her how to cook.

It was only as she grew older that she convinced herself she had always been alone, pushing him away, even when she needed him the most.

He had tried to be a good father, and even though she hadn't been as close to him as she would've liked for many years, she still loved him with everything inside of her. She didn't believe it could be any other way. She adored him even though the darkness had seemed to claim him more than anyone realized.

"I forgive you," Eva placed her hand on the side of his head and pulled it down on her shoulder. "You've been just enough, and you've been good to me."

She could feel him crying and she shushed him as though he were a small child. "We can get you the help you need, Dad. I'll help you and we'll get you through this darkness and through this pain."

Adam shook his head, against her. "No ... no," he said, his voice muffled.

"Why not?" Eva said, pulling his face up so that he could look at her.

"I just ... I can't ... I'm sorry, Eva," Adam said, wiping his face with the back of his hand, trying to compose himself.

"You need help, Dad. I can help you do this. We need you." Eva gripped his arm tightly, trying to keep the desperation out of her voice.

"It's too late, Eva. There's nothing else that you can do for me." Adam stopped suddenly as though he wanted to say more. Instead, he asked about Chris. "I need to know about Chris. I need you to tell me what's been happening."

Eva knew he was changing the subject, but she needed him, and for the first time he was truly listening to her. She slowly told him everything she knew about Connor Michael Martin. She marveled at how he listened so intently, and as she talked, she discovered that he was finally the father she had always wished he had been.

32

Redemption
~Brynn
September 23rd, 2016

The footsteps to my room are quiet and slow. I can hear them outside the door, waiting and pausing. I wait, wondering if anyone will come in. I can hear the clearing of a throat and know immediately that it is Adam.

The door opens slightly and I try to sit up as best I can in my chair.

I look up expectedly and see Adam slowly walking toward me, hesitant and shy, looking more like a little boy than the man he has matured into.

I wait for him to speak but instead he just stares, his beautiful blue eyes rimmed with red, his hair entirely too long and a tousled mess. The memory from long ago, of my fingers in his hair comes crashing back on me like an ocean wave, and I feel my lips respond to the memory with a smile.

He smiles back at me, his teeth still straight and white, his face even more handsome than when he was a younger man. When he smiles, his face transforms instantly and I can see the boy I fell in love with. Then the smile falls away and suddenly he becomes a tragic shadow. I can see the lines of age and heartache etched into his skin like a road map and my heart aches for him. As he comes closer, all the bitterness that was once between us slowly melts away.

As he sits down in the chair next to me, I can see that he is uncomfortable so I motion for him to move his chair closer. I want him to be nearer because I feel as though I haven't seen him in so long, and at that very moment I realize how much I have missed him. I can see by how his blue eyes widen, and by the somberness of his expression, that he is terrified to be too close to me.

"Hi," he says finally, his voice quiet and deep.

I smile at him again, trying to get the words to come out. Eventually, much to my relief, they come. "Hi."

The heaviness around us begins to dissipate until we fall into a more comfortable silence, though his shoulders and jawline remain tight and tense.

He finally speaks, breaking the silence. "I've missed you so much, Brynn. Nothing in my life has been the same since you've been gone." Before I know it, Adam is kneeling before me with his arms around my waist as he holds me close to him.

I circle my arms around him, holding him, though not as tightly as I would like, the strength gone from my arms and hands.

"I'm so sorry I haven't come to see you." His voice is muffled in my nightgown as his head is buried close to my chest. "I've been … afraid. Completely terrified, if you must know the truth." He wipes his nose with the back of his hand, which makes him look even more vulnerable than he already appears to be.

I look down at him, questioning. *Why would you be afraid?*

"I've been afraid because I don't want you to hate me for what I've done, or rather, what I haven't done. I've been afraid because I've loved you all these years, but I've been a mess, and I knew that the moment you saw me you would know immediately. I've never been able to hide from you. I knew you would know everything about me because you're the only person who ever has."

I try to tell him that I do know, but instead I nod, afraid the words will sound silly, or not come out at all. Only this time, the fear is not unfounded as my body rebelliously refuses to cooperate with my brain.

He holds me tight and I hold him back, the time going slowly yet quickly at the same time. I begin to feel very tired, and, as though he can sense it, Adam stands up and lifts me onto the bed so I can rest. He moves his chair close, grabbing my hand and holding it tight.

"I have to tell you this because it's been eating me up inside. You may hate me, but you have a right to know. I didn't tell you when I should have and then ... the accident happened." I watch him take a deep breath, summoning every ounce of courage from within. "I never signed the papers ... the divorce papers. I hid them like a coward and I ... never divorced you. I know that's what you wanted and it's what I thought I wanted. The papers had already been drawn up when I realized I didn't want it, and then you had the accident and it was too damned late. I'm so sorry."

I grasp his hand tightly, his words a muddled mess in my head, and I look at him with confusion. *What?*

"I'm sorry," he says over and over.

I hear him and the anger wells up in me, bubbling slowly.

I know that he has been here and I know that he hasn't left me, but I wonder why he would do such a thing. He betrayed me and the anger floods through me, hot and slow. I know that he can feel it and he shrinks away from me, afraid.

"I couldn't let you go, Brynn. I loved you too much." Adam's voice is barely a whisper, but when he speaks, I think of Nick. I wonder why he isn't here and then I slowly realize that it must be because Adam is here instead. I imagine that Nick has moved on with his life, probably married with a lot of children, and I know that he must have forgotten all about me by now.

Adam looks so sorry. I can't help but soften and feel sad for him and all that he has been through over the years.

I know that I've always loved him, our love fading into a softer, hazier version of what it was so many years ago. I feel the fuzziness of our love in my heart and I realize that, as much as I want to be mad at him, I can't be. The anger that began to well up simply refuses to consume me. What's done is done, and, as beautiful and intense as it was, Nick and I were never meant to be. I don't have it within me to be angry and I can't fault Adam. He's suffered enough.

He looks into my eyes for a long time and I realize that he knows what is in my heart, like only Adam ever could. For the first time I watch him relax, his shoulders letting go of the weight that is crushing him.

It doesn't matter anymore. We can let it all go now.

He kisses me sweetly on the cheek, his lips lingering the way I always liked them to. He clears his throat and when he finally speaks, his voice is thick with emotion. "I'm so happy you are finally awake. Everyone told me that it was impossible, but I *knew* you were still here. I could tell, I could sense you just as I always could … like I always did. I couldn't give up, ever. I always knew you were in there." Adam's tears flow freely and easily down his face as I put my hand on his cheek.

The blue in his eyes is beautiful as he stares down at me, and for a moment I feel like the fifteen-year-old girl who loved him with all her heart. He rescued me, saved me, and has been loyal to me my entire life. He has stayed by my side and protected me, especially when I told him about Thomas and how he had abused me. He loved me with all of him even when I was unlovable and broken.

I squeeze his hand and he places his palm against my cheek. For a moment we slip back in time to a moment when there was nothing between us but the love that saved me. I smile at him and he smiles back and I can see that boy, buried deep down inside, fighting hard to resurface. I know that he isn't gone completely. Instead he is right here, begging me to remember how he was once so strong and loving, always protecting me.

I look at Adam and open my mouth, speaking slowly and praying that the words will come out the way I intend them to. "I. Remember. You."

Adam looks at me, his mouth open wide, stunned by my clarity.

"I remember you," I repeat, and he leans over and kisses me gently, his lips familiar and soft. I lean into him as though I had been waiting for this moment my entire life.

"I remember you, too." Adam smiles wide and I see nothing but joy in his eyes, the sadness and pain dissipating in an instant. I realize that I feel the same happiness.

As he leans over to kiss me once more, his body jerks and he falls to the floor. Pain floods over his features, and an agonizing scream comes out of his mouth. I struggle to reach out to him, but there is nothing I can do, my body fighting desperately against me.

He reaches out his hands to me as though begging me to save him. I try to hold onto him to no avail. I watch his eyes open and close, his face distorted in pain. He has been rendered helpless and cannot get up or move. He tries to speak but only gurgles and cries come through his lips. His body twitches uncontrollably.

"Help! Help us," I scream out, my voice lost in his cries. It feels like hours, but I know it is only moments until there are the sound of feet running down the hall and the door crashes open. Kelly's voice cries out, "Adam!" as I hear her scream for someone to call 911.

I watch as Adam falls to the floor, writhing in pain with Kelly holding tightly to him, tears running down her cheeks. Adam looks up at me and our eyes lock just as the paramedics rush in and start their work on him.

"Brynn, Brynn ..." Adam cries, his voice reflecting his agony.

"Adam," I call out, my voice thin as paper in the flurry of activity in the room.

"I love you." Adam's voice echoes down the hall and I realize that my chance to tell him that I love him, too, is gone.

All at once, the room becomes quiet and I am left completely alone.

I realize that the emptiness I feel is more than just the stillness of the room. The emptiness is separation, and, with slow realization, I know that Adam must be gone too, because for the first time in many years I can't feel him at all.

33

The Visitor
September 23rd, 2016

As the gates opened and the ambulance flew out of The
Harper House, the small silver sedan smoothly drove in.
Nick drove slowly down the long, familiar driveway, his
mouth dry as he remembered the last time he had been to The Harper
House; how he and Adam had fought, his visit with Brynn, and the
twin freckles on Eva's arm.

Nick felt his heart pounding with fear at the sight of the
flashing lights and wondered if he should turn around and follow
the ambulance out of the gates. He took a deep breath and parked
the car, leaping out of the driver's side and onto the front steps of
the home as quickly as he could. His long legs covered the steps
two by two until he found himself at the front door, his palms
sweaty.

He rang the doorbell, his chest heavy with anxiety until a kind-
looking woman of about sixty with soft blonde hair and a tiny frame
answered the door.

"Can I help you?" she asked, cracking the door only wide enough for him to see one quarter of her face, her light blue eyes squinting suspiciously.

"Hi. I'm an old friend of Brynn Michael's and I was hoping I could see her," Nick said trying not to appear too anxious.

"What is your name?" she asked, stiffly.

"Nicholas Easton." Nick shuffled his feet.

"Please wait," she closed the door and Nick stood there wondering what she was doing. The door reopened and Nick jumped.

A somber looking man in a dark suit stood nearly toe-to-toe with Nick. At six feet five, Nick wasn't accustomed to being looked in the eye by many and was taken aback.

"Who are you?" the man said, staring Nick down.

"I'm Nicholas Easton. I'm an old friend of Brynn's and I want to see her," Nick repeated, trying not to sound intimidated.

"Let me see your ID." The look on the man's face let him know that it wasn't a request but a demand.

Nick pulled out his wallet and fumbled for his license which he gave to the man who disappeared with it back into the house. The door reopened a few moments later. He handed the license back to Nick without saying a word. He opened the door wide enough for Nick to enter. "Wait here," he said, his voice absent of expression.

The older woman who had answered the door stood just beyond the foyer and motioned to him. "I'm sorry for the security, but we just can't be too careful," she apologized.

"That's okay," Nick said trying to sound more gracious than he felt.

"We've just sent Mr. Michaels to the hospital, so Brynn is distraught," the woman said as she wrung her hands, nervously. "Please ... don't upset her."

"I promise, I won't. Is he okay?" Nick asked, curious.

"I can't say," the woman said motioning for Nick to follow. They walked into an elevator and she pushed the button for the second floor. "How do you know Brynn?"

"I ... uh ... we were old friends," Nick said, careful not to give his feelings away."

"I don't know how long ago you knew her, but you do know that she's been in a coma for a very long time? She doesn't get around very well yet, though she's doing better than anyone ever thought." The woman's voice was full of pride and Nick could tell that she cared about Brynn a great deal.

"Yes, I knew that," Nick said smiling at the woman.

"Good," she said, as they got off the elevator and walked down a long hallway. Nick was impressed with the beauty and simplicity of the house. It was just as he always imagined it would be, a reflection of Brynn, gorgeous but classic. He could see her in everything as though she had designed it herself, and though he couldn't understand why, it gave him hope.

He wondered for the thousandth time whether she would remember him. It had been so long since he had last seen her and he worried that she might've possibly forgotten about him completely. He had never been able to forget how she'd made him feel. When he was with her he imagined that anything in the world was possible, and the thought that she could forget him made his heart ache.

The woman slowed down as they approached a set of large double doors. She hesitated and knocked gently. Nick wondered impatiently if anyone on the other side could even hear her.

The woman knocked again, a little louder.

The door opened and a young, pretty, blonde nurse in pink scrubs opened the door with a big smile. She had taken over for Anne, the night nurse, who had finally retired. Becca had been a great addition to The Harper House and fit in well with the rest of the staff.

"Is it okay if Brynn has company?" the woman asked the nurse.

The nurse gave her a long look. "She's pretty upset right now about Mr. Michaels getting rushed to the hospital. We just gave her a mild tranquilizer to try and calm her so I don't think that company is the best thing right now. She really needs to rest."

Nick's heart sank to his toes and he prayed she would see the desperation on his face. *I'm so close. Please!*

"If you think that's best," the woman said, turning around.

The nurse looked at Nick's face and hesitated. "Who are you?" she asked staring directly at Nick.

"I'm Nick, I'm an old friend of Brynn's. Please, if you'll let me see her, I've come so far … I'm sure she would be happy to see me." Nick hesitated, shifting from one foot to the other anxiously.

The nurse looked at him for a long, intense moment with scrutiny well beyond her years. She turned around and listened as though trying to decide. Nick held his breath until she finally opened the door and motioned for Nick to move closer. "You can come in, but only for a little while. If you upset her in any way, you'll need to leave immediately." The young woman stared at him evenly, not in the least bit intimidated by his height even though Nick knew he could pick her up and move her out of his way without much effort.

Nick nodded obediently, letting his breath out slowly.

"Whatever you say." Nick was grateful for the opportunity as he walked slowly into the room, nodding at the older woman on his way. She smiled encouragingly and closed the door behind him. As he walked toward the figure that lie still on the bed, he tried to prepare himself. He had dreamt of this day for almost two decades. Now, he was finally going to see the woman who had stolen his heart so many years before.

Brynn lie still, except for her breath, which came slow and even. Nick tried to mask his surprise as he took in her face, still scarred, yet beautiful. He could see that the years had stolen her youthful glow, but she had been transformed into a softer version of the woman he had once known. He reached out his hand, aching to touch her, but pulled back at the last moment. He didn't want to frighten her as he sat down carefully in the chair next to the bed and waited for her to wake up.

He fought the urge to awaken her and chuckled at himself, running his hands through his chestnut hair that had grayed over the years. He thought about when his daughter was a baby and he would watch her sleep, wanting to wake her up just so he could hear her giggle. He felt like that again as he watched Brynn sleep. His stomach churned as he wondered if she would know him if she were to open her eyes.

He thought about the last time they had been together. The details had grown fuzzy over the years, but he never forgot how his heart stopped when she looked at him with her large, dark eyes. Nobody in his life had ever looked at him like that, as though he was the only person in the world, and he longed to see her eyes once again. He stared at her intently, unable to believe that he was finally sitting in the same room with her. She stirred slightly and Nick felt his heart quicken in his chest. He wanted her to wake up but he had to admit that he was terrified.

What if I didn't mean as much to her as she meant to me? What if she doesn't remember me? He had asked himself the same questions over and over, afraid that the connection he felt to her had only been in his own mind. He had never been a romantic man, but when the question arose about soul mates, Brynn's name always came to mind. Even though he had loved, nothing had ever come close to what he felt for her.

He cautiously reached his hand out once more and this time, didn't pull back. He gently traced her jawline with his thumb, careful not to wake her. He could feel the slight bumpiness of the scars and winced at the thought of how much pain she must have experienced. He wondered if she'd suffered, and his heart ached at the thought of it. It was the first time in many years he had been this close to her and even the smell of her skin intoxicated him. He marveled that he had been able to stay away so long. He cleared his throat without thinking, and Brynn jumped.

Nick held his breath, waiting for her to fall back to sleep, praying inside that she would. Instead, she turned her head toward him and Nick's heart fluttered as he watched her slowly open her eyes. She stared at him for a long moment and Nick was frozen, unable to breathe.

After what felt like an eternity, she began to blink rapidly as though trying to clear away a bad memory. He watched as her eyelids fluttered slowly, trying to bring him into focus. Suddenly, her eyes grew wide, and after what felt like an eternity, she opened her mouth to speak.

"You ... how?" Brynn said as she struggled to sit up but finally fell back onto the pillows, groggy from the sedative they had given her.

"Y-Y-Yes," Nick said, letting go of all his breath at once, relieved that she recognized him. "I'm finally here."

"You ... forgot?" Brynn said, her breathing labored and slow.

"No, never. I could never forget you," Nick said, his voice full of emotion.

Brynn laid her head on the pillow and closed her eyes. "Good," she said, her voice barely audible. "Good."

Nick leaned back in the chair and tried to control the tears that streamed down his face, afraid that his sobs would awaken her. He had been terrified that she wouldn't know him, but she knew exactly who he was.

"I'm so sorry I never came for you sooner. Please forgive me," Nick cried out, his heart emptying itself of all the guilt and pain he had wrestled with for so many years. Brynn's recognition of him healed him almost immediately.

"Don't ... cry." Brynn struggled as she whispered, slowly falling back to sleep. "Don't cry, Nick. Eva ... is ... o-o-okay."

34

Innocent

September 20th, 2016

"I'm telling you for the thousandth time, I didn't kill anyone!" There was a large vein popping out of Connor's forehead as he yelled angrily at the lawyer sitting across the table from him in the stark room. This lawyer was new and replaced the pathetic little man who looked like he was going to piss his pants every time Connor looked at him. This lawyer was much younger and looked expensive with his rich suits, manicured nails, and leather briefcase, but no matter how many times Connor asked who had hired him, he refused to tell. Connor knew that someone was looking out for him, but he didn't know anyone other than Eva with that kind of money, and he doubted that Eva would pay for someone to get him out of jail. "I swear, man. I didn't do anything so there is nothing for you to prove. I swear. I wouldn't have killed anyone."

The lawyer sat calmly, not at all affected by his client's outburst. According to them, they were all innocent, none of them committing the heinous crimes they were accused of. He knew when he looked in to the case that Connor Martin wouldn't be any different. The story read like a classic *little rich girl meets bad boy*, and before the lawyer even got started, he was already bored with the case.

The lawyer looked at him evenly.

"Listen, Mr. Martin, you're in here because they found you at the scene, covered in blood, with the murder weapon inches from your hands. Despite the fact that your fingerprints aren't on the weapon, there's been enough to hold you. If you add to that your violation of probation, the drugs they found in your system and the RAP sheet the police have on you that's a mile long, I wouldn't be very optimistic if I were you. If you don't tell me everything about that night, then I'm going to have a very difficult time proving your innocence. Now, somebody wants you to get out of here because they've paid me very handsomely, but I can't work with you if you don't at least tell me what happened and why Nora Symon is dead."

"But I didn't do anything, dammit. That's what I'm trying to tell you. We did get into a fight but I left and went to a bar and got shit-faced. The next thing I know, I woke up lying in a pool of blood in her apartment. I swear, I wouldn't have hurt her. Dammit, I ... l-l-loved her." Connor put his head in his hands and shook it back and forth in disbelief. *How could this have happened to Nora? How did I get myself into this mess?*

"You admit that you were in a relationship with Miss Symon, then, even though you were married to Eva Michaels under an assumed name?" the lawyer asked, leaning forward, repositioning the recorder in front of Connor.

"Yes ... I was." Connor's face turned red and he looked away from the lawyer, embarrassed.

"Did you love Eva Michaels?"

"Yes ... God help me... I did. She was ... kind ... to me." Connor admitted, his voice barely audible.

"Who were you involved with first?" The lawyer almost sounded bored as he asked the obligatory question.

"Nora. I was involved with Nora first. ... I've known her for a long time." Connor paused, as though there was more, but closed his mouth before he said anything else. "I met her in high school. When we met, I remember she said 'Finally' and we've been together ever since. She was a good person, she was just … a little messed up. I loved her, man. I wouldn't have hurt her. We were going to be together forever, but then …"

"'But then …'" the lawyer repeated as he leaned forward, his dark eyes suddenly glittering with interest.

"N-n-n-nothing," Connor stuttered, hesitant.

"It doesn't make sense why you would change your name, then date and marry Eva Michaels within a few short months while you were involved with Nora Symon the entire time. Then suddenly, Nora Symon ends up dead and you're lying in her apartment in a pool of blood with the murder weapon right next to you." The lawyer stared at Connor trying to read his face.

"I know! I know what this looks like. I know that it doesn't look good for me … and Nora and I did intend to … to … hurt Eva, but only in the beginning. Only to get back at Adam Michaels for how he hurt my mother, but then I couldn't do it. I didn't want to hurt her. She was so nice to me and cared about me and she was pregnant with my baby, and I just couldn't do it. I couldn't hurt her even if it was for the money. I swear."

"Your mother was Jessie Martin?" The lawyer flipped through some pages of notes and then fixed his eyes on Connor.

"My mother *is* Jessie Martin," Connor said, correcting him.

"According to these notes from your former lawyer, your mother took her own life a week ago," the lawyer said, his brows furrowed.

"What? No. No! That can't be true!" Connor buried his head in his hands, then ran his fingers through his hair, tugging at it in frustration, not wanting to believe it. "No! You're lying! You're fucking lying!"

"Oh … I would've thought your other lawyer would've told you. I'm sorry," the lawyer said, not sounding a bit apologetic.

"Oh, God no … no … how … why?" Connor already knew the answer. He had been rescuing her for years, and since he hadn't seen or talked to her for weeks, she had likely become unstable. Connor knew that he had himself to blame for her death and he suddenly felt nauseous.

The lawyer looked at him with a mixture of intrigue and disgust.

"I'm sorry about your loss, but I want to make sure that I'm clear with what we're looking at here. What you're saying then is that you tricked and impregnated Eva Michaels, even though you initially planned only to hurt her. Then you took pity on her and changed your mind, so you decided to kill your lover instead?"

Connor's face turned white, his hazel eyes bright red as his bottom lip trembled. Snot ran from his nose and he continually wiped it with his sleeve. After a long while he spoke, his voice broken and quiet, muted by the tears that ran down his face. "Yes ... I suppose that's what it looks like, but I swear to you, I didn't kill anyone! I didn't mean to care for Eva or get her pregnant, but she loved me and she thought I was a good person. Technically, I didn't do anything wrong because I decided not to hurt her. I loved her. I mean ... nobody has ever thought that I was a good person before."

The lawyer looked at Connor, trying hard to suppress his disgust for his client. "I'm going to do the best I can to figure out how to represent you, but nothing short of a miracle is going to get you out of here."

Connor closed his eyes and bowed his head quietly, Jessie, Nora and Eva's faces floating in the darkness of his mind, taunting him angrily. They all hated him and he deserved it for the despicable things he had done. He was a disgusting person. He saw himself reflected in the eyes of his new lawyer, repulsive and dirty, a man without character or worth, and he couldn't help but agree. He knew that nothing in his life mattered anymore as he silently surrendered himself to his fate.

35

The Truth
September 23rd, 2016

The hours passed like days and Eva was happier than she wanted to admit when she saw Jack walking down the hallway of the hospital corridor toward her. Relief seemed to flood over her and she was surprised that he had that effect on her after such a short time. Somehow, he made her feel safer in a world that she had never realized was so dangerous. That is until she discovered Connor Martin.

As they rode in the ambulance with Adam, the first person that Eva thought to call was Jack.

Eva was devastated as she held his hand and begged him not to leave her yet. After he was admitted, she waited patiently for Jack.

As Jack walked toward her she watched as his lean muscular body commanded the hallway. *Why couldn't I fall for a man like him and not someone like Connor Martin?* She felt guilty as the question popped into her mind, beyond her control. It felt inappropriate after all she had been through, and as Adam lie in a hospital bed, dying.

As Jack walked down the hallway of the ICU, Kelly came into the hall and motioned for them to follow her into Adam's room. The usual routine had already been done, and Adam was resting quietly, an IV firmly placed in his arm with oxygen lines and tubes weaving around his body. They were giving him medication for the pain and he was finally sleeping restfully.

Jack approached Eva and she hugged him, squeezing him harder than it looked like she could. He held onto her, enjoying their closeness and breathing in her sweet scent that he found so intoxicating. He took her in, silently assessing her, then quietly placed his hand on Eva's back and guided her into the room, unsure of what to expect. He tried to hide how nervous hospitals made him. After the death of his grandfather, he had made it a point to avoid them as much as possible. Eva looked at him and attempted a small smile as though to let him know she was okay. Concern was etched all over his handsome face and he stayed as close to her as he could, one hand remaining protectively on her back.

A young-looking, dark-haired nurse came in to check on Adam and asked impatiently if they had any questions. Eva wanted to ask her how long it would be and whether he would ever go home again, but she couldn't bring herself to say the words. Eva watched as the nurse took his vitals, quickly and efficiently, her dark eyes intent on her work. Eva thought briefly that the girl would be pretty if she smiled, but as she watched her work she knew there was no chance of that happening. The nurse quickly left the room and Eva followed her out, motioning for Jack to stay behind.

"I don't know ... I want to help if I can. My blood type is AB ... but I'm pregnant. If I'm allowed, if you need blood for him, I can give it. I don't know if you can do something to help him. A transplant ... surgery, something, but I can at least do that." Eva stammered as the nurse busily typed on the keyboard of a small computer.

"Oh, thank you, but we don't advise that pregnant women give blood," the nurse said abruptly, without looking up. "Are you his adopted daughter or step-daughter?"

Eva looked at her, confused. "I'm neither," she said, her voice wavering. "I'm his biological daughter. Why would you ask me that question?"

"Oh!" The nurse stopped typing and looked up at her, her eyes large. "I'm sorry. That was completely inappropriate and I wasn't thinking. I shouldn't have asked you that. It's none of my business."

"No! I mean … why would you ask a question like that? Why wouldn't you think that I'm his biological daughter?" Eva's voice was low but demanding.

"It's just that … you can't be his biological daughter," the nurse said quickly.

"Of course I am! Who are you to tell me that he's not my father? How dare you even say something like that to me?" Eva was angry, her voice elevating slightly with each word. Jack heard Eva's voice and rushed into the hallway looking for her. When he found her he saw that all the color had drained completely from her face.

"It's just … y-y-your blood type is AB, that's all." The nurse stammered, her face turning bright red as she looked from Eva to Jack and then back to Eva. "Please don't tell anyone I asked you that question or I could get fired. I'm already on thin ice around here. God, I'm so sorry. I can't keep my big mouth shut!"

Jack spoke up, his voice deep. "What does an AB blood type have to do with anything? What are you telling us?"

"It's just … I should'nt even tell you this because I've already said entirely too much, but with his blood type … it's scientifically impossible for Mr. Michaels to be your biological father. I'm so sorry."

Eva looked at Jack, and in an instant she realized that everything she thought she had ever known about her life had completely changed.

36

Answers
September 23rd, 2016

The news the nurse had given them about Eva's blood type was devastating, and Eva knew she had to get to Brynn to find out what was going on. Her entire life had been spent knowing that Adam had been her father, but with her blood type it just wasn't possible.

Jack had held onto Eva in case she might collapse, but she stood strong, holding herself up. He wondered how much more she could possibly take. *First Chris, then Adam, and now this. How is she still standing?*

Jack watched her carefully, but Eva showed no sign of breaking down. She stayed strong, not mentioning the conversation with the nurse, even to Kelly. Eva wanted to talk with Brynn first. They sat silently in Adam's room watching him carefully, each wrapped up tightly in their own thoughts. After a few hours, the doctor came in and let them know that if they could stabilize him they would also treat his pain. There was nothing more they could do other than make him comfortable and call hospice to go to The Harper House.

Kelly sent Eva home, volunteering to stay at the hospital with Adam for as long as he was there. She was used to long nights. "I don't want Adam to be alone and you need to take care of yourself," she said, hugging Eva tight. "Please, go. I'll let you know when he'll be coming home. It could be days until they've stabilized him, and I don't want you here in the hospital every day. It'll wear you out and it could hurt the baby."

Eva reluctantly agreed as she prepared herself to let Brynn know what was happening. She had a lot to talk to Brynn about and tried desperately to figure out how to do it. She looked at Kelly, her eyes large and fearful. "It's going to be okay," Kelly said, looking her in the eyes. Eva nodded, biting her lip to stop the tears from flowing.

"Please ... will you drive me home?" Eva asked as she grabbed Jack's arm gently, her eyes large and pleading.

"Of course, Eva," Jack said, smiling at her gently. Jack winced as he realized that Adam's coloring had gone from bad to worse, and he guessed that it might not be much longer. "Anything you need."

As they got closer to The Harper House, Jack could feel Eva tense up in the seat next to his. He reached for her hand and held it tight.

"What do you need me to do?" he asked, worried he would upset her.

Eva was quiet, the words caught in her throat. She opened her mouth to speak, but then closed it again, afraid to say the words out loud. Jack pulled over to the side of the road, the moonlight streaming in through the windows, making Eva even more beautiful.

"Please, tell me what I can do to help you," Jack implored, holding her hands together tightly in his. "I'm here for you Eva. I'm here to help you with whatever you need."

Jack marveled at his concern for her, and even as the words came out of his mouth, he felt as though they were coming from a complete stranger. He had never said anything like that to anyone in his entire life, or felt comfortable holding anyone's hands in his before. Something about Eva was changing him, and for the first time he felt his heart opening up to someone else. It was hard for him to admit that he hadn't stopped thinking about her and that his heart flipped when he was near her. She needed him and she brought out something in him that he never knew existed. He liked it.

Eva tried to speak again, Jack's eyes urging her on. "I-I-I'm just afraid, Jack. I don't want to be the one to tell my mom that he's going to die. I don't want to watch him die, and from the way things look, it won't be too much longer now. I don't want him to know that he's not my father. I thought I would ask my mom all of these questions about who my father really is, but now I don't think I can. I can't stand for him to die thinking that I'm not his little girl! I just can't!"

Eva was distraught, her mind racing back to her childhood and how Adam had been all she had. He had often held her close, reading to her, talking to her, and just happy to be near her. Eva knew that her childhood hadn't been perfect, but he had loved her, and every one of her memories was wrapped up in him. She knew with certainty that she couldn't bear to let him go knowing that she didn't belong to him.

As they pulled up to The Harper House, Eva threw her door open and burst out of it angrily.

"How could she do this to me? How?" she yelled, her voice rising, as she paced the length of the car.

Jack jumped out and kept pace with her. He was careful not to get in her way, to give her the space she needed to express her rage. He had never seen this side of her and, while it alarmed him, he understood it more than anything else. He had been full of rage toward his father for many years, and he recognized the same in her.

"My entire life, I grew up with this understanding that I was alone. Dad did the best he could to be a father to me, but he often failed, so I had nobody. Kelly loved me and so did Aunt Jane, but it wasn't the same, Jack! It wasn't the same at all, so I gave into my loneliness and embraced it, allowing it to become a part of who I was, until I met Chris. I gave him my heart because it was desperate and he knew that. He preyed on my loneliness and knew that I was vulnerable. All of this makes me feel stupid and angry and small! If my dad isn't truly my father, then who is? Why didn't he want me? Did he even know about me? Did she ever tell him about me?"

Jack let her rant, careful to listen and not respond. He hadn't known that Eva wasn't Adam's daughter, but he was sure that his father or grandfather had to have known. *Why wouldn't he have told me? Why would he have buried that information?* Jack knew the answer to his questions before he asked them because he knew that the number one priority was always to protect the family and this information could be devastating. This information was dangerous to both the family and their fortune.

Eva paced and yelled for an hour until her voice became hoarse. She knew there was nothing more she could do about any of it other than surrender to the inevitable. Jack watched as she began to slow down, exhausted by her outburst and tired of listening to the sound of her own voice. She leaned against the car, silent.

Jack leaned next to her, close enough to her that he could feel her body trembling from the cold as he pulled her closer to him.

Eva looked up at him, her embarrassment evident even in the moonlight. "I'm so sorry," she said, her expression quickly changing from angry to mortified. "I shouldn't have gone on like that in front of you. You don't even know me that well and you've seen me in every horrible situation you possibly could. I'm so sorry that you've had to experience all of this with me."

Jack looked down at her, a funny expression on his face. He had never understood the devotion his grandfather had to the family, though he always knew that his own father's interest was strictly monetary. Jack suddenly realized that his grandfather had *loved* the family, and he realized that taking care of Eva gave him a sense of purpose and pride that he never experienced before. In that brief moment, he understood the devotion that his grandfather had for Eva's great-grandfather, John Palmer, because he felt the same way about Eva.

Jack pulled her closer until she was in his arms. He knew she could feel his heartbeat because he could hear it beating wildly in his ears. He was pleasantly surprised when she didn't fight against him, and even happier when he felt her sink into his arms and lean against him with all of her.

"Don't be sorry, little one," Jack said stroking her long, dark hair. It was something he had been aching to do since the very moment he first met her. "I meant it when I said that I would be here for you. I'm not going anywhere. If you need anything, no matter when, I'll be here for you."

They held each other for a long time, both of them enjoying the stillness of the moment and neither of them ever remembering a time they had held anyone else so close. Eva closed her eyes and for the first time, her mind was blank, and she reveled in it for as long as she could. The anxiety rushed out her until she was empty of it all. Jack gave her a sense of calm that she desperately needed, and Eva knew the baby must somehow appreciate it too.

"Should we get going?" Jack asked, pulling away from her ever so slightly.

"Kiss me, Jack," Eva said, surprising herself as the words came tumbling out.

Jack looked at her cautiously.

"I-I-I don't know that is a good idea. I don't think that I should, Eva. You've been through so much." Jack looked at Eva, wanting to believe that he could kiss her, but not sure if he should.

"Please, kiss me. I've never wanted anything more than this right now." Eva looked up at him longingly, pulling him to her.

"Eva, you're confused. You don't know what you want right now. You've been through so much and I don't … don't … want to take … advantage of you." Jack ran his thumb down Eva's cheek and loved the silkiness of it. It took everything inside of him to hold himself back, but he didn't trust himself to kiss her when she was under so much duress.

"Jack, you are the one person that I know is right in my life right now. Everything else is crazy and wrong, but the only thing that I *do* know is you're here with me for a reason." Eva's blue eyes were large and glistening and Jack fought to stop himself from staring into them. He stepped back, distancing himself from her intentionally.

"Eva … I want to kiss you. Believe me, I want nothing more right now than to …" he paused, searching for the right words. "… to kiss you for hours. But I need to know that you want this for the right reasons. I need to know that this won't complicate things for you. You're going through too much, and I think you need some ... time."

Eva pulled away from him, the silence falling like a thick, dense fog between them. She felt herself falling into a cloud, and she suddenly wanted to cry. She knew that Jack was right and she kicked herself mentally for throwing herself at him.

When she finally spoke, her voice was so low that Jack had to lean in to hear her. "You're right. I ... I have a lot to deal with right now. I have a lot to face. I need to talk to my mom, and I need to see Chris and find out why he would do this to me. And I have to say 'good-bye' to my dad." Eva sobbed at the thought of saying good-bye to the only dad she had ever known, the thought of it tearing her apart from the inside.

"Yes." Jack said, relieved that she finally understood. "But I will be here for you. I'm not going anywhere. I don't think that seeing Chris is a good idea, Eva, but if you need to, then I'm not going to let you do it alone."

Eva smiled at him through the tears that refused to fall.

"I promise you, Jack Palmer, that when all of this is said and done, you will kiss me. I just hope you'll still want to," Eva said, her voice hopeful.

Jack smiled at her, pulling her close once again and happy to feel her body relax in his arms. "Believe me, Beautiful. I'll still want to."

From that moment on, Jack knew there would never be another woman for him. He held her for as long as he could until he was worried she would be too cold. Finally, he grabbed Eva's hand and led her to the warmth of The Harper House. Just as she was about to walk in the door, Eva looked up and gave him the brightest smile he had ever seen. For the briefest moment, he knew she was no longer thinking about telling Brynn that Adam was about to die.

37

Confession

September 23rd, 2016

Nick watched Brynn as she slept peacefully. He hadn't been sure what to expect, but just being in the same room with her, being able to touch her again, was enough for him. He didn't even mind that her beautiful, brown eyes were hazy with the sedatives she had been given to keep her calm. He was thankful for the opportunity to sit quietly and study her for a while.

Her beauty remained, the scars on her face visible, but many of them faded over the years. There were still long scars and burns on her arms, but what alarmed him most was the frailness of her body. She had always been slim, but now Nick felt that if he touched her the wrong way he would snap her in half. He cringed at the thought of hurting her and he stroked the back of her hand lightly with his index finger.

"If only I could tell you everything I've done to come back here to you," Nick whispered, staring at her face for any sign that she might be listening. "I divorced Melanie because after I got home, she had become quite unstable, which I know you experienced some of. I can't tell you how much it broke my heart to have her lash out at you the way she did, but it was one of the reasons I was trying to get away from her. After we divorced I lost track of her. Even though I tried to convince her to get help, she refused. She was a lost soul who had sunk into alcoholism and addiction. I had heard rumors that she had a child and a string of broken relationships after we divorced, but I never heard from her again. She made my life hell and if it hadn't been for her, I never would've left you to begin with. I never should've left you, Brynn. Never.

"Over the years, I tried to stay away from you, Brynn, but I just couldn't. I've come back here nearly every year with the hope that I might be able to see you, but I cowered, knowing that Adam was here. I know that I shouldn't have. I know that you wanted to be with me and that I shouldn't have let him stand in my way, but I was weak and afraid. I regret that I didn't try and that I missed every chance that I ever had to be here for you. I hated looking at myself in the mirror all those years, knowing that I was living without you and wondering if you had woken up yet. Every morning I woke up and thought of you immediately until I finally realized that I would never be able to live with myself if I didn't come back here for you. Now … I just hope that it's not too late."

Nick placed his hand gently on her face and continued confessing, realizing that he was doing it more for himself than he was for her. He had ached to talk to her for so long that he couldn't stop himself once he started.

"I don't know why I did it, maybe I was lonely and trying to move on, but I got married to a woman named Fiona. We have a little girl. Her name is Mandy. I didn't love Fiona, though I swear, I did try. She's a good woman, really, and she was good to me even though she knew that I couldn't love her the way I loved you. She knew that I came back here every fall. She never knew exactly why. I told her one night when I was drunk and stupid that I came here hoping that you had woken up, but the next year she let me come as though I had never told her. When I finally found the nerve to come in and see you, Fiona called me to come home because Mandy had been in a car accident with the babysitter, and nearly died. I ran out of here so fast, but I don't think Fiona ever forgave me for not being there. Eventually, she divorced me. She deserved better and should've done it years before, but for some crazy reason, she truly loved me. I didn't deserve her. I was a terrible husband, Brynn."

Nick paused to see if there were any signs that Brynn could hear him, but she remained still, her breath even.

"I fought for years to find the courage to walk back up to those steps again. I don't know what I was afraid of. I don't know if it was of you, or Adam, or … I don't know. And now that I'm here I don't know what I'm supposed to do next."

Nick could feel the softness of her cheek against his hand, and he closed his eyes, trying to think of what he should do next. He had never been able to get the twin freckle on the girl, the same one he had on his own wrist, out of his mind. He knew in his heart that she had to be his, but Nick wasn't sure that he was ready to claim her yet. Even though he had thought about it for ten years, he wasn't sure he knew how.

Nick stroked her cheek gently. He still couldn't believe that he could have such a strong connection with this woman after having spent such a short time with her, but even looking at her now, lying there so peacefully, he knew the connection remained. If he tried to explain it to anyone, he knew that it wouldn't make sense, but he was sure that he couldn't walk away from her again. Looking back, his life had seemed so short, but it felt as though it had taken him so long to get to this point, to get back to her.

"God, Brynn, I missed out on having this entire life with you and I feel as though I've been robbed of having you with me my entire life. But I'm here now, and I'm not going anywhere. I 'm never leaving you again. Ever. I swear."

Nick laid his head down on her bed, exhausted. He knew that he would have to tell her everything all over again once she had awakened. He knew that he might have to tell her many more times. But he was prepared. He had sold his home and moved his life, just to be near her. Nick closed his eyes as he held Brynn's still hand. He fell asleep in an instant, drained.

Nick hadn't heard the door open, nor did he see the small woman standing in the shadows behind him. He didn't know that she had been listening to him the entire time he laid his soul bare.

And he didn't see the angry tears coursing down her cheeks as she realized that he was the father she'd yearned for her entire life.

38

Bitter

April, Twenty-Five Years Earlier

The little blonde girl with the long lashes and bright green eyes sat on the steps of the beat up front porch, clutching Sadie, her favorite doll. She did her best to fight back the tears as she remembered how Momma had yelled at her to get out of the house as soon as the man had gotten there. Momma had started kissing him as though she forgot that the girl was there, and when Momma realized she was staring at them, she screamed angrily. "You stupid girl, what are you doing? Get out of here!" The girl knew that it shouldn't hurt her feelings because Momma always said she was sorry after she was mean, but it still made her heart hurt anyway.

The girl sat on the porch with Sadie for what felt like hours until the man left. The sun was beginning to go down and she shivered as the air started to get a little colder. She hoped that she would be allowed to go inside soon. She thought about the man and wanted him to leave. She had only seen him a couple of times, but she knew that he wouldn't be around forever. They never were. She didn't even bother to remember their names anymore until they had been to their house at least five times. Her rule was always five. One. Two. Three. Four. Five. The man inside was only on three.

Finally, she heard the door to the house open, and the man walked out on the porch and lit a cigarette. His clothes were wrinkled and his face was slick with sweat, and she thought that he wasn't handsome at all. He paused briefly, taking a deep drag of his cigarette, not realizing that she was on the top step watching him. He startled as he looked down and saw her, but didn't say a word as he continued to stare at her and smoke. After a few moments, he jogged down the stairs and walked away without saying a word. That was fine with her. She didn't mind. She didn't like it when they talked to her. Sometimes they tried to be nice, bringing her candy or toys as a bribe, and sometimes they were mean. There were a few of them that made her feel funny and afraid inside, especially when they wanted to hold her too close or too tight, or tried to kiss her on the cheek with stinky breath. But Nora knew that no matter what they did, or who they were, they never stayed.

She sat on the porch for a while after the man left, trying to remember all the ones who had been through that door. There had been the tall one with the brown hair, the bald one with the glasses, the plump one who smelled like cotton candy, the ugly one who smelled like cigarettes and stared at her in a way that made her want to crawl out of her skin. There had been the cute one who Momma said was as dumb as a box of rocks, and then there had been the one with the muscles who had tried to get Momma to stop drinking and smoking. Only two of them came around for as long as a couple of months. Most of them didn't last more than a few weeks. The girl hadn't cared much about any of them. She was always happiest when they were gone and it was just her and Momma, because Momma seemed to be happier when the men didn't come and go.

"Nora!!" Nora could hear Momma's voice through the tattered screen door. "Nora, get in here right now!"

Nora could tell from the thickness and high tone of Momma's voice that Momma had already been drinking a lot. It was earlier than usual, but this time of the day always came no matter what time it was. Nora was accustomed to the tone in Momma's voice that always signaled the change in her mood after she'd been drinking.

Nora walked slowly up the stairs and into the front hallway, her stomach tight. She dreaded talking to Momma at this time of the day and hoped that Momma might get sleepy soon and fall asleep like she often did.

"Nora!" Momma was nearly screeching. "Where are you, girl?"

"I'm here, Momma. I'm here," Nora said, breathlessly as she ran up the stairs and into Momma's bedroom.

"Aren't you a little old for that stupid doll?" Momma eyed Sadie dangerously.

Nora gripped Sadie and held her close to her chest. "Y-Y-Y-You gave her to me when I was little. I always have here with me."

"I s'pose I did," Momma said, lighting a cigarette and blowing the smoke in Nora's face. "You need to put that ratty thing away and not carry it around with you. You're too old to carry around a doll like a baby."

"Yes, Momma," Nora said, putting her head down. "I'll keep Sadie in my room."

"Good girl," Momma said opening her pill bottle and taking out two pills. She placed them carefully on her tongue and then took a big swig of the clear liquid in her glass. Nora knew enough to know that she wasn't drinking water and that the pills would make Momma even more drunk and sleepy.

"So ... tell me, little Nugget, what did you think of my new friend?" Momma asked Nora, taking another big sip of her drink and smiling at her expectantly.

"Um ... he was ... nice. He seemed like he would be ... okay," Nora said, careful with her words. She didn't want to make Momma angry.

"Okay?" Momma said, her voice taking a dangerous edge. "Just okay?"

"I mean, I-I-I didn't really talk to him," Nora said slowly, her voice faltering.

"Oh, well, you should, Nugget. I have a good feeling about this one. The rest have been ... well, you know, but this one ... there's something special about him. I can tell." Momma's eyes got a dreamy look in them as she smiled a little crooked smile.

"Oh ... that's ... good," Nora said, unsure of what to say She didn't like to talk to Momma about the men because she never knew what she should say and was always afraid to say the wrong thing. The edge in Momma's voice told Nora to tread lightly.

"Just good? That's all you have to say? Do you know how long I've been alone and how hard it is for me to take care of you? You know that I've been trying to find you a daddy, but you're too selfish to pay attention to how much I do for you and all you have to say is 'that's good?'" Nora cringed as Momma's voice grew thin and strained. Nora hated when Momma became this angry because it usually ended up with a few smacks to the face or a hard whack to the back of the head that made it hard for Nora to remember that Momma loved her.

"No, Momma. I mean ... I thought he was nice. I did! I swear!" Nora tried to make her voice sound happy because she knew that Momma would like that.

Momma smiled. "Good girl, Nugget. Thank you."

Momma's eyes glazed over even more than usual as she talked and Nora watched with dread as Momma talked about her new love with words that didn't make sense to Nora's eight-year-old brain. "This one may be the one." Nora had heard her say that before.

"The one for what?" Nora asked, her voice low, almost hoping that Momma wouldn't hear her.

"The one who will be your new daddy," Momma said yawning, her eyes growing heavy. "Come closer to me, Nugget."

Nora stepped closer to Momma the way she would get close to a snake. She thought Momma was happy enough not hit her, but Nora could never be too sure.

"Oh, stop being such a baby!" Momma said, grabbing Nora and pulling her close. "Why do you make that face? You act like I'm going to hurt you or something."

Nora tried to smile.

"Listen, Nugget ... You know that I love you, but taking care of you on my own is so damned difficult. You don't understand it because all you have to do is wake up and expect that everything is going to be done for you. It's hard for me and I'm alone. Your daddy didn't want anything to do with me ... or you. And you're going to have to do so much better than I did!"

Nora nodded, obediently.

"I'm trying to find a daddy for you. I'm trying to find someone to take care of us ... and take care of you. And when you're old enough, you'll need to find someone to take care of you, too. Someone who has money, someone you can make do what you want him to. Do you understand? You're going to need help because you'll never be able to get by on your own."

"I can take care of myself, Momma," Nora whispered, hoping Momma wouldn't hear her.

Momma grabbed her arm so tight that it hurt.

"Nora, you're such a stupid little girl! You would *be* nothing without me and you would *have* nothing without me. Your father didn't want you and he didn't want me, and now all you have is me." Momma pulled her so close that their noses were almost touching. "If you're lucky ... very lucky, you'll find a man with a lot of money. And then if you're smart, very smart, you'll take his money and get rid of him. But only if you get smarter and don't end up being the stupid little girl that you are right now."

Nora pulled her arm away and rubbed it trying to stop the pain. She wasn't surprised to see that a bruise was already starting to form. Nora knew that it usually didn't take very long.

Nora looked at the peeling paint on the walls and the smelly, worn-out second-hand furniture and promised herself that she would never be like her Momma. She knew that she would need money in order to escape this life, and decided that she would do everything in her power to make sure that she had it so she would never need anyone to take care of again.

39

Home Sweet Home
October 1st, 2016

Adam lie restlessly against the pillows of his hospital bed, blankly staring out of the window. The eight days in the hospital had been brutal. He'd been poked and prodded with needles, put through test after test, but everything came back with the same result.

There was nothing more that could be done and he knew it.

Adam had felt his body was dying for a long time. It was close to being over and the excruciating pain told him this every day.

"Please. I want to go home now," Adam said, grasping Kelly's hand tightly. "They've done what they can and you and I both know that there's nothing else that anyone can do here."

Kelly had been there, only leaving to go back to The Harper House to change her clothes. She refused to let Eva stay there overnight, protecting her from the pain of watching her father die. Instead, she carried the pain herself, unable to choose anything else.

Kelly looked at the nurse who had been checking his vitals.

"Will you please let the doctor know that we've decided to go home?" Kelly said, her voice low.

The nurse nodded and smiled a comforting smile. She had worked on the floor for quite some time and knew that these decisions were never easy.

Kelly held onto Adam's fingers tightly, fighting back the tears that threatened to erupt. She knew that she had to be strong and that she couldn't let him see that his end would also be her undoing. She had been hiding her love for him for so long, she didn't know what she would do without it.

The doctor had been in earlier and given Adam the news that his counts were poor. It was only a matter of time. This was something that Adam thought he had been prepared to hear, but the words still knocked the wind out of him. He thought he would be relieved, but when faced with the end, he was filled with an uncontrollable dread and a futile desire to live. He tried to force those feelings down as much as he could, but they were beginning to overcome him. He felt as though he might lose control if he stayed in the hospital any longer. Dying in such a stale and stagnant place horrified him.

Adam wanted to be at home for the end, with Brynn and in the comfort of the home she had given him for the past twenty years, even if she hadn't done it consciously.

Kelly looked down at Adam, his skin sallow and his cheeks beginning to sink in. She thought about how handsome he had been and how much she had loved looking at him, especially when he didn't know that she was watching. She had made it a habit to stare at him out of the corner of her eye, and her stomach dropped at the prospect of losing him completely.

"I'll take you home," Kelly said, kissing his hand softly.

Adam looked at her, tears glistening in his blue eyes.

"I'm sorry for what I've done to you, Kel. I meant to be a much better man than the one I ended up as. I thought ..." Adam's voice cracked, betraying his emotions. He took a deep breath and did his best to continue. "You deserved so much better than loving someone like me. You should've had more happiness. I wish ... I wish ..."

Kelly nodded as the tears flowed freely down her cheeks. Adam tried to wipe them away, his arm falling to his side weakly. "I wish you had loved me, too, but it just wasn't meant to be." Kelly attempted a smile. "You loved me as much as you could, and it was more than I ever should have hoped for. I was a big girl, Adam. I knew that I was in love with a man who couldn't love me back. But you've been my family, and for that I'm so grateful."

Adam buried his head in his hands, his body racked with pain and sadness.

"I ... just wish that things had been different. That we could've all been happy and gotten the life that we deserved. You deserved so much more than me. I don't know why this has happened to me ... to us. I'm sorry ..."

Kelly swallowed, trying to rid herself of the lump in her throat so that she could talk. "I-I-I wish that I could've chosen who I loved, but I couldn't. For some reason, my heart chose you, and nothing I could ever do was able to change that. I knew that you loved Brynn, yet my heart couldn't let go. But please, know that I don't regret that even for a moment."

She leaned in close to him as she spoke, placing her forehead against his and closing her eyes as she spoke. "My life has been centered around taking care of you and Eva and Brynn, and I love all of you so much. I would never want you to feel bad for loving Brynn the way that you have."

Adam smiled, gratefully, and Kelly noticed for the first time that the whites of his eyes were yellowing. "Please ... take me home."

Kelly arranged for a car to pick them up from the hospital as she sat quietly with Adam and held his hand. The doctors hadn't been very specific about Adam's prognosis, and said that it could take weeks or months. Judging by the way Adam looked, Kelly feared that it would be weeks, but she prayed for much longer. The thought of never seeing him again gripped her heart so tightly she felt as though she would never breathe again.

"Have you talked to Eva today?" Adam asked, lying his head on the pillow. He was becoming more tired as the morning went on and he hoped that he would be able to leave soon.

"I'm going to text her and let her know that we'll be bringing you home," Kelly said, reaching for her phone. She knew that the timing wasn't going to be good, but there was nothing she could do about it.

Today was the day that Eva was planning to go to the prison to see Chris. Kelly had tried to talk her out of it but Eva insisted, saying that she needed to do it.

When Eva told her about it, Kelly had been upset.

"Eva, you never have to see him again," Kelly said to her on the phone as Adam dozed restlessly in the bed. "Please don't do this. You don't need to torture yourself by seeing him."

"I have to, Kelly. I have to face him or I'll never know why he did what he did to me. I'll never know why he did this to me and I'll never be able to move on." Eva had sounded as determined as she ever had about anything her entire life.

Kelly understood, but she still didn't agree.

"You can't go alone." Kelly said, finally.

"I won't be alone. I'll have Jack," Eva said. Something in her voice caught Kelly's attention, but she chose to leave it alone. She knew that Eva didn't have any experience with men other than Chris, but something about her and Jack together made sense to Kelly and she didn't want to jinx it.

Now the day for Adam to go home and Eva to face her fear had arrived, and Kelly prepared herself for what was to come.

Eva had told her that telling Brynn that Adam would die hadn't been easy, but that she wasn't sure if Brynn fully understood what was happening. Kelly was shocked to hear about the arrival of Nick, and Eva begged Kelly to tell Adam about Nick before he came home. Nick was refusing to leave the house, and Brynn seemed to find comfort in having him there. Kelly had always anticipated that he would return, but hadn't heard anything about him since his confrontation with Adam ten years earlier. She had always known that there was a chance that Eva was Nick's daughter, but it had never been discussed with anyone aloud. Kelly had tucked it away in her heart until now. Kelly noticed that Eva's voice had grown tight when she mentioned Nick, but they had been interrupted before Kelly could ask her about it.

Telling Adam about Nick had been surprisingly easier than she thought it would be.

"I remember him," Adam said at the mention of Nick's name. For a moment, there was a fire in Adam's eyes, but the flame went out just as quickly as it had come. "He was there to see Brynn and I kicked his ass. But then I let him see her and afterward, he disappeared without a trace. I don't think he'd ever hurt her, and it was obvious that he really cared about her."

"Are you going to be okay if he is in the house?" Kelly asked, taken aback by Adam's strange acceptance of the situation.

"What can I do?" Adam asked, his voice strangely calm. "I always knew this day would come."

Kelly stared at him, filled with curiosity. "How?"

"When you love her, it's impossible to forget about her." Adam said, apologetically. "I could tell from the moment that I met him that he loved her, and when I let him see her, I knew that he would come back. It just took a lot longer than I thought it would. His timing really sucks."

Kelly marveled at how peaceful he seemed to be and it made her admire him even more.

"I don't like this. I don't like it at all ... but I've been selfish with Brynn her entire life, and I realize that now. I ... I ... don't want Brynn to be without love in her life when I'm gone," Adam said finally, and Kelly realized that Adam's love for Brynn ran far deeper than most people ever loved in their entire lifetime.

The house had been readied for Adam's arrival, and the plan was to make him as comfortable as possible for as long as he was alive.

When the private van arrived to take Adam back to The Harper House, Kelly left the hospital, grateful for the fresh air that filled her lungs. She took a deep breath in as they settled Adam into the van.

The ride home was somber and silent.

As Adam stared out of the window he thought with sadness that it would be the last time that he would ever get to be on this journey ever again. He had made so many trips to the hospital over the years with Brynn and for himself, that he knew the route by heart. He was thankful that it was scenic and that he had a good view to look out at. As they drew nearer to home, Adam sighed heavily.

He was nervous about seeing Brynn. He wasn't sure how much she would understand and wondered if she would even care that he was going to be gone soon. As they pulled into the long driveway, he was astonished to see that she was outside waiting for them with the new, pretty, young nurse, Becca, that Adam had only met a couple of times before he left for the hospital. Brynn waved as they drew nearer and Adam could see that she was smiling as well. He was relieved to see her, and his heart swelled as he realized how much he had missed seeing her. When he looked at her he still saw the girl he had fallen in love with, and he hoped that she would remember him, too.

As they helped him out of the van and into the wheelchair, Brynn approached him slowly with the nurse's help. Adam looked around for Nick, but was relieved to see that he wasn't there.

"I-I-I've m-m-m-issed you," she said, taking a long time to get the words out.

Adam's eyes filled with tears as he pulled her onto his lap as gently as he could and held her close to him. She was nothing but skin and bones and he was careful not to hug her too tight for fear that he would break her. Having her in his arms felt right.

"I've missed you, too," Adam said, kissing her softly on the cheek. Kelly stood by and watched them, a smile on her face, the sadness evident as she wiped the tears away. She convinced them to allow her to wheel them onto the large, spacious porch, where she left them alone to sit for a while wrapped up in one another.

As Adam held Brynn, he stroked her long hair and enjoyed the closeness of her.

After a long time, Brynn spoke.

"Is ... it ... t-t-t-true?" Brynn asked, her large brown eyes boring into his, searching. "Are you d-d-ying? Is this it?"

"Yes, it's true." Adam said, hating the effect that his words had on her. He watched as she seemed to crumble in his arms, her face full of devastation. "Please, don't ... don't ..."

Her sobs came heavy and long as he held onto her as tight as he could, willing her to stop. "Please, Brynn … don't … it's okay, it's okay."

She cried in his arms until she could cry no more, and when she was done, she collapsed against him exhausted. Adam's legs were beginning to fall asleep, but he dared not move her or ask her to move. He knew that having her close to him like this was something he wouldn't get to experience for much longer.

"Don't cry, Brynn. My life … has been worth every moment because of this, because of you." Adam kissed her softly on her cheeks, trying to kiss the tears away. The saltiness from her tears burned his dry lips and he searched for the right words to comfort her. "I've loved you every day of my life. There was never a choice about loving you. If I had never met you, I don't know what would've become of me, but I do know that nothing in my life mattered until you loved me. Nothing else matters now. Nothing."

Brynn nodded in agreement. "H-h-how long?"

"I don't know. It could be days, it could be weeks, it could even be months," Adam said, lost in the silkiness of her long, dark hair. "However long it is, all I wanted was to be home … to be with you. I hope that ... that is okay."

Brynn nodded, placing her hand on his chest. "Y-y-y-yes … it's okay."

As the evening got cooler, Kelly and Becca came out, brought them in and got them settled for the evening. As Kelly wheeled Adam into the guest room that they had set up, he was pleased to see that the hospital bed was very large.

"I thought that we might want to give Brynn the option of staying in here with you, if you'd like," Kelly said, as though reading his mind. Adam was struck with how well Kelly knew him as he gave her an appreciative smile.

Adam paused, overwhelmed by Kelly's kindness. He knew that if he had never found Brynn he would've been fortunate to have someone like Kelly to love him.

The nurse settled Brynn into the bed and then Kelly got Adam ready. As Adam got comfortable he tried to remember the last time he had slept in the same bed with Brynn and found that he couldn't. Adam was embarrassed as Kelly helped him undress and get his night-clothes on, but she talked pleasantly the entire time, trying to distract him from the awkwardness of it.

When Kelly and the nurse had left the room, Brynn and Adam lie in bed, the silence falling over them like a soft warm blanket. Adam was exhausted, but tried to find the strength to move his body over so that he was side-by-side with Brynn until he couldn't get any closer. He loved the warmth of her body and the way she instantly reached for his hand, like she used to so very long ago. He focused on the way her fingers entwined with his and tried to ignore the excruciating pain that shot through his shoulder. It was becoming more and more constant. His stomach was beginning to swell more and more, and he knew that it wasn't going to be too long.

"What about Nick?" Adam asked, unsure if he should.

"Nick is my ... friend," Brynn said gently. "He understands ... and he respects that I need this time with you."

She could feel Adam nodding above her.

"Adam," Brynn's voice was sleepy.

"Yes?" Adam said, thinking how much he loved her voice.

"I-I-I'm sorry," she said, her voice barely audible.

"Sorry? Why would you ever be sorry?" Adam said, surprised.

"I-I-I lost you," she said slowly. "I should've h-have n-e-ever l-l-et you go. My fault ... my fault."

"No, no, no," Adam said, rolling to his side so that he could look at her. "You didn't do anything wrong. I left you ... I lost you. I never should've let you go. If anyone is to blame, it's me. I'm the one to blame!"

"No. I ... l-ove you. I al-ways h-have." Brynn said.

"I've always loved you too," Adam said, tears filling his eyes as he leaned over and kissed her forehead. "Always."

Brynn's eyes were closed and Adam realized that she was asleep. He silently promised himself that no matter how many minutes or hours or days he had left, he would never again, leave her side.

40

Closure

October 10th, 2016

Eva took a deep breath as she stood outside of the prison.

"Are you sure that you want to do this?" Jack asked, his face full of concern.

"Yes … I mean … no. I don't *want* to do this, but I *need* to do this. I need to face him because I need to ask him why he would do this to me. Why he would have chosen me. I need to face him or I'll never be able to move past this and …" she put her hand on her growing belly and rubbed it slowly. "I just need to do this for me and … for the baby."

Jack nodded.

They walked slowly and checked in. Eva still thought it was strange that she had to check in for Connor Martin, but she reminded herself that her Christopher never existed. She had worked herself up to the visit and tried to remember that she needed closure and that the person she had fallen in love with wasn't real.

They sat in the visiting area, waiting.

Eva's palms were sweaty and her chest felt heavy.

How do I do this? How?

"Visitor for Connor Martin."

Eva stood up and saw Chris staring at her. His hair was longer and shaggy and his beard was long and unkempt. He looked like a completely different person and she was grateful for that. It made doing what she came here to do so much easier. She was astonished at the weight he had lost and alarmed at how empty his eyes looked. There was a part of her that enjoyed seeing him miserable, but even though he looked like a complete stranger, she felt her heart aching for him beyond her control.

He sat down at the table, heavily.

They stared at one another for a few long moments until Eva finally spoke.

"How are you?" Eva asked, trying to ignore the large bruise under his eye while a tiny voice inside of her begged to know how he got it.

"How do you think I am?" Connor said, his voice flat as he refused to look at her.

Eva looked at him apologetically, even though she had nothing to be sorry for.

"Who is he?" he asked, gesturing to Jack, his voice turning hard. "Why did you bring a stranger here?"

"He's a friend of the family," Eva said, nervously.

"Oh," Connor said, staring at Jack in disgust. The two of them sized one another up, until Connor's attention shifted back to Eva. "What do you want? Why are you here?"

"I just want to know … why … Why … Chr… Connor. Why did you … lie … to me?" Eva asked, her voice low but determined.

"Does it matter now?" Connor asked, angrily.

"Yes! Yes, it matters." Eva said, surprised at his anger and matching it with her own. "You lied to me and you took advantage of me! You used me and now I'm going to have our child. Why would you do something like this? What did I ever do to you to deserve having you treat me so horribly? Answer me, dammit!"

Connor finally looked at her, staring for a long moment, clearly stunned by her strength.

"Please … I need to know." Eva said changing her approach, her voice pleading.

"I wish I knew. I knew it was wrong … I knew that I shouldn't have done it, but I just got in too deep." Connor said, his head buried in his hands.

"Why did you pick me?" Eva asked. "Why would you want to hurt me?"

"It wasn't about you, Eva. It was never about you," Connor said, his voice tortured and full of conflict. "It was about my mom, Jessie Martin, and getting back at your dad … Adam. I wanted to hurt him for what he did to her … for what he did to us."

"Us? Who is Jessie Martin?" Eva asked, a feeling of dread growing deep in her belly.

"Jessie was my mom. She was Adam's girlfriend after he and his wife split." Connor said Adam's name with disdain.

"But … why … what …" Eva was confused. "Wait … are you saying … did you think that you're my… brother?"

Eva thought she would faint, the room spinning around her uncontrollably. The realization of what he was saying slapped her hard as the bile rose in her throat. She looked around the room desperately, knowing that she was going to throw up at any moment.

"God, no! No …" Connor said, his voice loud. He looked around the room uncomfortably and lowered his voice. "She always told me that he was my father, but I never believed her. One night when she was especially smoked, she admitted that Adam wasn't my father even though she didn't remember it the next morning when I asked her. She refused to acknowledge that she ever said anything at all, but I knew that she had told me the truth for the one and only time in her life. She had fooled around on him, getting pregnant with someone else, but she refused to admit it."

Connor looked at Eva, a look of disgust on his face as he thought about how indiscriminate his mother had been. "I never would've agreed to doing this if I thought you were my sister. Never for one second."

Eva breathed slowly until she began to feel as though she was no longer going to throw up. "Oh, thank God," she said, finally.

Despite the circumstances, Connor found himself amused with her, and he couldn't help but wish that things had been different between them. He resisted the urge to touch her, even though he wanted to. He still remembered how it felt to hold her hand and he desperately wanted to reach out and feel the soft silkiness of her hand in his. He knew that he would never have the opportunity to do that again.

Eva looked up at him, suddenly registering what he said. "What do you mean, you never would have agreed to this? Who made you agree, and what exactly did you agree to?"

Connor looked at her, realizing his error.

"Nothing ... I ..."

Eva felt that familiar tug on her heart as he spoke, even though she hated herself for responding to the sound of his voice the way she did. It was easier for her to forget about him when she didn't have to see him. She shifted awkwardly in her chair, feeling Jack's eyes on her and hoping he couldn't read her thoughts as she struggled desperately to forget what made her fall in love with Connor in the first place.

"You owe it to her to tell her what you were planning to do and why you hurt her the way you did." Jack's voice was sharp as he stared at Connor menacingly.

Eva held her breath, expecting Connor to react angrily. Instead he folded his head in his hands, his body shaking as he tried hard not to cry.

She looked up at Jack. She was at a loss.

"I never thought I would do something like this. I always thought I was a better person than ... I ended up being, and now ... I'm getting what I deserve by trying to hurt you. I'm sorry, Eva. Please believe that I did care about you very much. I did try to protect you, which is probably why I'm in here. I ..." Connor sighed, wiping the tears away, feeling the eyes of the other inmates on him and knowing that he had just made a dangerous mistake by showing his weakness.

"What did you do?" Eva said, staring at him evenly.

"I was in love, with a woman named Nora, the woman they are saying that I killed. And we agreed ... I agreed to ... I was going to ..." Connor struggled with the words, unable to believe that they were coming out of his mouth," ... kill you."

Eva gasped and stared at him, her blue eyes large as she imagined how she had planned to spend her entire life with him, his child growing large in her belly. She reached down and touched her stomach instinctively, the words stinging and unexpected.

"Oh, God. But why?" Eva said when she could find her voice.

"Money." Connor whispered carefully. "You had it and I didn't, and neither did Nora."

"So, you were going to marry me, get me pregnant, and then kill me so that you could have my money?" Eva's voice rose angrily as the reality grabbed her and gripped her so tightly she could barely breathe.

"Shhhh ..." Connor said looking around, his eyes meeting briefly with the inmate known as Scorpion, who was feared more than anyone else. Connor's face turned bright red, his voice suddenly fearful. "Jesus! Please, don't talk so loud, Eva. Are you trying to get me killed? You can't talk about money like that!"

"Should I care?" Eva said, her voice rising even more. Jack watched her carefully, impressed with how well she was standing her ground.

"No, you shouldn't," Connor said, desperation etched on his face as sweat began to bead on his forehead. "But I know you and you're better than this, better than me. Please... don't ..."

Eva could see the fear in his eyes and she realized that he was terrified. As much as she hated him, she couldn't bring herself to hurt him, and she tried to rein in her anger.

"What happened to ... Nora? Why did you kill her?" Eva said, trying to control her voice as she whispered in loud, hushed tones.

Connor's face turned white. "I swear, I didn't kill her. I know you won't believe me but I promise you," Connor said, his voice pleading.

"Why would I believe you or anything you say ever again?" Eva asked, her voice dripping with doubt.

"You shouldn't, but I swear, I didn't kill her. I would never hurt anyone, just like I could never hurt you. Think about it, Eva, have I ever harmed you? Have I ever even come close to hurting you?" Connor asked, reaching out to grab Eva's hand. "I don't know how to explain it, but I don't think she's dead."

Jack stepped forward as Eva pulled her hand back from Connor.

"I'm sorry, Eva. I'm so sorry," Connor said, his voice catching in his throat as he struggled to meet her gaze. "I ... I'm sorry for hurting you this way."

Eva stared at him, her blue eyes dark like an angry storm. "Is that what you want me to tell your unborn child? That you're sorry?"

Connor's face suddenly became blank.

"No. I don't want you to tell my unborn child anything," Connor said, his voice empty. "I'm never getting out of here, and I don't want my child to know anything about me. I don't deserve that child to know who I am or anything about me."

"If you didn't kill Nora, then who was that woman in her apartment? Who exactly is it that ended up dead? Wouldn't they have found that out during the investigation?" Jack's voice startled Connor and he lifted his head to look at the older man, his eyes narrowing.

"I don't know anything, but I know that I'm still in here so they still think that the dead woman is Nora." Connor said, never taking his eyes from Jack's. "Nora and I got into a fight after I told her that I had changed my mind and wasn't going to ... hurt you ... and then I got plastered and woke up in a pool of blood. That's what I know."

Eva stared hard at Connor, the part of her that thought she once knew him wanted to believe, even though her head warned her not to. She looked around the room and saw that a vicious looking inmate wearing a patch over his right eye was staring directly at them. When he saw Eva staring, he smiled, displaying a mouth full of gold teeth that sent a shiver down her spine.

"I just ... I had to know why you did this to me." Eva said trying to tear her eyes away from the man she had once promised her heart to. She stood up slowly. "I had to look at your face and know that you are no longer a threat to me and to my family. Mostly, I needed you to know that I'm not afraid of you."

"No," Connor shook his head, sadly. "I'm not a threat to you, Eva. And even if by some miracle I ever get out of here and see the light of day, I promise that you'll never see me again. But it's unlikely that will ever happen."

Eva's heart ached as she stared at the stranger in front of her. Less and less he resembled the man she had fallen so much in love with and so quickly. As hard as she tried not to cry, she felt a tear slip down her cheek. She knew that it was the last time she would ever see him. As the reality sat heavily inside of her chest she felt as though she would be sick.

Jack stepped forward and put his hand gently on her back. He saw her expression change. The gesture was not lost on Connor, either, and the two men caught one another's eyes briefly.

"Good-bye, *Connor*," Eva said, her blue eyes glistening with the rest of the tears that she refused to let fall.

"Good-bye, Eva," Connor said, his chin trembling as he tried hard not to show any weakness. "Please, know that in the end I did do what I could to protect you, even though I have a horrible fucking way of showing it."

Eva turned around and walked away, her hand on her belly. She suddenly felt naked as she realized that the eyes of the other inmates were on her, a palpable danger suddenly in the air. She felt certain that they must have heard her comment about the money and she thought about how careless she had been to talk about it with Connor.

"Don't worry. They can't hurt you," Jack whispered, noticing the goose bumps on Eva's neck. She had done so well up until this point, and Jack steered her quickly and carefully out of the prison and back to his car.

"Why wouldn't that one inmate with the patch stop staring at me?" Eva asked once they got in the car. She was visibly shaken.

"He probably heard you ... about the money. Any talk of money is unsafe, but you didn't know. I should've warned you about it, but it'll be all right. Connor will be fine." Jack said, giving her a small smile.

Eva wasn't convinced as she envisioned the inmate with the eye patch staring at her, and she knew that she wouldn't be able to get him out of her mind for a long time.

CONNOR FELT danger everywhere he walked throughout the prison, and no matter where he was he knew that he would never feel safe again.

He was a prime target and he had no way of defending himself. He had only been in a few bar fights, but nothing prepared him for what happened to guys like him where he was, locked in maximum security with violent offenders, murderers, and rapists. He knew the moment Scorpion saw Eva that his fate was sealed, and there was nothing he could do about it. He had already made the mistake of looking into Scorpion's good eye, the other one covered with a black patch, and knew that it was only a matter of time until he came for him.

He waited for days, sweating it out in his cell, huddled against the wall and barely sleeping. He knew what was coming because he'd seen it happen to too many inmates since he'd been put inside. Connor had kept his head down and tried to stay out of the way as much as possible, but he was marked now. Now that they thought he had access to big money he would be an even bigger target, and they wouldn't believe him when he told them that he didn't. Court was coming soon, but not soon enough for Connor. His lawyer told him that they had enough to keep him locked away for a long time, but Connor knew that the outcome in court wouldn't matter. He knew that he was never going to walk outside of the prison walls ever again. Deep down, Connor knew that if he called Eva, she might help him. He knew that she was kind and generous and that she wouldn't want to see him get hurt, but he had already tortured her enough.

As he walked in the yard, keeping to himself, his head down as usual, he saw a large shadow on the ground as it approached him. He looked up to find himself face to face with Scorpion, his good eye cloudy and horrifying to look at. Connor's eyes rested on the large, faded Scorpion tattoo on his massive forearm and shuddered. The stories about him that circulated throughout the prison had sent chills through Connor, and he knew that his time was up.

"I saw your pretty little girlfriend. She looked like a rich, sweet, little thing," Scorpion said, making an obscene gesture at Connor while standing way too close to him. "How come you didn't tell us about her?"

Connor tried to back away from him, but he was flanked by two of Scorpion's companions.

"Are you ignoring me, you little bitch?" Scorpion stepped up until his nose was touching Connor's, his one eye glaring at him. Connor shivered in fear, sweat popping up on his forehead.

"No," Connor mumbled.

"I think you're ignoring me," Scorpion said his voice angry and dangerous and he ran his hands over his own naked scalp in frustration. "I don't like to be ignored!"

Connor found himself struggling to breathe.

"I'll forgive you if you can get your little girlfriend to send me some money. Or maybe you could call her and she could come and give me one of those conjugal visits," Scorpion said, smacking his lips, the vibration of them tickling Connor's ear.

"No! She can't help you. Leave her out of this," Connor said, his voice louder than he intended it to be as he tried to step back once more.

"Ain't nobody says 'no' to me!" Scorpion said, his face twisted up angrily. "What's a little bitch like you going to do about it?"

Connor didn't realize he'd been punched until he felt the blood flooding from his nose. He put his hands up, but the blows came fast and furious, the pain catching up in slow motion.

"Nobody tells Scorpion 'No'!"

The dirt began to sting Connor's eyes before he registered the fact that he'd fallen on the ground in a heap. He could barely see a crowd forming around them chanting, but he couldn't hear what they were saying as the pain became even more intense, his belly exploding as he felt the heavy blows from Scorpion's feet.

He tried to open his eyes, but could tell that they were swelling shut, grateful that the tears were washing away the stinging from the dirt.

Connor felt himself fading in and out of consciousness, and wished desperately that the pain would stop. He didn't think that it was possible to feel this much pain at once, but his entire body hurt and he couldn't tell if it was just Scorpion beating him or if there were others. He groaned and tried to keep from crying out, but there was nothing he could do about the sobs that escaped.

He thought about Eva and what he had done to her and he knew that he deserved everything he was getting. If he had never gotten involved with Nora, none of this would have happened and Connor couldn't help but feel sorry for himself. He silently cursed Nora for letting this happen to him, and he regretted the day he ever laid eyes on her, even though he had loved her so much. He knew that it was too late for regret and that nothing could be done about what was about to happen.

The faint sound of a whistle and more shouting assaulted his ears, but he tried to give into the darkness that consumed him. Everything had nearly gone black and Connor remembered thinking how relieved he was to let the pain go.

He didn't feel the blade plunge into his side the first time, but when it went in the fourth time it went in deep. That's when Connor knew he was going to die. He lay on the ground and thought about Eva's beautiful blue eyes and nothing else. He began to pray as he felt the blood gurgling up into his throat, nobody coming to help him as he lay on the dirt, drowning in his own blood. He couldn't remember the last time he prayed and he wondered for a brief moment if there was even a God to hear him.

As he fought for consciousness, he thought he heard his mother calling his name. He closed his eyes and listened for her again and knew that there had never truly been another voice that had ever sounded so sweet. Soon, he could no longer hear anything at all.

41

Settling In

December 1st, 2016

As Adam grew weaker, Brynn grew stronger, walking and talking as though her life depended on it. She spent every waking moment with Adam, and they cared for one another as though they were the only two people on earth. All of Brynn's sadness and torment seemed to lift from her.

Nick was a frequent visitor to The Harper House and was relieved to see that Brynn continued to get better and become stronger. She often met him on the large wrap-a-round porch, each visit feeling like the first time.

"I miss you so much," he said, caressing her cheek with the back of his fingers.

She smiled as she leaned into his hand, but then pulled away.

"I've … missed … you," she said her speech still slow, but getting better.

They sat on the porch in silence, his arm around her as he waited for her to speak. He knew she had something to tell him by the way she looked at him anxiously. Finally, he turned and looked at her.

"You can tell me, Brynn. I know you have something you want to tell me and you can say it. You can tell me anything." Nick's heart was beating in his chest as he watched her struggle with the words. He prayed that she wasn't going to tell him that she never wanted to see him again. That had been his biggest fear since he'd moved to be near her.

"Adam ... is dying." Brynn said simply, as she looked at Nick with large brown eyes the size of saucers. Nick could see that it was tearing her apart inside as he began to realize what she was telling him.

"I know, Honey. You need to be with him," Nick said, saving her from having to say the words. He always knew that despite his love for her, Adam would always be first in her heart and that he could never replace him. While he wanted to be angry with her, he knew that he couldn't. He felt the same about her, having walked away from his life just so that he could be near her. He understood what her heart was saying even though he hated that she still loved Adam as much as she did.

"Yes," Brynn said, leaning her head against his chest. "I'm sorry to put you through this."

Nick was silent for a long time trying to find the right words.

"Brynn ... don't be sorry. I'm here for you and I'm not going anywhere. I'll still be here when you're ready."

Brynn looked up at him gratefully. Nick had imprinted himself on her heart and she was astounded by his love for her.

Adam had grown weaker, but was holding on to meet his new grandson. Eva's stomach had grown rounder with each passing day as she waddled around The Harper House, getting ready for the baby to come. Jack had become a permanent fixture in the home, claiming that he was there as a monitor, but the entire household knew that he was completely in love with Eva.

The house was full of life for the first time in many years. Becca and Kelly were there night and day, and Kelly added more help to ensure that Adam stayed as comfortable as possible. Kelly knew that the end was rapidly approaching. As the days went on, she tried to ignore the break in her own heart.

Even though she knew that she wouldn't have Adam for much longer, Brynn felt at peace for the first time since she could remember. Her family was together, and her body was healing.

But Eva was distracted as Adam faded away and the baby began to grow larger inside of her.

Ever since her visit to the prison, things between her and Jack had been different. Eva had been different. She was afraid and Jack could sense it, even though he stayed near hoping she wouldn't be so fearful. The banter and the closeness between them had all but disappeared, and he missed it. The only thing he could do was to stay close to her, close to the family. No matter how much she pushed him away, he stayed near, knowing that she would need him again one day and ready to be there when she did. He had never met anyone like her, and he wasn't going to let her go easily. Jack was a patient man. He was willing to wait it out. Wait for her.

As Eva's due date approached, Adam, Brynn, and Eva spent as much time as they could together, and Eva marveled at the love between her parents. For the first time, she saw what had bonded Adam to her mother so completely, and why he never let her go. The love between them was palpable and strong. Eva wanted desperately to live in it for the rest of her life.

"Dad, feel! The baby is kicking!" Eva grabbed Adam's hand and placed it on her belly just as the baby moved inside of her, her stomach rippling as he touched her.

His smile was weak but his eyes shone as he felt his grandson moving against his hand.

"Wonderful," he said, simply.

Eva smiled, fighting the tears, praying once more that Adam would live long enough to see his grandson. She knew it wouldn't be much longer until he arrived, her belly protruding so much that her skin felt as though it was stretched as far as it could go. She was glad to have the pregnancy nearly over, as well as her marriage to Connor Martin annulled. That last part Jack had gotten started as soon as Connor had been sent to prison. She no longer had any ties to Connor, and after her visit to the prison, she no longer worried that he could hurt her or their son. Jack had taken care to ensure that she would never hear from him or the prison again, and she knew that she had nothing to fear now that Jack was protecting the home. Jack was intercepting the mail and had security fielding phone calls to the home, but thankfully, Connor hadn't tried to contact her.

The prospect of motherhood excited her and she did her best to let go and be happy. She found it difficult to ignore the tiny, nagging feeling that refused to let her be completely at peace.

I'm losing the only father I've ever known, the little voice in her head reminded her every waking moment as she struggled to smile and breathe through the pain that she knew would come when Adam drew his last breath. Eva loved Adam with all her heart, and even though he hadn't been the perfect father, he was paying for it with his life, and Eva could no longer be angry with him.

As Adam lie in bed with Brynn and Eva at his side, he looked as though he was finally at peace. Eva loved how much stronger her mother looked, and Eva finally began to see how much she resembled her. She was happy that her baby boy would know her, and thankful for the chance she had been given to know her as well.

"Noah Adam, will be his name," she had told her parents happily.

She planned to name him after her uncle and father, and Eva smiled as she rubbed her belly and thought of holding him. She couldn't wait to meet her baby. Her entire life she'd wanted nothing more than a family of her own, and now she would have what she had always wanted, and the excitement bubbled up inside of her.

Jack stayed close, afraid to leave the family for fear that he would miss some unknown threat, even though Brynn and Eva both tried to get him to relax.

"We are safe," Brynn said, patting Jack's arm as he sat in the kitchen, sipping coffee and enjoying the promise of spring from his view in front of the large bay windows.

"I know," Jack said, smiling at Brynn. He had come to like her so much over the past few months, and could see why his grandfather had been so fond of her. She was much stronger than she appeared, and his grandfather had always admired strong women. "I just want to make sure it remains that way. How is Adam doing?"

Brynn shook her head as she got herself a cup of coffee, moving slowly, but purposefully. "Adam is … surviving but when the baby comes, he will go."

Jack was silent, no words coming to mind, unsure of what he should say.

"It's okay," Brynn said, sitting down at the kitchen island across from Jack. "He's ready. He's just waiting. For Noah."

Jack smiled. They were all waiting for Noah.

"How are you?" Jack asked Brynn, worry creeping into his voice as he saw how tired she was.

"I'm good," Brynn said, smiling a weak smile. "Tired, but good."

They sat in silence sipping their coffee.

"Eva is good, too," Brynn volunteered, her brown eyes staring into Jack's.

Jack flushed, taking too large a sip and choking on it, coffee spilling all over the granite countertop.

"Good," he said, when he had finally recovered. "Can I talk to you about something?"

"Yes," Brynn said, leaning forward.

"Why … I mean … do you know why … why she has pushed me away? We were getting close and then … she … it's almost as though she is afraid of me. I thought she felt the same way about me as I do about her, but then …" Jack threw his hands up in the air in exasperation.

"She's been through a lot," Brynn said, understanding his frustration. For a moment, she felt as though she was looking at Adam years ago, frustrated that she refused to return the love he tried to give her. Brynn understood her daughter more than Eva realized because she was just like her. "Give her time. She'll come around."

Jack looked at her, embarrassed. "I know. I'm sorry. It's just that … I …"

"You love her." Brynn said, smiling. "I know. I can see it."

"Is it that obvious?" Jack flushed.

"Yes," Brynn said covering his hand with hers. "I was very much like Eva when I was younger. I had been … abandoned and hurt by everyone who was supposed to love me the most, and I was terribly afraid. Just give her some time, but don't give up. Never give up."

Jack smiled as he stood up and enveloped Brynn in a hug. "I won't. I can't. I don't know that I can ever feel about anyone the way I do about her."

Brynn stood up just as Eva walked into the kitchen, holding onto her belly, her face white.

"I think we need to go to the hospital … now," she said, her voice strained.

Jack and Brynn stared at her in shock as the red seeped down her pants and onto the floor.

"Oh, my God," Brynn yelled, moving as fast as she could. "Kelly! Becca! Somebody, help!"

Jack moved quickly, picking Eva up as carefully as he could, yelling for Brynn to open the door. Just as he cradled her in his arms, Eva lost consciousness, her head rolling back and finally resting against Jack's chest.

Becca arrived first and when she saw the blood, she startled, but regained her composure quickly. "Go," she said to Jack as she followed him to the car, grabbing towels from the kitchen as she did so. "I'll go with you."

Brynn stood in the kitchen, helpless as she watched Jack's car speed away.

She fell into a chair as tears streamed down her cheeks. The memories came flooding back to her as she thought about how so many years ago she had lost her first daughter, Sophie. She prayed with all her heart that Eva wouldn't have to go through what she had, and that she would be able to bring Noah home to them.

Home to Adam.

42

Coming Home
March 15th, 2017

Becca sat in the back seat with Eva, holding her tight, trying to keep the blood from flowing all over Jack's car with the hand towel she had grabbed on the way out.

"How is she?" Jack yelled back, driving as fast as he could toward the hospital.

"She's hanging in there, but you need to hurry," Becca yelled as she held Eva's wrist. Her pulse was getting weaker, and Becca could tell that she was barely holding on.

Jack had memorized the route to the hospital and got there in record time. As they wheeled her in, Jack tried to follow, but the nurses refused to let him go in with them. "You'll have to wait outside until we know what we're dealing with, Daddy," the nurse said giving him an apologetic smile.

"Dammit!" Jack swore, as he paced the length of the waiting room.

Becca sat silently in one of the chairs. "She's going to be okay," she said.

Something about her voice grabbed Jack's attention. He looked at her with irritation and wondered for a second if he had heard her tone correctly. Her voice sounded flat, unconcerned, but when he looked at her he saw a look of worry on her face.

She met his eyes briefly, and he relaxed a bit seeing the same concern on her face that he often saw when she was caring for Adam. I'm just going out of my mind, he thought, shaking his head.

The minutes passed like hours, and the hours felt like days. He texted Brynn and Kelly, but there was no news to tell them and he knew they were just as anxious as he was.

Finally, a nurse came out and looked around the waiting room. "Family for Eva Michaels?"

Jack jumped up, the nurse approaching them with a kind smile.

"She's okay. We had to do an emergency C-section, but the baby is healthy and she's resting. She lost a lot of blood, but she's going to be alright."

Jack blew out a sigh of relief as he grabbed Becca and hugged her.

"What happened to her?" Jack asked the nurse, trying to get the sight of her blood out of his mind.

The nurse hesitated, "That's not for me to say. The doctor will come in and talk to you, but she is doing well now and is resting. She should be just fine."

"Thank God!" he said, his entire body finally relaxing.

"Would you like to see your baby?" the nurse asked, smiling.

"Oh ... he's not ... I mean, I'm not ..."

"Come on," the nurse said, grabbing his arm gently. "Miss Michaels wanted you to see him."

Jack followed up, happily, as though in a dream.

Becca shook her head and refused to follow as Jack left her behind in the waiting room.

As he walked up to the large glass in front of the nursery, he knew immediately which baby was Eva's.

"That's him," he whispered, as he stared in awe at the tiny person with the head of dark hair like his mother's. "That's Noah."

Until Eva, Jack had never imagined that he could love another human being so much, but the moment he saw Noah, he knew that nothing about his life would ever be the same again.

When Eva awoke in her hospital room, she looked up to find Jack asleep in the hard, plastic chair next to the bed, his body contorted in a way that was not possibly comfortable.

"Jack," she said, her voice weak.

Jack jumped, his neck snapping. He grimaced as he opened his eyes, confused. The moment he saw Eva he was awake and alert.

"Eva! What do you need? Are you okay?"

"Yes. I'm fine," she said hoarsely.

"Have you been here this entire time? Go home," Eva marveled at Jack's commitment to her. She didn't know what she'd ever done to deserve his dedication.

"No way. You should know by now that I'm not leaving you in here like this," Jack said, smiling at her and making her heart flutter.

"You don't have to be here. You don't have to do this for me," Eva said, knowing that she was pushing him away but not sure why.

"Eva, please. Stop doing this. You and I had ... have a connection, a strong connection. You and I both know it. Please stop." Jack's deep voice was pleading as he watched her carefully to see if he had any effect on her. He saw the tears fill her eyes as she refused to look at him.

"Yes, we do," she said, sniffling. "But, you deserve so much more than me, so much more than raising a child that isn't your own, the baby of an idiot and a ... a murderer. Do you really want to be here for that?"

"Yes! I do! I want to be here for that," Jack said, picking her chin up so that she was looking at him. Even in the hospital he was in awe of her beauty, and he knew that he was completely in love with her. "Yes, I want to be there for you and Noah, for all of it!"

"How can you say that? You barely even know me," Eva said in disbelief. "I'm a sheltered little girl who married a murderer and has no idea how to navigate through life. How can you want someone like that? You can have your choice of any woman you want. Why me?"

Jack looked at her long and hard, unsure where her doubt came from.

"How can you think so poorly of yourself, Eva? You made one mistake by falling in love with the wrong man, but that's not your fault. You can't punish yourself for that for the rest of your life." Jack placed his hand on her cheek and felt her resolve begin to loosen as she listened to him. "When I look at you, I see a beautiful, strong, and amazing woman. You've kept your family together. You've been your father's purpose your entire life. You are ... the most ... unbelievable woman ..." Jack's voice caught as his emotions got the better of him.

Without thinking, he leaned over and kissed her, losing himself immediately. The moment he felt his lips on hers, he felt her respond to him and his eyes grew wet with happiness and relief, the tears flowing freely down his face.

"God, I just love you so much," he said, holding her face with both of her hands.

Her large blue eyes glistened as she stared up at him. Relief and happiness flooded out of her. "I love you, too. I've been trying not to love you, but it's not working. I don't know what I ever did to deserve you, but I am so thankful for you," she said, kissing him over and over again. "Please don't ever leave me."

"I don't intend to," Jack said holding her close, finally able to breathe normally. "It'll always be you and me and Noah, and I'm never going to leave your side. Ever."

As the week went by, Jack was amazed at how easy it was for him to hold Noah in his arms. Noah responded to the sound of his voice and Jack realized that soothing came naturally to him. He had never been able to picture himself as a father until he met Eva, and now that is all he wanted to be. She made him want more than he had ever imagined in life, and he promised himself that he would always keep her and Noah safe, even if she wasn't completely ready to let him yet.

Eva was anxious to get home. Adam had been declining and Brynn and Kelly refused to leave his side. Once they were finally cleared, the ride home seemed long and unsettling as Jack drove below the speed limit. He had never driven with a baby in the car and the thought of it terrified him. Jack was never as grateful to pull into The Harper House as he was with baby Noah for the first time.

Brynn and Adam met them in the driveway, both anxious to meet their grandson. Adam had suffered through a difficult week, and Brynn knew that it was only a matter of time until he decided to let go for good. She watched him like a hawk every second of the day, not wanting to miss one moment with him while he was awake. As Jack's sleek, black car pulled into the driveway, Brynn smiled with amusement. His car was not very child-friendly, which she figured he would soon realize.

Adam was nervous. He hadn't held a baby since Eva was one, but he was eager to. He didn't want to leave, but he knew the time was coming. His body was growing weaker and he was asleep far more than he was awake. He fought to hold on for as long as he could.

As Eva got out of the car, Adam marveled at how beautiful and strong his daughter was, and how much she resembled Brynn in every way. He admired her strength and goodness, and he reminded himself to tell her before it was too late.

"Daddy!" she said, walking quickly toward him with the baby, her blue eyes sparkling at the sight of him. Adam gazed at her and the baby taking a mental snapshot in his mind, vowing to always remember how she looked at this very moment. She approached his wheelchair and carefully laid the tiny bundle in his arms.

The baby awoke just as Eva laid him down, looking Adam directly in the eyes as he did so. Adam's eyes filled with tears as the emotion overcame him. He found as the days went on he cried easily. "Meet your grandson, Noah Adam," Eva said proudly, kissing Adam on the cheek.

Adam stared down at the baby lost in eyes that were bright and alert, realizing that he had never felt so much love for another human being in all his life. Noah stared up at him with quiet curiosity as Adam cried helplessly. At that moment, he understood that he would miss every important moment in Noah's life, and he hoped with everything that was inside of him that Eva and Brynn would make sure the baby knew who he was.

"Hi Noah, I'm your grandpa. I'm so happy that I got to meet you and that you're as healthy and beautiful as everyone hoped you would be. I ... wish you so much happiness and love. I only wish that I could be here to see it, but... I'm leaving you in good hands."

Adam looked up to see Brynn and Eva holding one another, the sight of Adam and Noah tearing them apart as they gripped one another tightly, unable to let go. Adam sighed, wiping the tears from his eyes and surrendering himself to a reality that was far beyond his control.

He gestured for Eva to take the baby.

"I love you," he said to Noah, planting a kiss on his forehead as Eva carefully took him from his arms.

"Please take me inside," he said quietly to Becca, putting his head down. "I need to lie down."

Becca pushed his wheelchair up the ramp easily. Adam was barely skin and bones and wheeling him around had become much easier.

Brynn looked at Eva and Jack, her bottom lip quivering.

"I'm so glad you've come home. Your dad can go home now, as well."

43

Jealous

March 20th, 2017

Nora watched Eva and the baby for days, her skin tingling with jealousy and anger.

She hated that little rich bitch for everything she had taken from her, first Connor, and now his child. She blamed Eva for everything and knew that the time was coming when she would take everything that was important to her. First, Nora planned to take her child and then her life, although she didn't care which order she did it in. If she could take her child first and make her suffer, she knew that would be much sweeter, but she was willing to accept whatever she could get. Nora smiled as she gazed at Jack under her long lashes, imagining what she could do to him if she ever got her hands on him for even just a moment. She let her mind wander to thoughts of him naked, sweaty, with her on top of him, until she was interrupted by the sound of Adam's voice.

"Becca, can you help me get to my room? I need to rest." Adam's voice was beginning to grate on her and she was starting to regret that she hadn't found another way to infiltrate the house. He constantly called her name and she hated how hard it was to put him in bed, even though he couldn't weight more than one-hundred pounds now. Taking care of him had to be the most unglamorous job she had ever imagined, and she thought that even housekeeping would have been better than being Adam's personal nurse day and night. She wondered why that lazy bitch, Kelly, had relinquished most of his care to her, instead of just doing it herself. Nora hated Kelly's weakness, crying anytime she was anywhere near Adam or the rest of the family, and she wondered how she had managed to stay employed for as long as she had.

I wish he would just fucking die already!

"Of course," Nora said, smiling her sweetest smile at Adam "I'd be happy to help you."

Nora always knew that she was a good actress. Her entire life, everyone had always believed her lies.

No, Momma, I didn't take the last cookie.

No, Mrs. Stephens, I would never pinch anyone! He pinched me!

No, Momma, I would never undress in front of your boyfriend!

Momma, he forced me do that to him, I would never do anything like that with someone you liked that much, ever!

Connor, you are my one and only love, I promise.

Detective, I'm terrified of my boyfriend, Connor Martin. He's extremely violent toward me and I don't know what he'll do next so please, I need a restraining order.

Nora wondered why she had wasted all that time killing herself in nursing school when she should've gone into movies or television and made it with her acting skills. But Momma had insisted that she do something more than work in a bar like she had, and with her grades in school, it had been easy for her to get a full ride scholarship.

"You've got a brilliant mind, Nora. You've never even tried and you get perfect grades, so going to school will be free and you can get out of living in a shithole like this one. Get a good job because God knows that you'll never find a man to put up with you for too long."

Even Connor believed every word she had ever told him, following her every instruction. She had stumbled upon him accidentally, and when he had told her the story about his mom and the rich guy, Nora knew that he was her ticket to an easy life. Getting him to seduce and marry that pathetic weakling had been easy. Nora had even anticipated that he would end up feeling sorry for the spoiled brat, but hadn't imagined that he would love her or end up getting her pregnant.

Nora thought about Connor as she prepared Adam for a nap. Her chest tightened slightly as she thought about the lengths she had to go through in order to frame Connor for her murder. It had taken a great deal of time and planning, and seducing her look-alike had been fun, although shorter than she wished it had been. She thought about Hannah Leigh, and her heart quickened as she remembered how easy and incredibly sweet and innocent she had been. The first time Nora had kissed her, she knew that Hannah was something special, and the first time Nora touched her naked flesh and pressed it against her own, she realized she would regret what she had to do to her. In the end, it had been much easier to bash her skull in than Nora thought it would be. Nora found that she had actually enjoyed it. She had anticipated that he would return to the apartment after their fight, like he always did. He was predictable in every way. When he returned, she drugged him. Her only regret was that she hadn't gotten to have sex with him before he passed out.

Nora hated having to punish him so brutally, but she didn't have a choice. He had betrayed her and she couldn't allow him to treat her that way after everything she had planned to do for him. She was going to make him very happy, but he ruined everything. She was looking forward to seeing the look on his face when she went to the prison to tell him what she had done, but was shocked to find out that he had been killed by an inmate. There had been nobody listed as next-of-kin, and he hadn't even had a proper funeral.

Nora grieved as much as she could for Connor, but she knew that it would have to wait. She had infiltrated the house months before Connor had been sent to prison. She'd played the role of her lifetime as Becca, and nobody suspected her of a single thing. It was the only way she could get close to Eva and pay her back for ruining everything she had worked so hard for.

Eva had gotten everything that Nora ever wanted, and she waited patiently for the moment that she could look Eva in the eyes and punish her for what she had done. Nora knew the opportunity would present itself soon, and she was going to ready when it did.

44

Good-bye, My Love
March 25th, Present Day

Adam knew that the end was almost near.

He had been waiting for Eva and the baby to come home, unable to leave the house any longer to visit them at the hospital. He knew that he had to see Noah Adam just one time. The moment he laid his eyes on baby Noah, he was finally at peace. He thought it would be so much harder to let go once he saw him, but instead the baby had given him hope. He knew that life would go on, even without him there, and he decided that he was no longer afraid.

The doctor had been in to visit him and told him that the end was near. It had already been three weeks since Eva had come home with the baby, and he knew that he was living on borrowed time. His organs were failing and the family had been vigilant, staying by his side. Even Jack, who Adam had grown fond of, stayed close, clearly taking care of Eva and anything she needed. Adam could tell that he loved her deeply, and he hoped that Eva would someday reciprocate the love he had for her.

"I hope you will let yourself love him one day, Bitty" he said to her when she came home from the hospital, holding her hand as he spoke to her.

"Dad, don't worry about that," Eva said, her voice quivering. She was having a difficult time as his skin became more sallow and his strength all but disappeared. "I ... please don't worry about me."

"Of course ... I worry for you," Adam said, his voice barely above a whisper. "I ... worry ... for all of you. But ... you are in ... good hands."

"Yes, Daddy. I know that I am, and I do love Jack, but right now, I want to concentrate on making sure you know that I love you. So much." Eva hugged him as gently as she could, hoping his heart could feel the love that poured out of her.

Adam nodded and sighed. "Yes. Now ... please ... send Jack to me."

Eva looked at him, pausing. She hated leaving him, never knowing when the last time would be that she would see him. "Daddy, I can stay."

"No, Bitty I need to ... rest, but first ... Jack." Adam said grabbing her and pulling her toward him.

Eva rested in his arms, hesitant to leave the room.

"Please," Adam said, staring into the blue eyes that were so much like his own. "I love you, Bitty"

"I love you too, Dad," Eva said kissing him on the cheek. As she closed the door carefully behind her, a sense of finality overcame her and she couldn't hold the tears back any longer. She hated feeling this way and sought Jack out, knowing that she would find him with Noah.

When Adam's door opened and Jack peered in, Adam was sleeping soundly. Jack turned around to leave but then he heard Adam's voice call out to him.

Jack sat next to the bed reluctantly.

"I'm sorry if I woke you, sir." Jack said, clearing his throat. He liked Adam but was intimidated by Eva's love for him. He knew that it wouldn't be long before Adam was gone, and he desperately wanted Adam's approval, a feeling that was completely foreign to him.

"Do … you have … something to say to me?" Adam said, making Jack immediately uncomfortable.

"Um … I don't know," Jack said, suddenly feeling like a ten-year-old boy who had thrown a baseball through the window. "Do I?"

"Yes … you do," Adam said as Jack felt himself begin to squirm even more.

Jack sat and thought for a moment, hundreds of thoughts racing through his head. He didn't want to patronize Adam, but knew that Adam was looking for something specific from him.

"Yes!" Jack thought after a few moments. "Yes … I do."

Adam's expression was serious as he waited for Jack to find the words.

"You know that I … l-l-l-ove Eva," Jack said, awkwardly, his words finding a strange voice on his own lips. He sounded like a stranger, even to himself, but he pressed on anyway.

"Yes," Adam said, smiling.

"I would like …" Jack cleared his throat nervously. "I would like to ask your permission to marry her when the time comes, and to take care of her and your family."

Adam looked Jack over for a few long moments until Jack felt as though he would faint. He had never imagined himself in this situation, and hadn't even realized it was happening until Adam searched his soul and pulled it out of him.

"Yes", Adam said finally as Jack let his breath out loudly, relieved. Being a bachelor his entire life, he had never imagined ever facing anyone in this moment and was relieved when it was over.

"Yes, you can … marry Eva. But promise me … you'll take care of … all of them. Brynn … my love … please, don't abandon her. Don't leave her behind," Adam said, his voice imploring.

"Of course, of course," Jack said, the thought of leaving Brynn to fend for herself never even crossing his mind. He had fallen in love with the entire family and could never imagine walking away from any of them, ever.

Adam started to snore within minutes as Jack silently left the room, knowing that Eva would want to know what they had talked about. Jack decided that he would keep it to himself until the time came, even though he knew that Eva wouldn't be happy about it. Eva was everything Jack had never imagined wanting, and she had changed him for the better. She challenged him, excited him and mesmerized him in every way and he knew that loving her wouldn't always be easy, but he was ready for it. He just needed her to give into him completely.

I will wait for her for as long as I need to, until she realizes that I will never leave her or let her go.

Brynn lay on the bed next to Adam watching him snore gently.

She loved watching him sleep and had never told him how often she had done so during their lifetime together. As a younger woman, it was the only time she had felt completely safe with him, even though he promised her that he would never hurt her or harm her. Even after Sophie died, she watched him while he slept, but then it had become different. Brynn thought sadly that after Sophie died, everything between them had changed for the worse, and as she let her mind wander back, she wondered how much different their lives would have been if Sophie had lived. She sighed knowing that there was no way she would ever know as she once again tried to accept that this was the way their lives had been meant to go.

Brynn was thankful that most of her mobility and speech had finally returned. After countless months of therapy and hard work, she was finally close to being 100%, although the therapist had told her that she needed to be happy with anything she got back. Brynn fought hard and worked herself as much as she could, even on her own, and her doctors and therapists were amazed by her progress. Even though she knew that she would never be completely healed, she was thankful for what she had been able to do.

As she stared at Adam she thought of how unfair it was that she was about to lose him again. She knew that this time there would be no turning back. Once he was gone, she would never see him again. She shifted her body slowly, careful not to wake him as she fought back a sob that threatened to escape her. The emptiness she felt within threatened to consume her, even though she tried not to show it in front of Adam. He had been the only man to know her completely, and while he had rejected her after Sophie died, she knew that part of him had always loved her. If he hadn't, he never would've cared for her the way he did for twenty years, waiting for her to return to him.

Brynn realized that Adam's eyes were on her as she roused herself from the memories that had overtaken her.

"Hi, Love," Adam whispered, smiling.

Brynn smiled back, seeing him still as the fifteen-year-old boy who had stolen her heart.

"Hi, Love," Brynn said, touching his cheek gently. "Are you in pain?"

Adam lied. "No. I'm fine."

"Good," Brynn said, kissing him gently on the forehead. "You look good, today."

"You look ... beautiful." Adam said, his voice tender. He thought Brynn was the most beautiful woman he had ever seen in his entire life, and his heart warmed at the sight of her.

"Stop," Brynn blushed. She touched the faded scar on her cheek and frowned without realizing it.

"Don't ... don't do that," Adam said pulling her hand away. "I mean it, Brynn. You ... are beautiful."

Brynn could tell by Adam's breathing that talking exhausted him. She snuggled against him, loving the warmth of his body against hers.

She heard his voice above the top of her head as she closed her eyes, vowing to remember every moment they had left.

"You ... have been the best thing to ... ever happen ... to me. I'll never ... regret passing you... that note ... when we were fifteen. It was ... the smartest thing ... I ever ... did," Adam's voice reverberated in his chest as Brynn fought back the tears. She hated when he spoke like it was the last time he would talk to her, even though she knew that it might be.

"I'll never forget reading that note and giggling," Brynn said, trying to control her voice so that he wouldn't hear her heart breaking.

"You have been ... my greatest ... love," Adam said, squeezing her for a brief moment. His arms relaxed and the sound his breathing became slower and shallower as he fell quickly asleep.

"And you have been mine," Brynn said, hoping that his subconscious would hear her. She lay against him sleepily.

As she felt herself drift off to sleep in his arms, she thought she heard his voice in her dreams say, "Good-bye my Love. Good-bye."

45

The Final Farewell
April 2nd, 2017

Eva sat in front of her vanity, brushing her long dark hair, and staring at her red puffy eyes. She knew that no amount of makeup in the world would be able to conceal what she was looking at, and she didn't care. The dark dress fit her perfectly, her body almost back to where it was before she had Noah. She was thankful for good genes and thought that it was an odd thing to be thankful for on the day of her father's funeral.

She'd dreaded this day her entire life, knowing she would have to say good-bye to one of her parents. She had always been prepared to say good-bye to Brynn first, but not to Adam. Adam had been her rock, albeit, a spongy one. Still, he had been the only parent she had ever truly known. She looked at her watch, counting down the hours until she would have to stand in front of his casket. Four hours. Her heart thumped anxiously.

The thought of never seeing him again gutted her inside in a way that she couldn't prepare herself for.

Jack had been the only person keeping her sane. Even though he admittedly hadn't been close to his own father, he still experienced a lot of the same emotions when he lost him. Jack understood her and Eva realized that he always seemed to understand her. As she brushed her hair and thought of him, she briefly allowed a smile to touch her lips.

She went to Noah's nursery to prepare him and his bag for the long day ahead. Brynn had given everyone the day off as they prepared for the funeral. She and Kelly had gone out to make a few last minute preparations, and Eva was thankful for the near empty house. She worried about her mom who had fallen asleep next to Adam and then awoke next to him to find that he had died with her in his arms. Brynn had been by his side non-stop in the last weeks, returning the love that he had given her. He had spent so many years making sure she was given the best care in The Harper House, and she knew that she could never abandon him. Brynn had been heartbroken when she awoke to find that he had passed on, but didn't give herself the time to grieve.

She'd insisted on helping with the funeral arrangements, taking care of as much as she could on her own. She knew that nobody knew him like she did and she wanted the services to honor him.

Eva wondered what would happen to her mother when everything had finally calmed down. She desperately hoped that Brynn wouldn't break.

As she walked into Noah's nursery she was surprised to find Becca standing in the middle of the room, almost as though she was waiting for her.

"Oh ... hi," Eva said, stunned to see her there. "What are you doing in here?"

"I come here a lot." Becca said. The unexpected hardness in her voice made Eva's hair stand up on the back of her neck.

"Why? W-w-w-hy would you ever come in here?" Eva said confused. She noticed for the first time how close Becca was to Noah's crib.

"I come in here to visit Noah," Becca said taking a small step closer to the crib. Eva felt herself beginning to sweat, her nerve endings tingling as she looked around the room for something she could throw.

"But ... w-w-why would you come in here to visit my baby? When ... when would you come here?" Eva stepped closer to Becca, focusing her eyes on the dark piece of metal that Becca suddenly had in her hands. It was pointed directly at Eva.

"I come here because I want to see my baby, because I want to feel close to Connor. I come here because I can and because you've been too stupid to realize it and stop me." Becca's green eyes bore into Eva, enjoying the look of fear and confusion she saw on her face.

"*Your* baby? ... Connor ... what does this have to do with Connor? You knew him?" Eva's voice rose sharply as she felt terror replacing the fear that had been in her heart only a few seconds before at the mere sound of Connor's name.

"Yes, of course I knew him! He was my lover. He was the only love of my life. I was the reason that he was here. With you," Becca said waving her gun at Eva, carelessly.

The room began to spin as Eva fought to steady herself.

"Oh, God..." Eva's right hand rose to her lips in horror. "Are you ... Nora?" Eva asked, reality setting in slowly, her blood turning to ice.

"Yes," Becca said, her eyes bright and full of hatred. "You're finally getting it! You're not nearly as stupid as I thought you were."

"B-b-b-ut ... your dead. Connor killed you." Eva tried to step a little closer to the crib, but Becca motioned with the gun for her to back up. "Please ... please, don't hurt Noah!"

"I would never hurt Noah! Noah is going to be my son since you stole Connor from me! Connor was never supposed to get you pregnant! He was supposed to kill you, take your money, and then marry me. We were going to have a family together with all your money because we knew you would be too trusting for a prenup. But then you had to go and fuck it all up by making him fall for you. You ruined everything, you selfish bitch!" Becca's eyes glittered at Eva dangerously.

"No ... God, no. Connor didn't love me, he never loved me or he wouldn't have hurt me the way that he did. Please ... if it's money you want, I can give you money. Please, just get away from my baby," Eva begged, tears falling helplessly down her face as she struggled to think of a way to get Becca to move away from the crib. She could hear Noah begin to stir from his nap and she desperately wanted Becca and her gun to be as far away from him as possible.

"It *was* about the money, at first. But then he didn't want to go through with hurting you because he *cared about you too much,* and said that you were a good person. You wove some magic, rich girl spell over him, and then he shot our plan all to hell. So, I had to punish him and send him to jail. I was going to go in and tell him everything, but then I found out that he's dead and it's all because of you." Becca's voice was full of hatred as she waited for her words to sink in.

Eva's face turned white.

"Connor is dead?" Eva felt her knees go weak as she struggled not to collapse. "I'm sorry, I-I-I didn't know."

Becca snorted. "Of course you didn't know because you didn't really love him like I did. So, this is how it's going to go. I'm going to pick up my baby and then I'm going to shoot you and you're going to let me. Because if you don't, then I may accidentally shoot Noah, and neither of us wants that, do we?" Becca held the gun directly toward Eva's heart, enjoying every moment as she absorbed her fear and reveled in it.

"No. No. Please, don't touch my baby! Don't!" Eva screamed, anger welling up deep from inside of her.

A noise behind her made her turn, and for a split second all she could see was a blur as someone ran past her at full speed. Nora's eyes became huge as she shifted the gun toward her attacker, a loud crack exploding through the air. The attacker rushed toward Nora, knocking her over hard, flat on her back and onto the ground. As they struggling violently, another crack exploded from the gun and Eva realized that she could smell the sulfur assaulting her nose. She ran to the crib and scooped Noah up as quickly as she could, his sudden crying from the sound of the gun instantly breaking her heart. She inhaled his sweet baby scent, stunned, as she struggled to make sense of the pile of limbs in front of her. A thick pool of blood began to mingle onto the carpet, both bodies lying still. She felt as though the world was moving in slow motion as she held Noah as close to her body as she could, kissing the top of his head and over and over, trying to soothe his crying. She looked at his beautiful face, the thought of anything happening to him crushing her.

Eva could hear her name being called from a distance as she stood frozen to the floor, Noah miraculously asleep in her arms. She tried to replay what happened right in front of her, but all she could smell was the sulfur as her ears rang slightly from the sound of the gun.

"Eva!" Brynn's voice got closer as she and Kelly ran into the room, Kelly's phone in her hands.

"Eva!" Brynn grabbed Eva and pulled her close to her, holding her and sleeping Noah as tightly as she could. She stepped back and examined her for injuries, anxiously combing over every inch of her. "Are you okay? Are you hurt? What happened?"

Eva could hear Kelly's voice in the background calling 911 and she realized that she was barely able to breathe or move, the seconds moving like hours. She stared at the bodies on the ground, both unmoving, the sound of her own heart thumping in her ears. Brynn held her tight, waiting for her to speak.

"I think ... I think ... that Jack is dead," Eva said, her eyes refusing to leave the bodies.

"Oh, God," Brynn said, her eyes large. "Are you sure? What happened?"

Without saying a word, Eva handed Noah to Brynn as she walked cautiously over to where the two bodies lay, one on top of the other. She knew she shouldn't touch them, but she grabbed the top body and pulled it over, surprised by its heaviness. She cried out as she recognized Jack right away, his suit covered in blood from the large hole in his shoulder, his eyes closed. She kicked Becca's body cautiously with her foot, a large hole directly in her chest with blood flowing from it.

As the sound of sirens approached, Eva knelt next to Jack and cradled his head in her lap. "Please Jack, I need you to wake up. You can't leave me like this. You can't save me and then leave me. Please, I love you. Wake up." She wept above him, her tears falling onto his cheeks, unsure if she would ever be able to survive the heartbreak if Jack were to die.

As the sirens grew louder she felt Jack slightly stir.

"Are you alive? Please, Jack, are you there?" Eva leaned over his face, her hands on his cheeks willing him to be alive with everything she had.

His pallor was slightly gray as he struggled to open his eyes, his lids fluttering open and closed.

"I'm here." His words were gentle like a warm mist and she leaned in closely to hear them.

Eva sobbed in relief. "Please, don't leave me. Don't ever leave me."

Jack's lips turned up ever so slightly.

"Did I save you?" he asked, grimacing in pain and closing his eyes once more.

"Oh yes!" Eva said, kissing him over and over on his forehead and cheeks. "Yes, Love. You did. You saved me."

"Good. That's all I've ever wanted," Jack said, relief washing over him as he struggled through the pain.

"I love you, Jack Palmer," Eva said, cradling his head gently. "I love you and I'll never ever let you go. I promise."

A single tear squeezed out from the corner of Jack's eye as Eva finally did what he wanted her to do from the moment he first met her.

She finally gave her heart over to him, fully and completely.

46

The End

October 20th, Three and a Half Years Later

The bride stood in front of her mirror, brushing her long hair. It used to be darker and less gray, but she didn't mind. She liked the long white streak that was growing down the front of it, making her feel more glamorous. She admired her body that had grown stronger over the years with countless hours of exercise and hard of work. She had been determined to get back to where she had been before the accident. She was finally there.

She touched her face, the scars more faded than ever before. Now they were barely even visible and she reminded herself how fortunate she was. She smiled at herself and thought about Adam and wondered whether he would be happy for her. She decided that he would be.

It had been over three years since Adam had gone. The first year had been a blur. Brynn could barely remember it, lost in her sadness and grief. Nick had given her all the time that she needed to grieve, knowing that she needed it to become whole again. He had been as patient as he could until he could be no longer.

Brynn remembered the night he came for her, vividly. Nick

stormed up to the porch of The Harper House, flowers in hand and fire in his eyes. She met him at the door on her way out and before she could say anything, he had swept her in to his arms.

"I've loved you from the moment I met you and I haven't been able to forget you since. It's our time now, Brynn. Please." Nick gazed into her eyes and she was immediately swept back to the night they had spent together so many years ago, their hearts and bodies completely entangled together with an intensity that neither of them could ever forget. She was thankful that Nick had given her the time and space to love and grieve Adam. He'd shown his love for her by understanding what she needed to do. Brynn could never have imagined that he would be so kind and understanding, and when he finally came for her, she knew that it was time, and they found themselves inseparable.

As they sat on the front porch on that warm, fall night remembering their love, Nick had finally found the courage to ask her the question that had been burning within him for many years. "What about Eva, Brynn. Is she my daughter?"

Brynn hesitated. She had a difficult time imagining anyone other than Adam as Eva's father, but Eva already knew the truth. Brynn had told Eva the story about Nick shortly after Adam's death and Eva had been more accepting than she imagined she would be. Eva always suspected that Nick was her father, but wasn't ready to claim him yet. She was still grieving for Adam.

"Yes, Eva is your daughter."

Nick bowed his head and cried, the tears overcoming him unexpectedly. He had long since suspected that she was his, but never had any proof until now. His only daughter, Mandy, had succumbed to her mental illness the year prior, and Nick had lost her to suicide. There had been a deep emptiness within him ever since. The thought that Eva was his daughter both excited and unnerved him and he longed for a relationship with her, but he had been more afraid of her than he had of anything else his entire life.

After Adam's funeral, Nick asked Brynn if he and Eva could talk. Brynn agreed that it would be a good idea for the two of them to finally discover one another. She knew that, with Adam gone, Eva would need a father, though she was unsure if Eva would accept him.

"I have something to tell you," Brynn said as they sat in the library where Eva sought comfort from the ghosts of the past. "I hope you don't mind that I have Nick here as we talk."

"I already know," Eva said, staring at Nick's right wrist, her eyes resting on the freckle that was identical to her own. She stared Nick directly in the eyes and said, "I remember you. You were here for her, and then you left. But I remember you."

Nick embraced her and she held him tight, the connection between them immediate and palpable. She had always remembered her heart always waiting for him to come back for her.

Both Nick and Eva accepted their father-daughter relationship almost immediately. Eva had always remembered him from that night so many years before when he had sat at Brynn's bedside and cried. Something about his tenderness touched her even then at such a young age. Even then, she had known that there was something special about him, though she had been too young to put her finger on it.

Noah had taken immediately to his new grandfather, calling him Pa-Pa. Although he didn't take immediately to strangers, he allowed Nick to hold him within moments of meeting him. Nick and Eva spent a great deal of time together, getting to know one another. They found that they had many of the same preferences and dislikes, and the bond between them grew strong.

"I can't imagine ever living my life without you in it," Nick said, holding her close months later. He was proud to call this beautiful, strong daughter his own.

Eva had beamed at him, wondering how she had been so lucky to have two such wonderful men in her life that she had been able to call "Dad."

Over the course of the next year, with Brynn and Nick finally together, he was overjoyed to find that he was immediately accepted into the fold of The Harper House. Everyone was desperate to see Brynn finally happy. As Nick spent time with Brynn, Noah, Eva, and

Jack, he finally began to feel as though he were a part of a true family, and he knew that this was what he had been missing his entire life.

Three years after Adam's death, as Brynn readied herself for her wedding, Eva entered the room, remembering when she had gotten ready for own wedding to Connor. She shook her head at the memory and remembered how happy she had been at that time.

"Mom," Eva said, gently, careful not to scare her. "Are you almost ready? The guests are waiting for you."

"Yes," Brynn said, smiling. As she turned around she was struck once more at the beautiful woman her daughter had become. Regret picked at Brynn, and not for the first time, at the many years that Brynn had missed from Eva's life. Her dream had always been to have a daughter, and when she finally arrived, she had missed the whole thing. Even though Brynn knew it wasn't her fault, she still felt guilty, the darkness overshadowing her beautiful moment without warning.

"Why do you look so sad, Mom?" Eva said, noticing the immediate transformation in Brynn's face.

"Oh, it's nothing, Eva," Brynn said, smiling.

Eva stared at her mother's face, so much like her own, and took a step closer to her. "Please Mom, talk to me. I'm not a little girl. I'm a grown woman and I'm here for you." Brynn's tears began to fall as Eva's words rung true in her ears.

"Yes! That's just it, Eva. You aren't a child any longer, you aren't a baby, and you *are* a beautiful, grown, adult, but I missed it. All of it! I missed your first steps and first words. I missed your first crush and your school dances. I missed the girl talks and braiding your hair and buying your first bra. I wasn't there when you needed me the most. I lay in that bed, helpless and pathetic and I missed everything and I hate it!" Tears streamed down Brynn's cheeks as she grabbed Eva and held her close. "All I wanted was to be a mother, your mother, but we were both robbed of that."

"Yes ... we were, but we have each other now, and for the first time with you, Nick, Noah, and Jack, we finally have the chance to be a family. A true family." Eva held her mom close, enjoying the sweetness of Brynn's perfume and treasuring the closeness of her arms. She had always dreamt of a moment like this with her mom, and now, as Brynn held Eva tight, she understood how lucky she was to have a second chance at such a beautiful life.

The knock on the door startled both of them.

"Are you ready, Brynn?" Jack's voice came from the doorway. "Your groom is getting anxious down there."

"Mama," Noah's sweet voice came from Jack's arms, his little pudgy arms held out for Eva. "Mama, hold me."

Eva and Brynn smiled at the sight of Noah's face. His sweet, high voice was enough to remove the darkness from any day. He alone had saved Eva from falling into the abyss of her own sadness, and when she looked at him, she only saw love.

"Mama can't hold you Noah," Eva said, placing her hand on her swollen belly. "Mama has your sister in her tummy and you're too heavy, but I'll hold you on my lap in just a little bit."

"At the wedding?" Noah asked, anxiously.

"Yes, Baby. I will hold you at the wedding," Eva said, smiling at her sweet son.

"Not to rush you, but if we don't get moving, your groom is going to think that you got cold feet," Jack said, winking at Eva.

"Be patient, Husband, and let everyone know she'll be down shortly." Eva said, kissing him gently on the lips.

"Yuck," Noah said making a face.

"Mommy loves Daddy, Noah. It's not yuck," Eva said, planting a kiss on his cheek.

She watched the two people she loved so much as they left the room, her heart full. As she turned to look at Brynn, she caught a reflection of the two of them in the mirror and was struck by how lucky she was to finally have her mother.

Brynn had been the mother that Eva had always dreamt of, and she hoped that Brynn was proud of her too. There was nobody she had grown to love more than her Mom, and she wished that Adam had lived to see how much they loved one another. She imagined herself as the lonely little girl she had been and was struck by how different her life was now. She had a mother, a father, a husband, a child, and one child on the way, making her life far fuller than she ever imagined it would be.

For the first time in her entire life, the loneliness and fear had disappeared. Eva knew that the people she had ever loved the most had finally, saved her.

47

The Wedding

It's the day I've always dreamed of, only I'm not a young girl and this was never the dream of a young girl. As a young girl, I dreamt only of survival, not love.

But now I'm older. I've survived against all odds, and I have love that I never imagined possible.

As I watch Eva walk out of the room and I take one last look in the mirror, I realize for the first time in my life that I'm beautiful and I'm strong. I smile and I know that I should see an older woman, the scars still barely visible on my face, the lines etched in around my eyes and forehead where it was once smooth. Instead, I see the girl I once was with large brown eyes that reflect hope for the first time instead of sadness. I see strength that has been forged from years of endurance, created from the love of the people who surround me.

I am happy.

I open the door and I walk down the staircase of the home that was built for me by my grandfather into a grand ballroom and a sea of waiting faces, most of which I don't recognize. But there's only one face I'm looking for.

Nick.

I knew him the moment that he held me in his arms, and it's unbelievable to me that he is here now. That he's always been here for me. I never imagined a connection so powerful and real; the kind that weaves its way into your soul and rests, waiting patiently for you to discover it.

I know that I should feel as though I'm betraying Adam, but he would want me to be happy. He would want me to live a full life because he loved me and I loved him. Even though our love was far from perfect, we chose one another, and I am so grateful that I had his love. I know that he would be happy for me and in a strange way, his love for me allows me to love again.

As I walk toward Nick, the beautiful bouquet of lilies in my hand, I can feel my palms sweating, but when I look into his eyes, all I see is the man who has loved me with his entire being for two decades. He has tears in his eyes and he looks as though he might never stop crying.

"Hi," he whispers.

"Hi." I'm struck with how handsome he is as he towers over me. He makes me feel safe and protected. When I'm in his arms I feel as though nothing can ever hurt me again and I want to shelter in them forever.

"We're here," he says, looking only at me.

"Finally," I reply, smiling as the tears fall down my cheeks.

The ceremony is short and sweet, as we requested, but Nick and I feel as though we are the only two in the room, our eyes locked, our hands touching, our hearts finally one.

"To have and to hold …"

"In sickness and in health …"

"Until death do us part …"

I look down as he slips the band on my finger and I'm electrified by the warmth of his touch and know that with him I am finally complete. I slip the band on his finger and I grasp his hand, tightly. I don't know if I can ever let it go. I look into his eyes and I am beautifully lost.

"I'll never let you go, again, Brynn." He says.

"I'll never let you go, Nick."

He bends over and kisses me, not waiting for permission. Suddenly the entire world stops spinning and for the first time in my life, I know why I was allowed to survive through all of the horror and loss of my childhood, and the accident that nearly took my life, but did not destroy me.

It was for this very moment and all the moments that are to come. It was for Adam, Eva, Noah, and Nick. It was for the chance to finally have hope.

Most of all, it was for love.

The End.

AFTERWORD

Thank you so much for reading The Eva Series.

Please help others to find my book by leaving an honest review on Goodreads and your favorite book-buying platforms.

Reviews don't have to be long or detailed. They can be one or two lines that simply state how you felt about the book! It helps readers want to take a chance on a new-to-them author and we appreciate it so very much!

If you'd like to keep up with me, please join my email list and you'll receive a free eCopy of The Good One, the first book in the Happy Endings Resort Series, as well as updates and news about my author journey.

Thank you so much for reading!

X,

Jennifer

ACKNOWLEDGMENTS

This is the hardest book I've ever written, to date.

As the third and final in the *Eva Series*, I felt incredibly pressured to make the story perfect, even though I realized that I could write and edit for eternity if I wanted to. I'm happy with its completeness, and feel that it was fitting for
the story.

The *Eva Series* began as a way to exorcise my own demons. It has reminded me of who I am, and, like Brynn, how strong I can be. *Leaving Eva* was the book that I'd always hoped I would write, the story I wanted to tell, and the dream I wanted to fulfill. Writing this final book has been beautiful and bittersweet, but I never could've done it alone.

I'm so completely fortunate that I have such an amazing family. Surrounded by my boys, it's loud and chaotic at times, but I wouldn't have it any other way. My husband and two sons have taught me the true meaning of joy and the potential for happiness. They are funny, stubborn, and so incredibly good, and they make my heart burst with joy every day.

I am incredibly thankful for wonderful friends and readers like Suzy Conerly, Elizabeth Shuey, Patty Vowell, Keni Preston, Stefanie Lewis, Ebony McMillan, and Sarah Harmon, and many more, who have been with me and stayed with me since the beginning of this journey. I love and adore them like family, as well as my sweet friend, Tracy Johnson, who takes every opportunity to share my work with everyone.

I am perpetually grateful to be surrounded by so many amazingly creative and inspiring people in the book world. Absolutely nothing can be accomplished without my amazing friend and editor, J.C. Wing, or my cover designer and friend, Brenda Gonet. They make my work complete, and I am the luckiest woman in the world to get to have both of them in my life. Lastly, I am so thankful for Samantha Soccorso, my sweet PA and wonderful friend, who works tirelessly. It feels serendipitous to have such talented, dedicated, smart, and strong women in my life, and I couldn't ask for anything more.

All my life, I always dreamed of writing down my stories, but I never truly believed that I could. With the love and support of my family and friends, I get to live this amazing life and I am eternally grateful.

For all of it.

ALSO BY JENNIFER SIVEC

Leaving Eva

Losing Eva

Saving Eva

The Eva Series; the Complete Collection

I Run to You

The Forgotten

The Other Half of Me

The Good One, Part One

The Good One, Part Two

Grey's Harbor Series:

Grey's Landing (Book One)-Lark Griffing

The Grey's Harbor Anthology (Book Two)-JC Wing, Piper Malone, Carol Cassada, Lark Griffing, Jennifer Sivec

Hope Adrift (Book Three)-Lark Griffing

Harbor Tides (Book Four)-Lark Griffing

Perfect Seas (Book Five)-Jennifer Sivec

(Harbor Song (Book Six)-JC Wing)

A Grey's Harbor Christmas Anthology (Book Seven)-JC Wing, Lark Griffing, Piper Malone, Jennifer Sivec

ABOUT THE AUTHOR

Jennifer Sivec writes beautifully broken stories with heart. She is attracted to and writes stories with characters that are complicated, flawed and completely imperfect. Her books are often a reflection of life, encompassing difficult subjects such as cancer, addiction, abandonment, and abuse. She writes with a raw, complex, yet hopeful approach often weaving tragic stories with honesty and grace, creating unforgettable characters.

Jennifer's passion for reading and sharing stories is her therapy, which gives her perspective and peace of mind.

She lives in Ohio with her husband, two boys, and herd of dogs who create balance and levity for her. She loves her crazy life and wonderful readers, and is grateful for all of it, every day.

To find out more about Jennifer
www.jennifersivec.com
jennifersivec@yahoo.com

www.ingramcontent.com/pod-product-compliance
Lightning Source LLC
Chambersburg PA
CBHW030103260626
47156CB00008B/2498